HARD EXIT

A JACK DRAKE PRIVATE-EYE MYSTERY

BRUCE LEONARD

Eye-Time
Press

HARD EXIT

A Jack Drake Private-Eye Mystery

Book 1

Bruce Leonard

Published by Eye-Time Press

Copyright © 2024 Bruce Leonard

All rights reserved.

This is a novel, meaning it's fiction. The characters came from my imagination, so they're not based on anyone, living or dead. If one of the characters reminds you of your Uncle Ned, well, that's just coincidence. If you'd like to reproduce part or all of this book, you are not legally allowed to do so, either electronically or digitally. Doing so would violate the copyright, and then lawyers would have to get involved. Although some of my friends are lawyers, I'd rather not involve them because I probably owe them money.

Cover Design: Eva Spring and Getcovers.com

Cover Photo: Bruce Leonard

Connect with me at bruceleonardwriter.com.

First Edition

Printed in the United States of America

❧ Created with Vellum

DEDICATION

I dedicate *Hard Exit* to Sedonia Sipes, the most impressive wife anyone has ever known, to my parents, and to my brother and sister. And I'd like to send a special thank you to Mike Krentz and Jayne Ann Krentz.

OTHER BOOKS BY BRUCE LEONARD

Quilt City Murders, the first Hadley Carroll Mystery, named Best Mystery of 2022 by the National Indie Excellence Awards

Quilt City: Panic in Paducah, the second

Quilt City: Measure Once, Cut Twice, the third

Quilt City: Proving a Negative, the fourth

Quilt City Cookbook, a companion book narrated by Hadley at her funniest and most vulnerable

If you sign up for my infrequent newsletter on my website,

https://www.bruceleonardwriter.com

I'll let you know when I release new books.

My books are all available via my website.

CHAPTER ONE

I lifted the kayak onto the hooks under the house and knew the workout hadn't cleared my head. After releasing the stairs down to Broad Beach, I climbed them and rinsed off in the outside shower on the side of the house. Stepping out of my bathing suit, I dried off, opened the sliding-glass door, and pushed "play" on the stereo. Miles Davis' "So What" filled the room. I picked up my cell phone from the kitchen counter and listened to my messages.

"Jack, it's Mike. There's been a shooting in Oakville, near the school. Call me ASAP." The next message, from my neighbor and best friend, Jennifer, said, "It will be okay, Jack. You can dodge whatever Amanda throws at you. You always have. Let me know how it goes." Mike's second message said, "Where are you, jackass? Meet me at 164 Ivy." Followed by Amanda cooing, "Sweetbuns, I miss you. You better be home when I get there because I have a surprise for you. Kisses."

I headed to Oakville.

Why would Mike involve a private investigator, especially a lazy one like me based in Malibu, in a shooting in the inner city? That was police territory, although the Oakville police were notoriously incompetent.

If you committed a murder in Oakville, you had a seventy-six percent chance of getting away with it. Rape, ninety-three percent. Mike Sherwood knew this, which meant he had a personal interest in this shooting. He and I went way back, so I knew he wouldn't involve me frivolously.

On the drive, I was grateful for the distraction of the Oakville excursion. My girlfriend, Amanda Bigelow, a movie star, would return from two months in Italy that night. She'd been on location in Milan, staying in a magnificent villa, but I was willing to bet she'd visited the Ponte Vecchio in Florence. Her last visit to this famous bridge lined with shops had led to her spending $33,000 on a sapphire necklace that she wore to the Academy Awards, then claimed she could never wear it again in public.

Unlike most PIs, I'm principled, but only to a point. My job often requires me to find dirt on someone—ugliness I can use to blackmail a blackmailer. Almost as often, I bury unfortunate realities. The movie stars, with help from their public-relations flaks, have created their images—from squeaky-clean to seductively scandalous—and I help to prop up those images, regardless of the truth. Obviously, I can name my price because in Hollywood all publicity is not good publicity, despite rumors to the contrary.

Of course, you don't have to have talent to own a house on the sand in Malibu. The one I lived in with Amanda—the $30 million profusion of spires and turrets, surrounded by glass and topped with patina, all suspended by some architectural sleight of hand twenty feet above the breakers—is a showpiece owned by a woman who couldn't act surprised if she found a horse's head in her bed.

She and I lived near the gnarled finger of rock known as Victoria Point that juts into the sea. Our neighbor Jennifer Pearson hired me twice. She owns the architectural marvel two doors away. She's smart, educated, funny, gorgeous, and as broken as the rest of us.

As I passed Santa Monica High School, my cell rang. I hit the answer button on the steering wheel without looking to see who was calling.

"Jack Drake."

"Where the hell are you?" Mike asked.

"Passing the Lincoln exit."

"Well, hurry up. Game was hit, but superficially. Five others in the park didn't make it, though."

"Who's Game?"

"Wendell Jackson. Our point guard, remember?"

"Right. Quick as hell."

"Good kid, but in the wrong place at the wrong time today. Crispus Attucks Park. Borders on ironic. Game's been heading in a bad direction, so I can use your help. Step on it."

I headed east on the 105 until I reached Oakville. I saw many mom-and-pop eateries, and every major intersection was anchored by at least two fast-food restaurants. Korean grocers fought for space among the bail-bonds shacks, check-cashing stores, chop shops, and auto-parts chains. And every second block featured a liquor store.

I wanted to examine the shooting scene before I went to Game's house. I asked Siri the location of the park, then headed there. When I arrived, I saw a park nothing like the ones I grew up playing in. One basketball court didn't have a hoop at either end, only the remains of fiberglass backboards. The seesaw, monkey bars, swings, and slide sat on blacktop cobwebbed by ruts, and the entire baseball field was nothing but dirt.

I inched my way past the park. Half of the Oakville PD had set up out front. In the next row were the television crews doing stand-ups at the curb. The crews' vans were parked in the eastbound lanes of Mallory, and that side of the street had been blocked off by black-and-whites, so the news vans weren't impeding traffic. The police, however, appeared to be upset because the newscasters and reporters were badgering them for information about the shooting. And I'm sure the news chopper circling overhead didn't please any of the city officials.

Groups of three or four teens milled about, some of them being asked by the media what they thought about the events of a couple hours earlier. I stopped, rolled down my window, and saw a young, well-dressed blond woman extend a mic to a large male teenager I guessed was Samoan—wearing Osh Kosh overalls but no shirt. I heard him respond to her question by asking, "Would I a been in the park, lady, if I knew it was jumpin' off?"

I drove to the end of the block and turned left at the corner. The other cars checking out the scene turned right, heading out of the residential area the park was located in and into downtown Oakville. I followed the yellow crime-scene tape along the chain-link fence that bordered the two tennis courts without nets. Officers were posted at each corner. Plainclothes detectives wandered around, looking for the clue that would solve the case and get them out of the media's spotlight.

Lab techs had chalked the outlines of five bodies, which presumably had been taken to the morgue. Dozens of small white plastic markers with black numbers printed on them were scattered around, trying to establish order out of chaos.

But there was no way to tell in which order the bullets had landed, let alone to deduce anything about the shooters. Authorities could tell by the pattern of the spray where the shooters had been standing, which was relevant. But the exercise was nothing more than theater, performed for the sake of appearances.

I pulled to the curb and tuned the radio to KNX. After two minutes I heard a report on the shooting. A local gang was suspected. The five men who were killed ranged in age from nineteen to twenty-six. "It is a tragedy," a male newscaster on the scene said, "one that has become all too common. Today it was Oakville's turn. Which city or town will be next?"

The newscaster said, "The investigation is ongoing," then added: "Not much is known at this time, except the perpetrators were last seen leaving Crispus Attucks Park, heading west in an old, brown Honda Accord." Next, a male Latino who witnessed the shooting was quoted: "These guys in no hurry. They just walk fast away, no big deal." Then came a report on the status of the freeways. I turned off the radio.

Oakville's population was about sixty percent Latino, twenty-five percent Black, ten percent Samoan, and five percent Asian. The municipality's only real distinction was that twice in the last five years it had led the nation in gang-related murders. The school district was so atrocious that Mike had told me that many of the students in his tenth- and eleventh-grade English classes could barely read, let alone comprehend *Julius Caesar* and *Great Expectations*.

A tap on the window startled me. I lowered it to a young police cadet who asked, "You got some reason for being here, sir?" The "sir" obviously pained him.

"I'm a private investigator." I flashed him my license. "I'm curious what happened. Any progress?"

"Ain't you outta your jurisdiction?"

"P.I.s are licensed by the state. But I'm not from here, if that's what you're asking." I smiled to let him know I wasn't there to cause trouble. He didn't buy it.

"Well, okay, but this is a crime scene, so—"

"You mind if I look at something?"

"What?"

"The dirt between the court and the road?"

"That's part of the crime scene."

"Not trying to hassle you, but the scene's on the inside of the tape, and I just need to look at the outside."

"I guess. Just don't touch nothin'."

I got out of the car and began to walk in the street. The yellow tape that read Police Line Do Not Cross was strung around the four courts on the basketball stanchions, well inside the park. It took me about a minute before I found what I was looking for: fresh shoeprints in the dirt that the shooters could have made while leaving. A real police department—or a conscientious Boy Scout troop—

would have had the whole area cordoned off, at least to the sidewalk on the other side of the street. But this was Oakville.

The officer had been shadowing me. I asked, "Do you know if the techs made casts of these shoe prints?" I knew they hadn't because no residue and no other fresh prints existed around those of the shooters. But I figured I'd let him present the idea as his own to his superiors. He'd either be praised or sacked.

"Don't think so."

"Probably won't get anything off them, and they could be anyone's, but this guy wore Nike running shoes, size twelve or thirteen. And this guy wore what look like work boots. See the small slice there, on the heel? That could be useful, you find the guy. You'll call the techs?"

"Yes."

"All right. Good luck." As I pulled away, I saw him talk into the radio on his left breast, letting his superiors know of his discovery. How they would bungle the investigation, I could only guess.

CHAPTER TWO

Ivy Street was only four blocks long, beginning at Alameda Street and ending in a cul-de-sac that abutted a small park. There must not have been a homeowners association to enforce standards because the houses ran from nicely maintained, with well-tended lawns and cared-for flowerbeds, to run-down and decrepit, including one house with an ancient gray Oldsmobile Cutlass Supreme up on blocks in the driveway.

Game's house was of the well-maintained variety—small, painted sky blue with yellow trim. The lawn, bisected by a brick walkway, had been recently mowed. On the left side of the house stood a large sycamore tree. On the right, the driveway ran beneath a closed white gate into the backyard. A forest-green Toyota Corolla was parked in the driveway, outside the gate. I found a spot at the curb, got out, grabbed my jacket, and locked the car.

"You must be Jack," Rachelle Jackson said after opening her front door. She had a natural hairstyle that framed her face. The red in the corners of her big, brown eyes told me she'd been crying. She looked about forty. "Hello, I'm Rachelle, Wendell's mama."

"Nice to meet you, Rachelle."

We shook hands, then went inside. I set my jacket on the nearest chair.

"Sorry I'm late. I stopped by the park first. What a mess."

Mike and Wendell were inside the small living room. Mike held a bottle of Miller Lite and leaned against the doorjamb to the kitchen. He wore chocolate slacks, brown wingtips, and a silk rep tie that picked up the royal blue in his dress shirt.

Game was lying on the couch, his head propped up by pillows, his legs hanging out of sight over the far edge. He wore his hair shaved on the sides with an elevated flattop. He didn't wear a shirt and had a bandage on his left shoulder. He wore baggy jeans cinched below his waist with a thick, black belt.

"Did you forget the accelerator is the pedal on the right?" Mike asked.

"Hush," Rachelle said. "Can I get you something to drink, Jack? Soda, beer, something stronger?"

"A Diet Coke would be great, if you have it. Thanks. Hi, I'm Jack." I put out my hand, and Wendell surprised me by sitting up and looking me in the eyes as we shook. He said, "What up? I'm Game."

"Nice to meet you, Game. I like the way you run the point. Saw you dish twelve assists against Crenshaw last season."

"Thanks, man. Just finding the open man, like Coach Sherwood taught us."

"How bad's your shoulder?"

"Ain't nothing." He waited two seconds then added, "Thanks for asking."

I sat down in one of two flowered armchairs.

Rachelle reentered the room with my soda and handed it to me. She sat next to the couch in the other armchair. I looked around the room. The décor was minimal: a few large candles, souvenirs from not-very-distant locales, and three photos of boys on the shelves. The pictures looked like official school portraits, the kind in which subjects pose unnaturally. One was of Wendell.

"What did you find at the park?" she asked. "Forgive me for not getting to know you better before I start badgering you, but it's been a rough day."

"You think it rough? I the one got hit," Game said.

"English, Wendell. Is this what you teach him in that class of yours?" she asked, turning to Mike.

He opened his mouth to respond but rethought whatever he was about to say. He gestured with his head for me to follow him, and we walked through the kitchen and into the backyard.

Mike had been best man when I'd married Jami, my late wife, and I'd been there for him when his father died and when a drunk driver killed his sister.

A cinder-block wall enclosed the small rectangle of the backyard. A young peach tree didn't bear fruit yet in the corner farthest from the kitchen door. A transparent Plexiglas backboard was mounted on the roof, above the left side of the back door. We sat on the steps.

"What's going on?" I asked.

"Graduation was at noon today. Every year, the graduates pretend to be hopeful, but they know the deck's stacked against them. Anyway, summer's here, so Game's playing full-court pickup with older guys, members of his set, or gang, called the MLKs. Shooters pull up right at game-point, so the players' and onlookers' attention is elsewhere. Shooters get close enough to hit seven of the fifteen people on and around the court in a matter of seconds, then they walk away. Game got hit and was lucky because a much bigger guy stood between him and the shooters. The big guy didn't make it. We don't know much other than it's between da Uptown Posse and Game's MLKs, but he won't tell us any more than that."

"Because you're his teacher or because you're sleeping with his mother?"

"Probably both," he said.

"Is he cool with it?"

"Cool as any sixteen-year-old male would be."

"Does anyone at the school know?" I asked. "Or would they care?"

"We've only been seeing each other for a few weeks. But are you kidding? At Oakville? They'd just be grateful she's of age." He finished his bottle and set it at his feet. "That doesn't make it right, of course. Could compromise my objectivity. Grade inflation's bad enough as it is. He was one of my students."

"He's not as of today. Get over it and deal with the shooting."

"What'd you find out at the park?"

"Nothing you're not aware of. Oakville P.D. isn't going to solve this. The officers were as well organized as a hurricane."

"They'll put on a show," he said, "but it won't amount to much. One falls in their laps every so often, so who knows? Most cases, though, get solved by the gangs themselves, and that's why I called you."

"I was wondering if you were going to tell me."

Rachelle stuck her head out the door. "Can I get you boys something to eat? I have some leftover barbecue."

Mike shook his head and said, "I'm okay. You want anything?" The barbecue sounded good, but I wasn't going to sit there licking my fingers while Mike told me what was going on, so I passed.

"Okay. Let me know, though." She started to close the door, then stopped and said, "Jack, Wendell wants to know if you have LoJack on your Beemer, 'cause you're not in Malibu anymore." Obviously, Mike had told them something about me.

"We white folk just think positive thoughts."

She laughed, shook her head, and closed the door.

"You've never turned down food in your life," Mike said. "You okay?"

"Just tell me why I'm here so I can eat."

"Game's in the MLKs. Most people would guess this moniker is an homage to Martin Luther King Jr., but they're the Major League Killers, and they're the archrivals of da Uptown Posse, the ones he said did this."

"Are they the Hatfields or McCoys?"

"Exactly." He stared at his wingtips, then said, "Thing is, Game and the other MLKs intend to exact revenge tonight. We can't let that happen."

"Understandable."

"No, there's more. He's the last of Rachelle's boys. She lost his two older brothers to this shit. Despite the magnificent performance she's putting on, she's a complete wreck. Game's been involved for about nine months, and she's tried everything she can think of to convince him to get out. She asked me if I had a pair of handcuffs so I could keep him inside. Before you arrived, she was pleading with him to end all this today and stay with her because he's all she has left. He's calling her a traitor for even thinking he'd allow his brothers' murders to go unavenged. He's an excellent student, a tremendous athlete, and, except for the fact he's in this damned set, he's a quality teen. Exceptional, considering the cards he's been dealt."

"You're not saying that because you're dating his mother?"

"No. It was because he was a great kid that I met his mother. I called her to see if there was any way to transfer him out of this awful district into a city in which he might have a chance."

"No go, huh?"

"She's a nurse. Sorry, a registered nurse, as she keeps correcting me. There must be a bunch of rogue nurses out there who never completed their paperwork. She says she'd never send him to live with a relative, and she feels lucky to have a stable job, so she won't risk moving and having to wait tables somewhere."

"How long ago did his brothers get killed? If payback is exacted quickly among gangs, why haven't those scores been settled?"

"It's been about a year since the middle son, Terrell, was killed. But that doesn't matter. Remember, it's Hatfields and McCoys, so everyone in the rival set has to be eliminated for the slate to be clean. The war's still active if anyone's left standing. That's why it takes major players to sit down to effect a truce. For every banger gunned down, there's some poor, lonely kid being jumped in. They know the odds are against them, so they do what they think they have to do.

Sadly, it makes a certain sense. They're a part of something for a while. They have a purpose, at least until they're killed."

"Better to go out fighting than to suffer the slow suicide of the hopeless," I said.

"Something like that."

"Which takes us to a place where I can't believe we're going." I stood and stretched. I'd overdone it in the kayak and felt my misguided exuberance in my aging back. I wanted food and a massage.

"Look, Jack, you know I wouldn't ask if I could think of a better way. If he could just stay with you—"

Rachelle's screams interrupted him: "No! No! Wendell! *WENDELL!*"

We ran into the house and followed Rachelle through the open front door. She slowed her run to a walk as she reached the street and approached my car. The driver's-side door was open, and Wendell sat in the car, with his left Adidas basketball shoe on the pavement. By the time we reached the car, Rachelle's panic had turned to anger, and she was laying into her son.

"Why don't you just do it quick, Wendell? Take a gun and shoot me, 'cause that's what you're doin' to me every day, you know that? I'm sure you and your bad boys have plenty of weapons to choose from, so why don't we get it over with now?"

"Don't tempt me," he said. He'd put on a shirt and a leather purple-and-gold Lakers jacket.

I stepped past his mother and knocked the keys out of his left hand. The keys landed on the blacktop.

He let out a yelp of surprise and looked up at me with more fear in his eyes than hatred. I grabbed the collar of his jacket, lifted him up, glared at him, and said, "Don't ever speak to your mother like that again."

I let go of the jacket, and he said, "You're dead."

CHAPTER THREE

"I'm new to this gang stuff," I said, "but as I understand it, it's strictly Old Testament—an eye for an eye. What I just did to you was dis you, right?"

"Gonna kill you. Ain't be my first."

"Hold on, Wendell. What I'm getting at is that I want to square things up. If you accept my proposal, and apologize to your mother, then we'll call it even and proceed like men—no grudges, no harm done. If you decline my offer, it won't be beneath me to press charges against you for trying to steal my car and for making threats against my life."

"Man, you the one hit me. I should press charges."

"You mean slapping the keys from your hand? You think that was me hitting you? And do you have any witnesses?"

Mike and Rachelle laughed. She must have been conflicted, wanting to side with her son but also needing something in his life to change.

"Although it'll pain her to do so," I said, "your mother will act as a witness, as will Mike, when I accuse you of attempted auto theft and of threatening my life. The Division of Juvenile Justice will not be fun, but it probably won't kill you. It won't be a picnic, not with you weighing, what, 135, with the Adidas and the jacket on? They do their best to keep rival gangs separated, but you never can tell when the government's involved."

I reached down, picked up the keys, and put them in a pocket of my jeans. I'd left the keys in my jacket, which I'd left in the house. I gestured for Wendell to get up. I could see in his eyes he wanted to resist, to tell me to fuck off, but he knew he had no choice. He stood and stuffed his hands in his jacket pockets. Mike leaned against the car, then Rachelle did, too.

I turned to Rachelle and said, "Because you see the logic of sending him to juvie, you'll witness my complaint if Wendell doesn't agree to my terms?"

She hesitated, then nodded. Mike nudged her, and she said, "Yes."

Wendell took a step away from the car, his head down. A car approached slowly, then passed on the wrong side of the street, the driver's head swiveling to see what was up.

"You can do it any way you want, but I'd take off my jacket." He just looked at me. "It's not complicated. You get to pay me back now. I slapped your wrist and grabbed your collar. Let's call that two wrongs. You get two-for-one."

"That's it? That's your damn deal?"

"It's the first part of it, but by participating in this part, you agree to the second part."

"Ain't agreeing to nothing, don't know what it is."

"It's agree or juvie, Wendell."

"Ain't gonna send me to no juvie. No way." He looked at his mother.

"We're not joking. This is for real," she said.

"Why didn't the key work?" Wendell asked.

"Can't tell you. You ready?"

He took his jacket off and set it on the car.

"Three for one," he said, stepping closer.

"Six free shots? No, too many. Two-for-one, plus a bonus punch, just for being you."

"Anything I want?"

"Unless you have a razor in your shoe."

"Then you think we even? What if I still think I owe you?"

"If you try anything, I'll treat you as an assailant, not as a sixteen-year-old son of an acquaintance, and I'll put you in the hospital."

"What the rest of the deal?"

"Start hitting me, and you'll find out."

He stepped closer, put up his fists, and thought how best to use his five freebies. I cupped my hands in front of my groin, tucked my chin to my chest in case he went for the throat, and dropped my right leg back to brace myself. The first shot was an overhand right to my left cheek. He landed it solidly, but because I was five inches taller, he couldn't put his weight behind it, and it didn't hurt much. I didn't react at all, hoping he'd find the head shots futile and go for the body. He took the bait and delivered a two-punch combination to the gut. He flinched when he threw the left because of the bullet wound on his left shoulder. I clenched my abs, so I barely felt his fists, but I staggered back a step to sucker him. I must've overacted because he stopped the next punch to my gut before it landed.

"Two more."

"I know," he said. "Shut up." As if to help me do so, he caught me with a solid right-cross to the mouth. Even with our size differential, that one hurt. I'd have to ice it. But I didn't show him shit.

He looked toward his mother and Mike for help with the last one. To my surprise, Rachelle kicked her right leg up sharply. To my relief, Wendell took his mother's advice and kicked me in the shin. Adidas are fine basketball shoes but lousy weapons. My shin stung for a few seconds, but that was all.

"That's five. Let's go inside to finish our negotiations."

"Damn, you didn't even feel 'em, huh?" He picked up his jacket and started to walk next to me toward the house.

"The first one wasn't bad, and the shot to the mouth still hurts.

But let me show you something." I stopped and squared off with him. Tentatively, he took a fighting stance. "Two things. One, a punch is much more effective if you twist your fist when you land it, like this. You hit me straight on. If you'd delivered the right to the mouth like this, you'd have split my lip."

"Yeah, okay."

"Two, when you throw an overhand punch, think about your legs. Concentrate on pushing off with your lower body. You're just using your arms, throwing from the shoulder, not turning your hips to put your weight behind your shots. If you think about launching yourself through your opponent, you'll punch with your whole body, and he'll feel it much more."

"Damn, can I go again?"

"Not on me, you can't."

The four of us walked inside. Mike, Wendell, and I sat, and Rachelle went into the kitchen. This time I sat at one end of the couch, Mike settled into an armchair, and Wendell straddled the other side of the couch. Rachelle returned with a Baggie full of ice and handed it to me. I held it to my mouth and felt the sting.

"Because my stomach is beginning to consume itself, let's set the ground rules, then get something to eat," I said.

"Popeye's?" Wendell asked.

"I have leftovers," Rachelle said.

"I been shot. I deserve Popeye's."

"Fine," I said. "The situation as I see it is this: In the MLKs' crib, somewhere in Oakville, the guys are planning to hit the Uptown Posse."

"Da. It *da* Uptown Posse."

"Hush!" Rachelle said.

"That's enough," Mike said at the same time.

"Our objective is to prevent you from participating in any retaliatory attacks," I said. "Ultimately, we'd like to see you get out of the MLKs so you can pursue something that offers more longevity."

"Man, you just met me. Who you to say what I should do?"

"You're right, I don't know you, but that doesn't mean much. I'd like to believe I'd help any sixteen-year-old do what he had to do to free himself from a gang. But right now, we're talking about you. The plan is for you to stay with me in Malibu. Your mother and Mike are afraid they won't be able to stop you from joining the attack on da Posse if you stay in Oakville. Correct me, you two, if I'm wrong."

"No, that's it," Rachelle said.

"You got it," Mike said.

"Why I don't just head back? Ain't like I on the moon."

"Speak English in my house, Wendell."

"Or what you gonna do, send me to juvie?"

"I showed you earlier what you get when you disrespect your mother. I don't make a habit of hitting kids, but this is—"

"Who you calling a kid?"

"Despite your badass manner and smart lip, you're sixteen."

"Man, I'm gonna—" He got to his feet but without conviction.

"Sit down," I said.

"This kidnapping." He looked at his shoes, and asked, "How long?" He slid onto the couch.

"Long enough to let the heat die down. But because it doesn't look as though the shooting's ever going to end, maybe forever."

"Come on, Mama. This ain't fair."

"Is it fair I've lost two of my boys to this mess?" she asked. "And now you're trying to follow them into the grave. Is that fair? Tell me, is it? How're you gonna bring Lawrence and Terrell back to us by shooting someone else? Shooting someone else who didn't kill them, someone else who has a mama?"

"You don't know who did it."

"Exactly, and neither do you, which is what makes shooting people at random so stupid."

"Ain't random. Random what they did out there today."

"Quiet, you two," Mike said. "Let Jack finish."

"We're not planning to shoot anyone tonight or any other night," I said, "which makes us the adults. Instead, we're going to save your life. But I'll give you something in return. I give you my word I'll do what I can to put away today's shooters—not because I'm taking sides in this gang rivalry, but because people were killed today.

"Good, bad, or somewhere in between, like most of us, they were people, so someone's got to do something about their murders. The police department may luck out, but I doubt it, so we're going to need your help. You'll let me know what you know. You'll not only cooperate, but you'll also participate, offering up information, then tracking down leads. The drive between here and there will give us time to get to know each other." I smiled a big, goofy smile.

"Just what I need."

"Good, I'm looking forward to it, too."

"Why you think I'm not just gonna leave?"

"Because it'll be difficult. You already failed to take my car."

"I can take another one. Or catch a bus."

"Well, that's the sport of it, then. A little cat and mouse. Meeeooow."

"Mama, I gotta go with this clown, for real? He crazy."

"I agree with you, son, but his kind of crazy is what we need right now, so you're going. Pack some stuff."

"For real?"

"Go!"

Game slowly rose from the couch, his head hung low. He dragged himself to his room.

"Think it'll work?" Mike asked.

"I think I can keep him alive through the night. There aren't a lot of drive-bys in the Bu."

"What's the Bu?" Rachelle asked.

"It's the privileged white kids' slang for Malibu, like Oakville's the Ville or Crenshaw's the Shaw. And the Bu's a tough 'hood. Some people there actually have to drive Chevys."

"Do you think you can keep him safe, Jack?" Rachelle asked.

"Safe's no problem. Keeping him there's gonna be tricky, but I'll manage." I carried my bag of ice to the kitchen, dumped the water and ice in the sink, and threw out the Baggie. I could hear Game opening and closing drawers in his room.

I reentered the living room. Mike said, "He's a much better student than the average banger. He's never missed a practice, and, as far as we can tell, he doesn't do drugs. Maybe grass, but—"

"Who are we to judge, right?" I asked.

"Well, since we've managed to make it to adulthood," Mike said, "with varying degrees of maturity, I'll grant you, I think it's okay for us to assume we know what's best for him."

Rachelle asked, "But keeping him alive today, tomorrow, what's that do?"

"Don't get cynical on us," Mike said. "Sure, everything could still go wrong. The objective is to keep him out of harm's way for a while, to give him a change of scenery, maybe a chance to modify his perspective."

Game walked into the room carrying a huge blue-and-gold Oakville High School duffel bag. His downcast eyes told me he'd heard this last exchange.

"You think you got everything?" Rachelle asked. "Underwear? Toothbrush?"

"Yeah."

"Did you bring a bathing suit?" I asked.

"I'm not a good swimmer."

"Doesn't matter. Get a bathing suit, because I'm not letting you sit naked in the Jacuzzi with my girlfriend."

"Your girlfriend fine?"

"Yes."

"Very fine," Mike said.

"Hey!" Rachelle said, elbowing him.

"Ahhight," Game said. He went into his room and was back in ten seconds, stuffing some blue trunks into his bag.

"Say goodbye to your mama," Mike said, then motioned for me to follow him. We stepped outside. A police helicopter was flying in slow, giant circles, sweeping the neighborhood with a powerful shaft of light. Concerned Oakville residents would take this aerial surveillance to mean the police had their suspects pinned down, that it was only a matter of time before the shooters would be flushed from their hiding places and would have no choice but to surrender.

But I knew better. The three news-copters hovering on the periphery, edging into restricted airspace to get the best angles, needed visuals for the late newscasts. The police helicopter was giving it to them, while showing the residents of Oakville that its men and women in blue were hard at work. That it is standard operating procedure to employ a chopper only after a suspect has been sighted by officers on the ground—meaning only if they're almost certain he's in a defined area—would be lost on the public. This copter was sweeping practically all of Oakville, shredding tax dollars with every revolution of the rotors.

Mike said, "We're going to stay at my place, in case this thing escalates, and they start targeting the MLKs' homes."

"Smart," I said. "Make sure she has my number. In order to solve this thing, we'll be around."

"Good. I'll keep my eyes open, see what the cops are up to." He looked into the house. He turned toward me and asked, "How's Amanda going to take this?"

"Not well. She gets home tonight from Milan. Should be interesting."

"Yeah, can't wait to see it all on *Entertainment Tonight*."

"Nope, tonight it will be your neighborhood on TV."

He smiled, then Game joined us on the porch, followed by Rachelle.

"Ready to eat?" I asked.

"Yeah."

"Anything I should know, Rachelle? Medications?"

"No, just take care of his shoulder and don't be afraid to be firm with him. Let him know who's the boss."

"Tony Danza, right?"

"Or was it Judith Light?" Mike asked.

"I never could tell," I said. "That could be the eternal question."

"Get out of here, you two," Rachelle said. "Be careful—and have a good time."

"Yeah, right," Game said, as he walked toward the car.

As I walked away, I said, "Has Mike told you, Rachelle, he used to be a model?"

"Yes. He's shown me some of his work."

"But," I said, as Game and I reached the car, "has he shown you the campaign he's most proud of?"

"Jack, it's time for you to go," Mike said. "Let's go inside, babe. The man's obviously losing his mind." He gently tried to usher her into the house.

"Oh, come on, Mike, don't be modest," I said. "Game, I think you'll appreciate the artistic merit of this, too. Our friend Mike, that man right there, used to be the Fruit of the Loom purple grapes."

"Oh my God," Rachelle said.

"Naaah," Game said.

"Or was it the apple? I know it wasn't the currants. Don't have the range for those. No, you were the purple grapes, right, Mike?"

"Yep, the purple grapes. That apple was a hack. All surface and no depth."

We all laughed. Mike and I had done the Fruit of the Loom bit before, and I wanted to make sure I kept our parting light. I took Game's duffel off his shoulder and popped the trunk. As he got in the car, I set his bag in the trunk, unzipped the bag, and rummaged through it quickly, looking for a weapon. To my surprise, I didn't find one. I zipped the bag, grabbed two of the four aluminum bottles of water I kept there, then closed the trunk. When I got in the car, Game said, "You guys just playing, right? He wasn't the grapes for real?" I offered him a water and he took it, nodding his thanks.

"No, he was." I palmed my wallet, then reached under the seat, inserted the small key in the lock there and turned the key. Next to the lock, affixed to the bottom of the seat, was my Beretta. I pulled the wallet out from under the seat and set it on the console between us.

"There a trip switch under the seat, ain't there?"

I didn't respond.

"Your wallet was in your jacket with your keys."

"Okay, you got me. You need to release the lock beneath the seat before you can turn the ignition. But why don't we try something from here on. Why don't we be straight with each other, only tell the truth, and see how we do?"

"Why should I? You kidnapping me."

"I'm saving your life. Because Mike tells me you're a bright kid, I think in your heart of hearts you know that sooner or later you'll be gunned down the way your brothers were. And because you're smart, I'm willing to believe somewhere in that same heart of hearts you don't want to die. So, what do you say, do we have a deal?"

"Where you get this shit, heart of hearts?"

I wasn't sure my plan was going to work.

CHAPTER FOUR

"Where's Popeye's?" I asked as we pulled away from the curb. In the rearview mirror I saw Mike wrap his arms around Rachelle. Game didn't look back but instead seemed to study his right shoe.

"Did I bleed on you?"

"Scuffed my kicks." He pulled a toothbrush from his jeans pocket and rubbed it aggressively against a smudge I couldn't see on the front of his right sneaker. Then he put the toothbrush back in his pocket.

"Hope you brought another toothbrush."

"You gonna stick with the funnyman act 'til when ... 'til you get a laugh?"

"Why stop then? If people laugh, I'm officially funny."

"Man, this worse than algebra."

I liked that he was giving me attitude. After hatching this not-so-foolproof plan I'd worried he'd go silent and concentrate his efforts on how he could get away from this crazy man. I needed him to communicate.

"Left at the corner, right at the light. Popeye's the next block on the left, across from church."

"Got it, but I want to swing by the park."

"Why?"

Instead of taking the right at the light as he'd advised, I went left and took the same turn I'd made a couple hours earlier, heading toward the park. We rolled slowly down the nearly dark block. Groups of people still lingered, but far fewer than earlier. News vans were still parked along the curb, the newscasters probably off having dinner before returning in time to do live feeds for the eleven o'clock news.

He didn't make a big thing of it, but he slid down lower in his seat as we passed the groups. Everyone looked hard at the car as we drove by, and a few teenaged males turned to follow our progress.

"Pigs still stinking up the joint," Game said. The comment didn't warrant a response, but I liked that he was paying attention and wasn't lost in thought. I swung the car left at the corner, then left again at the next intersection. I parked where I had earlier.

"What we doing?"

I opened the car door and started to step out, then remembered the gun. I could reach under the seat and remove it, but then we could go in all kinds of directions, and I didn't want to launch into a sermon on the proper use of firearms and who can and should carry them when and where.

"I was going to have you stay in the car, but if we're going to be a team, then—"

"Team? Shit, you think we playing? This some game to you, Mr. BMW?"

"No, I know we're not playing."

I pulled the door closed and turned toward him. I was silent for probably thirty seconds, trying to figure out how to appeal to a sixteen-year-old who was filled with anger, grief, fear, and frustration. I didn't know him yet, but I guessed that anyone who valued his life so little that he would sacrifice it for a few seconds of glory and a special place in the memories of the fellow gangbangers who outlasted him was really looking for respect, for an acknowledgement that he mattered. It was only a hunch, but I decided to believe it was correct.

I reached under the seat and released the gun from its brace. I lifted the Beretta, reversed its position, and offered it to him, butt first.

He gave me a suspicious look.

"What, I reach for it, you do some quick-ass move and shoot me, claim self-defense? No way."

"Take the gun, Game."

"Why you doing this?"

I carefully set the gun down on the console between us, still with the butt toward him.

"It's loaded, a Beretta 92F, one in the chamber, fifteen in the clip. You can pick it up, shoot me, then disappear into the night. You could set up on a roof and pick off cops. Or you could do what you say you want to do: Hunt down a Posse member, or five, then start firing. Your brothers will high-five you from the grave, your buddies will hoist 40s in your honor, and a shorty or two might see fit to have sex with you.

"Of course, any one of these scenarios will end badly for you. You'll be killed very soon thereafter, or during your spree. You'll be a legend for a few months, maybe even get your portrait painted on a wall of honor somewhere. And occasionally your name will come up at get-togethers. But those mentions will quickly fade."

He picked up the gun slowly, then pointed it at me. He slipped his right index finger through the trigger guard and rested it on the trigger.

"I can't make any promises, Game. I can't tell you that if you stay in school you'll become a doctor, or that if you continue running the point as you do, you'll sign a multimillion-dollar sneaker deal when you turn nineteen. Hell, I can't even guarantee we won't get hit by a bus on our way home. But what I—"

"Why you ain't scared?" I didn't respond. Just looked in his eyes.

"Got a damn gun on you for real. Got no reason not to do those things you say."

"The safety's on. Push down on the lever on the left of the slide with your thumb, and you'll be ready to fire."

"See? I forget the safety, so the gun useless. Then you tell me how to kill you. I don't understand you."

I thought for a few seconds, then said, "Are you willing to believe that because you don't understand what I'm doing, there are other things you may not understand?"

"Yeah."

"You'll buy that because I'm willing to die trying to help you that helping you is important to me?" He nodded. He hadn't taken the safety off.

"You're almost a stranger. I saw you play ball once, then you tried to steal my car. But I'm entrusting my life to you. Why do you think that is?"

"Don't know. You crazy?"

The barrel of the gun dipped slightly. The Beretta weighs more than two and a half pounds fully loaded, and his arm was getting tired. He cupped his right elbow in his left hand for support.

"Are you planning to shoot me, Game? I'm not trying to rush you. You can take your time to think about it."

"Naw, ain't shooting you. But don't know why not."

"Because I believe you have enough sense to do the right thing, to weigh the consequences. It's not complicated." He nodded, as much to himself as to me.

He turned the gun around and handed it to me. He turned away and looked at his shoes. Finally, he asked, "Got kids?"

"No."

"Want 'em?"

"Not anymore." I put the gun under the seat and secured it.

"Let's go," I said. I reached across to the glove compartment, opened it, and grabbed a small flashlight. I got out and started to walk across the street. He got out and moved quickly to catch up.

"Where we going?"

"Nowhere exciting. I just want to check something."

Game and I reached the spot where the shooters had crossed from the court to their getaway car. I shined the flashlight on the area and saw many fresh shoe prints embedded in the dirt. Someone from Oakville PD had taken casts of the perps' shoe prints.

"What we looking at?"

"A miracle."

"You been to Popeye's?" Game asked.

"Many times. Couldn't get enough of it in college."

We sat in the fried-chicken joint, with Game about to dig into his spicy chicken and side of dirty rice. I'd ordered the mild three-piece dinner with dirty rice and beans and an extra biscuit.

"Of course, we had to drive across town to get there," I said. "Westwood wasn't considered a prime Popeye's location back then."

"Not enough Black folk there, you mean," he said, with his mouth full of chicken.

I nodded. Only a few customers were in the restaurant, including a table in a corner filled with three teenaged boys. Because I didn't know who we would encounter in the restaurant, I'd put the gun in a pocket of my jacket, then put the jacket on. The teens in the corner didn't seem to bother Game, so we devoured our food in silence. I asked, "How's the shoulder?"

"Okay. You gonna eat that biscuit?"

"Go ahead. I don't need it." He picked up the biscuit and took a bite.

"Why did da Uptown Posse shoot you guys at the park?" I asked. "Was there a precipitating incident?"

"Man, you sound like Coach. Like you ate a dictionary together. We jacked a drug deal a few nights ago from them. Payback."

"Was anyone hurt?"

"One fool. We trying to do it right, just business, keep things professional. We get the drop on 'em, so anyone with sense just do what we say—then get even later. But this fool think he Tony

Montana and try to knock the Glock outta C-Dog's hand, so C-Dog shoot him in the kneecap. The bitch scream louder than the shot."

I nodded. "What'd you guys get?"

"Their guns. Fools don't know shit 'bout guns, either. Idiot using a Colt .45, like he a cowboy. Other holding a sissy .22. But we got the green, too."

"How much?"

"It matter?"

"Not really."

We finished eating, left the restaurant, got in the car, then headed to Malibu.

When we hit the 110, he asked, "What I call you?"

"Jack."

"Last name?"

"Drake."

"Like the so-called rapper."

"Unfortunately. How'd you know da Posse had a deal going down?" I thought I might be pressing my luck, but he was cooperating, so I figured my ploy with the gun had worked. Of course, he could've been lying.

"TD's sister Tamara hooking up with a Posse fool."

"TD's in the MLKs?"

"Yeah. Tamara found out Posse Andy or Alfred or whatever his name is be stepping out, so she's pissed. He got a big mouth, and he bragging 'bout the deal going down. She figure they done, so she helps her brother and messes this fool up at the same time by letting us know when and where it's going down.

"We set six guys on the place early. Grab Andy Alfred from behind when he and the other fool show up, take his girl gun. Get the .45 off the other fool, cuz there what, five of us now drawing down on him. That's when C-Dog have to shoot the bitch in the kneecap when he go all Tom Hardy in *Venom*."

The freeways were unusually traffic-free, so we made good time. Near where the 10 becomes PCH, we passed the high school I'd attended, and I reminded myself how lucky I'd been only to have to deal with academic demands and the petty horrors of adolescence, rather than having to worry daily about gangs.

"Go on," I said.

"With us, we get our blow from a brotha called Arnold. Don't know where he get it, but he sell it to us, we sell it to anyone with the green. Some of that—maybe twenty percent—go to rich white kids roll up in Beemers looking to get sorority girls high so they can get some. What I'm saying is, only white dudes in our 'hood after dark are pigs or frat boys."

"Okay."

"But this skinny, old white dude show up in a piece-a-shit white van with the back all jacked from an accident, and he ain't buying no Franklin bag for a horny blonde. He selling the blow to Uptown. Or trying to."

"All right, so this supplier's the wrong color. If you say that's odd, fine, but that's not what I don't understand. When this skinny dude shows up and doesn't recognize the contacts, why does he get out of the van?"

"Maybe you ain't smart as I thought. Guy shows up at the right time and place to make a exchange with bangers. Think he's keeping close tabs on which gangbanger is which? Nah. He just does what he came there to do. 'Course, he don't know we gonna jack his stash and send him home with zip. Someone pissed off for real when he got home."

"Most likely. But I'm confused. Since da Uptown Posse are your enemies, and you've sworn to get revenge for your brothers by wiping them all out, why didn't you kill all of them on the spot?"

"If we kill 'em, Uptown would think the dealer shot 'em and jacked the cash. These some low-level nobodies. Bottom of the set. Otherwise we couldn't steal candy from babies like we did. And if they dead, they can't let Uptown know who punked 'em."

"Could've left one messenger alive. He'd have given you full credit for the heist."

"Yeah, that makes sense now. Didn't think of it. But kinda more humiliating they all get punked than get dead, right?"

"If that's not a rhetorical question, I'll answer in the negative, at least if I'm the one being humiliated."

I drove for a minute, thinking how little I understood about life—mine or anyone else's. Especially not Game's or his fellow gangbangers' or Rachelle's.

"You intentionally ensured you'd be retaliated against."

"Like Coach Sherwood say, Hatfields and McCoys."

"Hatred makes the world go 'round," I said.

"That and sex."

CHAPTER FIVE

We drove Pacific Coast Highway mostly in silence, passing restaurants with Friday-night revelers waiting to get in. If Game was impressed with or disappointed by the part of Malibu that PCH passes through, he didn't say. What he did say was: "When I was on the freshmen team, our small forward got invited to a fancy party somewhere in the hills near here. Four of us head out. We get about here when a sheriff light us up. Ain't stupid, so we doing everything like we supposed to. No speeding, no drugs, no weapons—acting like regular churchgoers. But *bam!* we lit up. He give us some crap about not signaling a lane change, but we been in the slow lane for ten miles, driving like a granny."

"Did he write you up?"

"Nah, just say if we turn 'round and head back to the 'hood—and he say it like this, *the'hood*, with contempt—then we cool. Otherwise, he'd ticket us for the lane change, then he threatened to search the car, and who knows what he'd find."

"The Sheriff's Department out here—and the Highway Patrol, for that matter—has plenty of stupid racists in it. Your story doesn't surprise me."

"Ain't you a cop?"

"No. Private investigator. I have a permit to carry a concealed weapon, but other than that, I'm subject to the same laws you are."

"'Cept driving while Black."

"Exactly."

"How'd you choose what you do?"

"I'd been a journalist, so I knew how to do research, and my dad was a cop, so I knew how to handle weapons and knew a little about penal codes and the legal system. My life went sideways. I needed something, so I reached for this."

"Like it?"

"It's allowed me to meet you, so how could I not?"

"You a clown."

"Yup. I need gas." I pulled into the gas station at the Malibu Country Mart, turned off the engine, then started to fill the tank. Game leaned across the car toward my open door and said, "Cool if I listen to music?"

"Sure."

A new gray Mercedes convertible pulled in and came to a stop. I heard Game running the stations and say "damn" when he couldn't pull in anything he liked. Malibu has lousy reception—too many mountains.

A guy I knew stepped out of the Mercedes, which had a vanity plate that read: A WRAP. Jason Gilson, a movie director, started to fill his tank. I left the nozzle running and approached him.

"Hey, Jason, how are you?"

"Okay, I suppose, Jack. How you been?" He was in his late forties, about five-seven, as round as a basketball, his hair mostly gray, his glasses thick. He wore a mustard cashmere sweater that I was certain was one-of-a-kind, his charcoal pants were probably custom-made in Hong Kong, and his shoes were made of what appeared to be butter-soft leather. Despite his sartorial ostentation, however, he looked terrible. His face was as gray as his car and his pants. He looked tired, and he didn't seem happy to have run into me.

"I'm fine," I said. "Amanda gets home from Italy tonight."

"That's great. Please say hello for me. She's doing *Tomorrow's News*?"

"Yeah. Says it's been a train wreck, but she'd worked with Goodwin before, so no surprise there. What are you working on?"

"It's tentatively titled, *Could Be*. There's an offer out to Amanda."

"Yes, she mentioned it."

Music suddenly exploded from my car.

"Lower it, Game," I shouted. He did. Jason ducked his head to see who was trying to blow out my speakers.

"What's going on there?"

"Too complicated to go into, but, so long as he doesn't play Ye, formerly Kanye West, things should work out."

"Okay. Be sure to give my love to Amanda."

"I will. Take care."

He turned to remove the nozzle and dropped his keys.

I finished fueling, then got in the car.

"Thanks for the serenade."

"No problem."

We headed up the hill, toward Pepperdine University.

"I like that song, man. Plus, you don't get shit for stations. Why you ain't got satellite radio?"

"Because I don't need satellite radio. Plus, I don't commute much, so it would be a waste."

"Who was that?"

"A director. You've probably seen some of his movies."

"He do *Avengers: End Game*?"

"No. The Russo brothers directed that. Gilson mostly does romantic comedies. He made two good movies, or what I consider to be good movies, about fifteen years ago, but now he's mostly a dump-truck director, according to Amanda."

"Who's Amanda?"

"My girlfriend. You'll meet her tomorrow. Or maybe tonight."

"That right, the fine one. She an actress or something?"

"Or something."

"What that mean? She ain't no good?"

"She's not an actress—she's a star. In most cases, there's a difference."

We passed Paradise Cove, where I'd gone scuba diving many times.

"She been in anything I seen?"

"*Twice Shy. Unvarnished. Never Forget.*"

"Hold on, she ain't Amanda Bigelow?"

"Yes, she is."

"Damn! You banging America's Sweetheart."

"Watch your mouth. If I can treat a sixteen-year-old like an adult, the least you can do is show me some respect."

"My bad. Surprised me. I mean, Amanda Bigelow. Didn't know something like that even possible—a regular nobody getting together with a big-time movie star."

"That's what she likes most about me, my regular-nobody-ness. Able to leap small nothings in two or three bounds."

Seeing Jason reminded me I was supposed to go hiking with my friend Chris Cerveris early the next morning. I called him to cancel but got his voicemail. "Chris, it's Jack. Taking a raincheck on tomorrow's hike. When this case is resolved, probably in a couple days, we'll hike or kayak. Hope you're doing well."

I took a left off PCH at Trancas Canyon, turned right onto Broad Beach Road, passed the public-access beach entrances, then drove up the hill toward Amanda's house. I took a left into the driveway and turned off the engine. Game said, "Amanda Bigelow. Fierce."

Yes, Amanda Bigelow, sometimes referred to in the tabloids and trades as AB. Star of the silver screen. A Hollywood hottie for twenty-four years—almost certain box-office gold. Sure, a couple of her movies had flopped, but whether she was in runaway blockbusters or limping disappointments, she was always America's Sweetheart. She'd managed to retain the adolescent, girl-next-door charm she'd displayed in the teenager-in-jeopardy Disney flick that had launched her career yet commingled it with a femme-fatale's carnality. That combustible combination kept her in-demand. She had an unmatched string of $100 million grossers when that number still meant something, and the public has never tired of AB's high-profile, off-screen entanglements.

Tabloids have linked her to every leading man she's worked with, relationships that existed for the most part only in the press releases her publicists sent to the fan rags.

"Contrary to the rumors being bandied around town, Amanda Bigelow and her co-star in the certain-blockbuster *Blue Wedding*—hitting theaters May 18—Justin Billingsley, are only very good friends. Yes, they were seen together entering Bungalow 4 at Chateau Marmont late one October night, but they insist they were only running lines." That Amanda's and—surprise—Justin's reps at HHH Public Relations had paid a photographer to capture this spontaneous late-night rehearsal was beside the point.

Amanda has, in fact, been linked to me for seven years, an eternity in this town, and I've accompanied her through the gantlet of microphones that inquire from the edges of red carpets at premieres in Westwood, Hollywood, and New York.

If I were a small-town private investigator forced for financial reasons to tail some poor slob's wife to cheap motels to see if she is in fact doing to her boss what she stopped doing to her poor-slob husband long ago, my career would be over as soon as I was seen on red carpets and in the tabloids. Stealth and anonymity are usually essential to private eyes. People have generally exhausted all hope when they call a P.I., but L.A. is different. I may as well be handing out business cards each time I walk those red carpets.

I popped the trunk to get Game's bag, and he said, "Damn" when he saw the gear inside—the wardrobe I used when I needed a disguise, the camera equipment, the night-vision goggles, the empty pee bottle for stakeouts, and the black Mossberg 500 Bullpup 12 gauge shotgun with pistol grip and eighteen-and-a-half inch barrel—all neatly organized.

"I like to be prepared," I said, handing him the duffel and closing the trunk.

He nodded and looked at the house. He saw the relatively unimpressive street side, with the three-car garage supporting only one elevated story, albeit a story with a turret, then said, "We ain't in Oakville, Toto."

It was 10:15, and other than the light above the front door, the only illumination came from the almost-full moon. He couldn't see the views of the ocean or the coast that arced gently off to the left or the rocky promontory, Victoria Point, to the right.

We walked to the front door, and he asked, "What that smell?"

"The ocean."

"People pay for that?"

"Millions."

I opened the door, disabled the alarm, and flipped on the lights.

I'd expected him to cuss when he walked in, run from room to room, something. But he dropped his bag and turned in slow circles, his eyes wide. His jaw moved, but no words came out. I wasn't sure if the pictures of Amanda, framed in silver and sitting on almost every level surface, had rendered him mute, or if it was the conspicuous wealth.

Amanda had decent taste, true, but she also had oodles of money, and she had parted with gobs of it to ensure that her home was as comfortable as it could be. She spent so much time in temporary settings—in on-set trailers, in hotels on location—that she felt compelled to create an atmosphere that all but shouted, "Lie down, relax, luxuriate. You deserve it."

Silk pillows the size of Shetland ponies—thickly striped in emerald green and silver, to interplay with the house's exterior patina and trim—lined the area against the left wall that wasn't punctuated by the emerald-green sectional. Game stood in front of the wall-to-wall plate-glass window, staring at the slick of white light rolled out by the moon across the ocean. One large pane had to be removed to get the sectional in, and while the glass was airborne, a second crane had delivered the silver Steinway concert grand piano that allowed anyone tickling the ivories to stare out to sea for inspiration. That neither Amanda nor I could play much more than "Chopsticks" didn't lessen the impression the gorgeous instrument had on people.

He walked from the window to the floor-to-ceiling bookshelves that ran the length of the right wall. The shelves that weren't filled with books held either the various pieces Amanda had acquired on her worldwide travels—candlesticks from Egypt, platters from Mongolia, a carving of a naked couple embracing from Nairobi—or glasswork, either Steuben crystal or Venetian masterpieces so delicate that they seemed only to have been imagined. The art was valuable, certainly, but Amanda had chosen each piece because it made her feel something—worthy, most likely. Game reached for a book, then thought better of touching it.

"It's just a book," I said. He made a dismissive gesture, then turned back to the sliding-glass door. I walked over, unlocked it, and slid it open. We stepped onto the large deck. He looked at the ocean, then shook his head.

"You live here? This your damn house?" He put his hands on the railing and looked down the beach, toward the moon's shimmering alley of light. "Every morning you wake up and look at this, and this your view at night."

I stepped inside, pulled out my phone, and checked my messages. I'd silenced my phone when I'd arrived at Rachelle's house, and the unexpected turn that my life had taken since had caused me to forget to turn the ringer back on.

"Hello, Jack. It's Rachelle," said the first voicemail. "This feels kind of pointless, since I don't have the words to thank you for what you're doing. But I'm hoping you'll understand. So, thank you from the bottom of my heart. I'm sure you will, but please keep my baby safe. Please tell him to call me, no matter how late. I'm at Mike's. Thanks again, and we'll be in touch soon." The next message was from Amanda. "Hello, Sweetbuns. The driver should get me there by 10:30 or so. I can't wait to see you. All my love."

I grabbed two waters from the fridge and brought them outside. I handed one to Game and said, "If you want something else, the fridge is full. We have three kinds of juice, all kinds of soda. Whatever you want." He gave me a look, and I said, "Don't even ask. I'm not giving you a beer or anything else alcoholic. In fact, there's nothing in the house."

"Big Hollywood movie star? Thought it be like a Crystal fountain here twenty-four–seven."

"Neither of us drinks."

"Don't mean you can't be good hosts and serve a brother a beer."

"It's not a question of manners. It's a personal decision. The house is dry."

"Then that's the only thing ain't perfect here. Where the TV?"

"Yours is downstairs."

"How many downstairs are there?"

"Four from here, because there are six levels."

"Six? This place unbelievable." I nodded. "I mean, I know what AB do to get a place like this. She a big star, maybe the biggest. At least biggest female. But what did you do to deserve this?"

"I'm a regular nobody, remember?" I looked at him for a second. "Your mom wants you to call her. She left a message." My comment revealed to him that something was wrong, and he reached in his pocket and took out his cell phone. He seemed perplexed.

"Why I ain't got no calls?"

"Who's your provider?"

"AT&T."

"Useless in the house. Only T-Mobile works, and that's spotty. You have to be on the sand for AT&T to have a chance to work."

"That messed up. Two things wrong with this palace."

"I'm sure you'll find others. We have to travel thirty miles one way to buy a piece of plywood, and the baristas at the Trancas Starbucks are very slow. Let me show you your room."

We took the outside steps because the glass elevator might have shocked his system. I unlocked the outside door on the next lowest level. Before Game followed me inside, he made a show of waiting until I looked, then shook his head at the eight-seat Jacuzzi that sat on the deck. I didn't mention the other one on the upper deck.

I opened the door to the room he'd be staying in, and he said, "This a guest room, and it bigger than my mama's house." He was exaggerating but only slightly. I figured he'd appreciate the 65-inch flat-screen and the pool table.

"That couch is comfortable," I said. "I've fallen asleep on it watching TV. Or that one pulls out into a bed. If you want a regular bed, you can stay in the room next door. But it's too girly for my taste."

"I'll manage here."

From upstairs I heard, "Sweetbuns, where are you? I'm home."

"Sweetbuns?" Game asked.

CHAPTER SIX

"Wait here until I explain things."

"Should be fun." His sarcasm made him chuckle.

I handed him the remote, then headed outside and up the stairs. As I stepped inside, Amanda was closing the front door, presumably behind the driver. Six Louis Vuitton suitcases sat near the front door. She wore a beautiful cream-and-tan sweater I hadn't seen before and milk-chocolate, skin-tight pants, the kind fashionistas wear to yoga classes. The gold silk scarf that her famous mane of blond hair was piled under complemented the soft tones of her sweater, and she wore a pair of exquisitely embroidered slippers—black beadwork and golden curlicues dancing across her toes. It was footwear designed for a genie who had flair and a sense of humor. In her hand she held a small package, wrapped in green-and-silver paper to match the room in which I would receive her gift. She was thoughtful that way. When she looked up and saw me across the room, she smiled. That's all it took. That's all it ever took.

Her teeth were perfect, and her gorgeous green eyes lit up like a pinball machine on tilt, but what was behind her ebullient expression rendered her America's Sweetheart. Her charisma and magnetism had paid for the mansions of numerous producers and directors, yet when she regaled me with her smile that night, something was different.

I didn't realize what it was until she glided across the floor and leaped into my arms. She clung to my neck, her legs wrapped tightly around my waist, then she began to kiss me frantically, first on my neck, then my cheeks, then my forehead. Between the kisses she whispered, "I missed you," over and over. Her signature perfume was too strong, as though she'd just doused herself, and when I returned her kiss, mouth to mouth, I could taste the alcohol behind the green-apple Tic-Tacs.

I wanted to push her off me, to confront her. I wanted to walk away, this time for good, because I didn't think I could go through all the drama again.

She had nearly two years clean when she left for the shoot—712 days—and I'd hoped she'd found some peace this time, bought into an image of herself that she could tolerate while sober. The misery that had preceded this latest stretch of sobriety had included temper tantrums, a car crash, two rehab stints, and a sympathetic, star-struck Highway Patrolman who drove Amanda home instead of arresting her for DWI. And she'd spent a lot of time in therapy. Her drug of choice had been cocaine, but alcohol was always in the mix.

While still kissing me, she removed her scarf and dropped it to the floor. I wanted to pull away but couldn't face what rejecting her would bring. She tried to take off her sweater but realized she was still holding the gift, so she tossed it on one of the giant striped pillows. With her still wrapped around me, I took three steps to another huge pillow, bent at the waist, and set her down on it. I tried to straighten up, but she grabbed my collar and pulled me down, rotating out from under me, then climbing on top of my face-down body, straddling my back and giggling.

"There they are, my sweetbuns," she said. She beat on my ass like bongo drums. "I thought about you and your sweetbuns a lot, you know." She nuzzled my neck and gently bit my left ear. "I thought about them while naked."

She sat up and pulled off the sweater, which she tossed on the other pillow, next to my present. "Do you want me to show you how I thought about you?" My arousal indicated I did.

"Turn over, you." I did, then admired her perfect, tan, surgically enhanced breasts as she undid my belt and slid my pants and boxers off. America had seen her breasts in her third film, the one she did in an attempt to shatter her girl-next-door image, the movie she hoped would turn her into an actress to be taken seriously. I don't think she achieved this aspiration.

She pulled my shirt gracefully over my head, licked each of my nipples once, and stood up. She started to roll her clingy pants down. Her body was perfectly toned and tanned, thanks to her five-days-a-week workouts with her trainer in the gym downstairs and the tanning she did on the roof, out of view from the tabloids' lenses, although drones were occasionally a problem.

She stepped out of her pants and straddled me again, balancing on the not-quite-firm giant pillow.

I made a noise that probably doesn't exist in any language.

She slowly began to play her fingers between her legs, her eyes going from her increasingly insistent ministrations to my reactions. As she transitioned from heightened arousal to complete ecstasy, she closed her eyes, and I wondered whom she saw behind her lids when she needed to crest the summit. Whomever it was, he or she got her there, and she shuddered and gasped. She caught her breath, smiled, squatted, and slid me inside her.

After bouncing around that pillow for a while, when it was my turn, behind my lids I saw my wife, my former wife, my late wife, Jami.

After our pulses had slowed, Amanda and I leaned against the edge of the pillow and engaged in how-was-your-trip, what's-new-with-you talk. She let me know about the wonders of Italy and about how messed up the shoot was, because the director, Michael Goodwin, was an idiot. Then I said I had something I needed to discuss.

"No, wait a sec," she said, "you didn't open your present yet."

"You haven't given it to me yet."

"Oh, I gave it to you all right."

"Yeah, yeah. Let me have it."

"Just did." She winked. She handed me the small package, then looked pensive. Her expression changed again into a smile, in anticipation of my delight.

I hate to receive presents. Even if I like the gift, and I rarely do, I always feel awkward about the process. Why are you giving this to me? What do you expect in return? Am I supposed to be grateful or impressed? Why did you buy me a gift that you actually want? Am I supposed to include this with me in my coffin?

Awkward is the best I ever feel after receiving a gift. It would be one thing to feel this way about gifts while partnered with someone who rarely gave them, but feeling this way with Amanda—who inundated me with one-of-a-kind baubles because it was Tuesday—was the height of absurdity. I'd tried to make it clear to her as diplomatically as I could that all of her gifts were just stuff to me, expensive clutter, money better spent elsewhere. "It's my money," she'd replied, "and I enjoy spending it on you."

I unwrapped the package, suspecting she'd dropped a bundle again. Please don't be another watch, I thought, certain that fashion rules dictate a man must wear only one watch at a time. She'd given me at least five over the years.

"Before you make one of your faces, I want you to appreciate the spirit with which I give it."

"Okay," I said. I removed the lid and pulled back the tissue paper to reveal a baseball card of Ed Delahanty wearing a Phillies uniform. It appeared to be a facsimile, not an original card from the 1880s.

No words came to me. Instead of speaking, I hugged her. I respected her at that moment because this gift actually related to me, indicating she'd given it thought, not having simply thrown money around. But I also felt betrayed because she'd broken our agreement.

When we first got together, Amanda agreed to my one condition: That she never mention Jami, my dead wife. In return, I wouldn't ask her about her sexual activity while on location. It was a pact forged of denial, resignation, and weakness, a concession to the fact that life is messy, honesty is subjective, and love often isn't enough. I knew I was deeply flawed to make such a demand, but I didn't want Amanda to sully Jami's memory by making catty or demeaning comments about her—or even by complimenting her. I wouldn't share Jami with Amanda, who had honored our arrangement for seven years.

But then she gave me the baseball card. The day Jami died, I'd received an offer from a publisher to write a book about Ed Delahanty and other unsung sports heroes. I hadn't written since that day.

I wanted to shout, "Who'd you screw you weren't supposed to?" I wanted to confront her about the alcohol on her breath, to remind her she'd just stepped back onto the same slippery slope we'd stepped off of two years ago. I wanted to smash something valuable, to run until I couldn't breathe, to feel physical pain to match the emotional torment I'd worked so hard to bury.

Instead, I said, "It's a thoughtful gift but completely inappropriate."

"Damnit. You and your stupid agreement. Jami, Jami, Jami. There, I said her name: Jami, Jami, perfect, angelic Jami."

"Don't. You're drunk and way out of line. I should've called you on it as soon as you came in, but I didn't want to fight. Obviously, you do."

"No, I don't. Damnit, Jack, I knew you'd mess this up. You're not normal. Most people like getting gifts. What's wrong with you? We both know you're just coasting. Not even that. More like stuck, and I thought maybe you'd start writing again if I gave you a nudge."

"I'm a private investigator, Amanda. Have been for a long time. I'm not going to argue with you now, but I will let you know we have a houseguest."

She looked confused, then waited me out.

"His name is Game, and he's downstairs. He's the son of the woman Mike's dating, Rachelle, and I'm keeping him safe for a while."

"Safe from what?" I was surprised she wasn't acting out more, protesting loudly, but I'd called her on her drinking, and she probably knew that making a stink about a short-term visitor would worsen the situation.

"'From himself and his youthful idiocy' is the easy answer. But I guess 'from participating in a gang shooting' is more accurate."

"You're kidding! He's a gang member?"

"His two older brothers were killed, so he joined to get revenge."

She got up and gathered her clothes. It must have occurred to her that she was naked in the great room with a stranger in her home. Carrying her clothes, she headed to the elevator.

"I gave him the chance to get away," I said, "but he didn't take it."

"You're his bodyguard, and he's supposed to try to escape? That makes perfect sense. I'm going to bed. It's been a long trip."

She stepped into the glass elevator and pressed the button for the penthouse. As the doors closed, she said, "Sorry about the gift."

She rode one flight up. I wanted to go after her to reassure her we'd get through this drinking episode as we had the others, to tell her the gift was thoughtful and she was right to try to jumpstart my life. Instead, I quickly put on my clothes, headed down the front steps, and said, "Game?"

No answer. I walked into the room I'd put him in, but he wasn't there. The TV was on, and his stuff was there. I walked to the bathroom, and he wasn't in it. I checked the two other rooms and the second bathroom on that level. I figured there was no need to panic because he'd left his stuff, but he would've been smart to leave it if he was making a run for it.

I'd figured he was bright but misguided. Maybe I'd overestimated him. Maybe he was naive enough to think he could travel forty-five miles without benefit of a bus line that late at night. And was he foolish enough to steal a car in this neighborhood? The homes had security systems, most of the cars were equipped with LoJack, OnStar, or another tracking device, and the Los Angeles County Sheriff's Department deputies would become giddy at the prospect of shooting a fleeing Black gangbanger. I hoped he wasn't that delusional. Maybe he was simply checking out the rest of the house.

I went downstairs to the home theater, another bedroom, and the study, as Amanda called the cozy room that contained a floor-to-ceiling bookshelf, then down again to my office, the gym, a bathroom, and the indoor lap pool and changing room. And he wasn't on the bottom floor, the one with the dance studio and the two storage rooms where Amanda kept items she'd never need. Game was in none of them.

I grabbed a flashlight from a storage closet, switched on the outside light, and shouted his name as I unlocked the steps, then lowered them to the sand. I saw where he'd landed after jumping off the railing and saw that his footprints led away from the house to the right. The light from the nearly full moon revealed Game standing forty feet away, near the mean high-tide line. I turned off the flashlight.

As he heard me approach, without taking his eyes off the house, he said: "Dawg, I come out here to check out the beach but see a sister in that house over there unbelievable. Tall, tight, and fine. She on the balcony with that short, fat dude we saw at the gas station. I was taking in the view, cuz who wouldn't, when I look up at this joint and see Amanda Bigelow in the elevator bare-ass nekked. Ain't never leaving."

CHAPTER SEVEN

"Yeah, this place has its advantages," I said. Game continued to stare up at the elevator, hoping Amanda would return, but she was out of sight, preparing for bed.

"I'm feeling antsy, and I'm not going to sleep tonight," I said. "I was thinking about heading out in the kayak and going night diving. Nothing serious, just tinkering with a spear gun, no tanks. I'm coiled up."

"You a strange man, Jack. Rest of us, we get busy with someone, we good for the night. But you do it with Amanda Bigelow and that bothers you. And you the one looking after me." He shook his head.

"Want to join me?"

"Do I have to swim?"

"No, I'll put you in a life-vest, and the worst that'll happen is you'll have to bob around. Best case, you'll barely get wet. Unless you want to dive with me."

"You want me to swim in the dark?"

"Didn't say I wanted it. I asked if you wanted to join me."

"Ain't gonna sleep either, so's let's do it. Gotta get my trunks."

He walked back toward the house, and I pulled the yellow, two-person sit-on-top Wave Skimmer kayak down from the hooks next to the hooks that held the sky-blue one-person kayak I'd used that afternoon. Then I pulled my fins, mask, and snorkel from the front hatch, followed by a life-vest for Game. I left the spear gun in the rear hatch, so there would be no chance of either of us getting jabbed if a wave wiped us out. I stepped inside, found a bathing suit, and put it on. It was knee-length with a loud, obnoxious floral pattern in blue and white—a suit a Miami Beach octogenarian would have worn in the late '60s, trying to show he was simpatico with the hippies. I wore it because Amanda hated it.

I pulled the kayak to the water, letting the incoming waves lap at the nose of the boat. I looked down the long arc of sand that encompasses Broad Beach and Zuma Beach and juts out into the ocean at Point Dume—an unbroken sweep of expensive real estate and public beaches that stretches for about five miles. House lights, mostly external at that hour, shined onto the dunes that buffer the private homes from the section of sand the public is allowed to walk on. That publicly accessible strip, however, now only exists at low tide, because severe storms obliterated most of the beach, and now many of the multi-million-dollar homes are separated from the sea by a jumble of rocks or a sea wall that grants the beach the feel of a demilitarized zone.

I waited for Game too long, then checked on him. I found him sitting in a chair in his blue bathing suit. He'd taken his shirt off. His left shoulder was still bandaged, and I reminded myself to check his wound later.

"Ain't going," he said without looking at me.

"Why not?"

"Ain't going in the ocean at night."

"Game, have I misled you?"

"Kidnapping count?" He turned and looked at me. "Nice trunks."

"Thanks. Knew you'd like them. But I didn't kidnap you. I'm your bodyguard, hired muscle, as they say. Just another of the lackluster components of the P.I. arsenal. I do this kind of work more than I'd like. It's how I met Amanda."

"For real? You her bodyguard?"

"Not anymore, but yeah, that's how we made contact. She had a stalker, and she hired me to protect her."

"Did you?"

"From the stalker, yes. The rest is debatable. Now get off your ass. I told you I couldn't promise you anything. We could've gotten hit by a bus on the way home. But now that we're here, I can promise you nothing bad will happen to you in the water. If we get dumped, you'll have a life-vest on, and I'm a great swimmer. Nothing worse will happen than your shoulder stinging in the saltwater."

He didn't move.

"The moon's nearly full," I said, "and I'll bring a waterproof flashlight for you and an underwater light for me." He started to stand, then sat down, but I suspected he was milking it for effect.

"Okay, if you don't get up now, I'll put up a webpage stating that Game Jackson, aka Wendell, refuses to face his fears and has cooties."

"You a sick dude. Worst part, you think you funny. A clown like you banging Amanda Bigelow. The world messed up, dawg." He got up, grabbed his shirt, and walked out the door in front of me.

"You may want to wear your shirt for warmth," I said. He shrugged it on, and I helped him slip into the life-vest. I tightened the straps, then ran back up the steps and grabbed the waterproof flashlight and my underwater spotlight from the storage closet. I jumped the steps into the sand, then removed a paddle from the Bungees that secured the paddles to one of the house's crossbeams. I walked back to where Game stood and clipped the lights to the hooks on the kayak.

I said, "All you have to do is hold onto the rails. I'll paddle from the back seat. The waves are small, so we shouldn't have trouble getting out. But on the chance I mis-time our entry, lean as far forward as possible when we go over the wave. But we'll be fine. Got it?"

"Got it."

"Get in the boat." He did, and before he could think too much, I grabbed the front handle, hoisted the bow, and hauled the boat into the water, running until an incoming wave reached my waist. I let go of the handle, stepped quickly to the back, and scrambled into my seat. I paddled like hell, and we glided over the crest of a small wave, then down the backside into the smooth water.

"See, piece of cake."

"Okay, that was fun."

I paddled in the moonglow another seventy-five yards so we would be clear of the outside sets, then turned to the right. I steered the kayak to a patch of kelp I knew about off the rocky point, about two hundred yards in front Jennifer's house. I used to dive in that spot as a teenager, before all of the overdone, I-Me-Mine houses cluttered the point.

I tied the back of the kayak to the kelp, which then acted as an anchor and held us in place. As I unbuckled the rear hatch to retrieve the spear gun, Game said, "Now what? I just sit here while you swim with the sharks?"

"I have another mask and snorkel in the hold."

"I'm good. Just shoot something so I can go back to that big-ass TV."

"Did you call your mom?" I asked as I pulled out the spear.

"Yeah, she cool. Acting like this all good for me and shit."

"We'll see."

I spat into my facemask, wiped the spit around, flooded the mask with seawater, then emptied it and pulled it onto my forehead, securing the strap behind my head and adjusting the snorkel.

"Why'd you spit in it?" he asked while craning to see me over his shoulder. He was still clutching the rails, despite the water being very calm, rocking the boat gently. I turned sideways so my feet dangled in the water, then pulled on my fins.

"To prevent the mask from fogging. What did your homies say?"

He twisted farther in his seat, letting go of the rail with his right hand.

"Why should I tell you?"

"Because you don't swim well, and we're a long way from shore." I jostled the boat with my hand, and he turned forward and clutched the rails as I stopped the spear gun from slipping in.

"What with you?"

"I had a privileged childhood. That shit stays with you."

I made sure the spear snapped into place, then rested the butt of the gun against my stomach for support. I carefully loaded the gun by pulling hard on the rubber tubing with both hands. I did the same with the second band. Because I'd forgotten to do it earlier, I reached to the end of the gun and made sure the spear tip was secure.

"What did they say?"

"They gonna pop some fools tonight."

"Anyone in particular?"

I slid into the water, which had ten degrees or so to go before it reached its late-summer high, but the brisk bite felt good. I reached up and released the dive light from the hook that secured it to the back of the boat. I flipped the light on.

"You want the flashlight?"

He shook his head. "Just dive."

"Sir, yes, sir."

I held onto the boat with my left hand. The light dangled from its cord on my left wrist, and I held the spear gun in my right hand. I pulled the mask on, took a deep breath, pushed away from the boat, jackknifed, then kicked hard as I descended. The tunnel of light spread out in a cone, diffusing at about fifteen feet. The visibility was fairly good for Victoria Point, and it felt great to be doing something that required specific thoughts. I followed the undulating copper-colored stalks of kelp downward, equalizing the pressure by pinching my nose, and blowing until my ears popped. The cold increased dramatically every few feet. I saw a cloud of tiny baitfish scatter when my light hit it.

I spun gently in a circle, saw a large calico bass about fifteen feet below me at the edge of the cone of light, moving slowly. I aimed the spear tip two inches in front of the fish's head. I pulled the trigger, and the spear shot through the gills, the line playing off the gun. The calico swam hard to the left, heading for the kelp. I pumped my fins, trying to reach the surface, trailing the gun, the extended line, and the bleeding fish behind me. I hit the surface and gulped air.

"Shit," Game said. "Made me jump."

"Sorry. Couldn't telegraph my arrival. Got one. About a five-pound calico." I treaded water and pulled the line up from underneath me, panting. When the top end of the spear hit my hand, I grabbed it and hoisted the fish on the other end out of the water. I swam toward the boat, holding the fish high because I had forgotten to bring a net. "We'll have it for breakfast."

I reached the boat, handed the light to Game, and asked him to shine it on the back hatch. He carefully twisted around, shined the light, and saw the fish.

"That gun tight. You nail a fish like that through and through in what, thirty seconds?"

I banged the fish's head hard against the boat, worked the spear tip back through the gills, and slipped my left hand into them so I could stuff the fish into the hold. I secured the hatch and battened down the gear.

"Could I shoot that gun?"

"Think you could say please?" I put my hands on the rail and carefully hoisted myself into the boat.

"Man, we going there? What, I gotta wash your car next?"

I settled into my seat. "Politeness and subservience are the same to you?"

"Just saying fellas don't say 'please' and 'thank you' when it's just them."

"Careful, because certain people might interpret that as a declaration of friendship."

I stuck the butt of the gun in my gut, pulled back the first band until it popped into the groove, and did the same with the second.

I tapped him on the shoulder with the barrel of the speargun. He grabbed it and maneuvered the gun in front of him slowly.

"Anything I gotta know?" He put his finger on the trigger and raised the butt of the gun to his shoulder.

"It has a big kick, so be—"

A huge splash sounded just off starboard, startling Game. He shouted and jostled the trigger, and the spear shot into the front of the boat, piercing the plastic near the handle with a loud squeak. The rear of the shaft pointed back at us.

"You okay?"

"Shit. I messed up your boat. My bad."

"It'll be fine. You're sure you're okay?"

"I'm good. Just jumped."

"A sea lion checking us out," I said, swinging my legs off the side of the boat and slipping into the water. I swam to the front. The point of the spear had pierced the top layer, poked through an inch or so of the front hold, and punched through the upsweep of the hull, the tip of the spear sticking out two inches. It looked like a macabre hood ornament. We wouldn't have a problem getting to shore because the seal looked to be watertight. And even if it weren't, we could make it to shore without being swamped. I removed the line that connected the spear to the gun. I unscrewed the spear tip and put it in my pocket, leaving just the shaft sticking through the front of the kayak.

The next morning, I'd visit Big Bill Watson, the inventor of the Wave Skimmer.

CHAPTER EIGHT

After stowing the gear and throwing the fish in the sink, I went downstairs, gave Game a towel, brought him sheets, a blanket, and a pillow, and told him where the snacks were. I examined his wounded shoulder, put antibiotic ointment on it, and refreshed the gauze and tape.

"If you want to use the Jacuzzi, pull the cover on when you're finished. Need anything?"

"I'm cool."

"Amanda will probably sleep late. Have a good night."

I turned to leave, but he said, "You doing this for your friend—and that righteous—but something else going on. I think you doing this more for you than me."

I waited to see if he had anything else to say. He paused for about five seconds, then said, "You got some dark places inside you, bro."

"Goodnight, Game." I closed the door and headed upstairs. I went through the great room and into the garage. I opened one of the three garage doors, pulled the BMW in, closed the door, then popped the hoods and pulled the rotors from the distributor caps on the BMW, the Land Rover, and the classic Porsche 911. I stuffed the rotors in the closet with my tools, shut the closet, and locked it. I used Kryptonite locks to secure the front wheels to the frames of Amanda's and my bikes. If Game could make a grand getaway in a kayak, more power to him.

I went upstairs to our room, walked quietly past the sleeping movie star, showered, dried off, and pulled on a pair of well-worn UCLA basketball shorts and a t-shirt.

I went to the kitchen sink, pulled a filet knife from the rack, and lifted the fish onto the cutting board built into the ecru-colored Italian-marble countertop. I filleted the fish as I had hundreds before, rinsed the fillets, put them in a large Ziploc bag, and set it in the refrigerator. I cleaned up and washed my hands three times with fresh lemon juice to remove the fish smell.

It was a little past 1 a.m., but I knew I shouldn't bother to try to sleep. I'd already tired myself out physically, with two kayaking sessions that day, as well as the interlude with Amanda. I could read, which usually settled my mind enough to let me feel that life is occasionally worthwhile. But I wouldn't be able to concentrate. I could stare at the ceiling and wait for the Big One, the earthquake that seismologists had been predicting for as long as I could remember. I'd already alphabetized my regrets, and killing something else seemed desperate. I really wanted a drink, but I'd given up booze when Jami died, and that was one promise to myself I intended to keep.

I went down a flight to the main room and heard Game turn off the TV on the floor below. I grabbed my cell phone, put in my earbuds, scrolled to Miles Davis' *Kind of Blue*, then let "So What" fill my ears. I walked onto the balcony.

The clean opening chords of the song give way to the backbone laid down by the double bass, and by the time Miles enters delicately, then unspools his genius, any listeners should know they're in the presence of greatness. Usually, artistry such as theirs was enough to pull me through tough days. Usually.

I looked down and saw Jennifer waving up at me from the edge of the diaphanous glow of the floodlights, trying to get my attention without waking the neighbors by yelling over the music in my ears. She was wearing dark sweatpants and a man's gray sweatshirt that hung down nearly to her knees. She wore a ponytail and was barefoot. I pulled the earbuds out and said hello.

"How'd it go?" she stage-whispered.

"Too complicated to go into, but thanks for asking."

"You look like shit, Jack. Come over."

Because I couldn't tell if she wanted to talk for her sake or mine, I told her I'd be right there.

I've known Jennifer Pearson, a bi-racial model and businesswoman, for decades. While she was getting her Ph.D. in English at UCLA, I was working on my doctoral dissertation, a nearly incoherent attempt to prove that in America only the winners are remembered.

The good-hearted, kind, or merely great among us fade to obscurity while those who stand atop podiums, hoist trophies, or quaff champagne in locker rooms live on in the collective memories of Americans, despite the moral failings, prison sentences, or prickly natures of many of the celebrated. To bolster my point, I researched, explicated, and distilled the story of Ed Delahanty, one of five Delahanty brothers to play professional baseball. Known as Big Ed, he played for four teams during his sixteen-year career, beginning in 1888 and continuing each season through 1903. He was primarily an outfielder, and the right-hander amassed one of the highest batting averages in Major League history: .346. Three times he batted .400 or better, and he led the league in slugging percentage and doubles five times each.

"Do you know who Ed Delahanty is?" I had asked the gorgeous woman who sat at the next table in the courtyard in North Campus. She was eating a salad and looked breathtaking while doing so.

"He pours a mean martini at the Tuck Room, right?" she'd responded, looking over at me with eyes as big, brown, and alluring as any I'd seen.

"His Manhattans aren't bad, either," I said.

"There's more than one?" she asked. She smiled, and I almost lost the thread.

"At least two, but the one in Kansas gets all the ink."

"And that's what's worrying you—Ed Delahanty isn't in Kansas anymore?"

I laughed and said, "Actually, he's kind of stuck there, in the hinterlands, never getting his due. Not to mention he died under mysterious circumstances at the age of thirty-five by falling into Niagara Falls."

"Wow. Too many of his famous Manhattans, perhaps?"

"There's been speculation to that effect."

"Are you always so passionate?"

"Only about important stuff."

We introduced ourselves and talked about our doctoral dissertations and our lives. Despite having started modeling at twelve and rising steadily to prominence—eventually doing runway shows, gracing magazine covers, and posing for the annual *Sports Illustrated* swimsuit issue three years in a row—Jennifer knew she was a lot more than a pretty face, so she set out to prove it. She juggled modeling and the demands of earning her B.A. in English, then turned down a lot of money by deciding not to pursue modeling full-time. She chose Dickens as her doctoral field of study "because I had no interest in law school," she said, "and because I've always had a thing for the Artful Dodger." She found the Russian Lit professor she was "seeing" to be fascinating, although blocked creatively, and she grew weary of being hit on by students in the freshman English classes she taught.

She asked: "Do you mind if I say something bold for someone who just met you?"

I raised my left hand and said, "As I said, I'm married."

"Yeah, okay. But you're sure you won't get offended?"

"You haven't said it yet, but I don't offend easily."

"Your dissertation doesn't sound like one to me. It sounds like a book." She looked at me, and I tried not to detect pity in her eyes.

"Don't worry. I'm not offended ... because you're right. That's what I was brooding about when I looked up and saw you. My advisor obviously shares your view but is afraid to point out that I've wasted far too much time sniffing around the *Baseball Encyclopedia*."

"So, change directions. Only those who lack creativity fear change, and you don't strike me as that type."

"The all-but-dissertation type, you mean."

"Let's just say, you appear to have plenty of options."

Those options somehow led me many years later to Jennifer's deck at 1:40 that moonlit June morning. By the time I walked up the steps from the sand, she'd settled into a teak chaise lounge that was covered by comfortable gray padding, a glass of red wine in her hand.

She stood as I reached the landing, set the glass down behind her, and wrapped her arms around me. She smelled of sea salt and lavender, with a hint of what I took to be Cabernet. Her long, dark hair tickled my left arm when she tilted her head and looked up at me. Her large brown eyes scanned my face, then, before our eyes met, she snuggled back down against my chest. I listened to her breathing between the crashing of the waves. We stood there a while—a minute, two—without words, and I wasn't sure whether her embrace resulted from sympathy or pity. I gently steered her back to the chaise, sat her down, and settled in sideways by her feet, my back against the teak rail. She knew better than to offer me wine and knew if I'd wanted something else to drink, I'd have gotten it.

She looked me in the eyes before she asked, "How bad was it?"

"Let me put it this way: What would you say would be the worst that could've happened?"

"She's drinking and using again."

"Yes, I'd have guessed that, too. And as soon as she walked in, I knew she was drunk. Two years thrown away. I know no one's ever really past it, but I was only expecting strained silences, miscommunication, and undelighted and servile copulations."

"Part of your problem may be you drop Milton into your speech."

"Only around those who will appreciate it."

"Or at least acknowledge it," she said. "So, you feel what—cheated? overwhelmed?—by the prospect of having to lead her back to sobriety again?"

"That's part of it. The tantrums and the rehab and the day-to-day sneakiness that her drinking and using are accompanied by seem childish. I know that's not a rational belief because age and maturity do little to quell those kinds of demons. But that's how I felt when she leaped into my arms—as though I'm her guardian, not her significant other. Or life partner, as she says."

Jennifer placed her hand on my left knee. "That's not you, Jack. Empathy may be your longest suit, so I'm not buying your story."

"You're good. I wasn't consciously trying to mislead you, but I could be blurring my emotions. Maybe all I felt initially was disappointment."

"Then why the muddled emotions?" She smiled, and I felt something break loose inside me, a sliver of the denial that men are supposed to hide behind. I'd never been afraid to display vulnerability in front of her—we'd both been available for solace when times got rough and had cried in each other's arms a few times. But the day had been trying and emotional and bizarre, and I just wanted it to end without more tumult.

"The drinking wasn't the worst part, Jen. She broke the agreement."

She hesitated for a few seconds, then said, "No, she didn't." She changed position on the chaise, rose up on her haunches, and wrapped her arms around me. "Shit."

"She bought me an Ed Delahanty baseball card. As gifts go, it's a good one, considering I had written about him and was contracted to write more. But I never mentioned Delahanty to her because he's connected to the day Jami died, and I'd never told Amanda anything other than 'She died, and if you want to be with me, that's the last time we mention her.' So, that means Amanda has been going through my stuff, snooping. My *Esquire* story, all of my research, and the pen Jami gave me were in the bottom of a locked desk drawer. Obviously, I should've hidden the key better."

"That's not on you. She's the one snooping."

"I stopped writing that day, stopped drinking, and stopped living, according to her. I'm not saying she doesn't have a point, but I'm saying she has no right to make it."

"She agreed to the terms. Regardless of whether your definition of living and hers match up—and, let's be honest, that's iffy—she's wrong to breach the agreement. Did she say why she did it? Was she compelled to shoot things all to shit because she was drinking, or was she drinking because she'd shot things all to shit?"

"I don't know. I don't think she thinks that way. Cause and effect don't play out with her the way they do with us."

"We both know she's not dumb, and her self-absorption definitely leads to some whacky decisions. But I'm asking, why now, why poke into your past from the far reaches of Milan?"

"I think she considers it a peace offering. She probably banged someone she shouldn't have, or maybe it's the drinking. And if she's drinking, why not use? Let's say she's disappointed in herself, guilty about bringing her addiction home again, and she wants to try to show me I'm more than the guy who puts up with her and looks after her. I suppose in the right light, her gesture could be seen as a noble one."

"That's the compassionate Jack I know. But you're an idiot."

"Thanks for your support."

"That's why I'm here." She pushed away so she could look into my eyes. "When Jami died you made choices. They might have been right, they might have been destructive, they might even have been irrelevant, but they were your choices. You presented them to yourself and to the world directly. That's better than most people, who make decisions based on gut instinct, tarot cards, or the price of tea in

Cambodia. The point is, just as you can't make her stop drinking and using, because it's her choice to make, she can't make you write your book, or honor Jami in a way she feels is appropriate, or become a Red Sox fan."

"Will never happen."

"Never say never because life is an endless series of curveballs. You need to stop feeling guilty for feeling angry at her. If you must obsess over something, obsess over why after seven years she felt the need to bring Jami into the picture. Trying to sabotage the relationship? Trying to get back at you for something?"

"Lost her mind?"

"Yeah, that's it. That's why I love you—your keen analytical abilities. Speaking of men and their so-called thought processes, I had a weird experience tonight."

I nodded.

"Jason Gilson called and asked to come over, but he arrives, and something's not right."

"Such as?"

"Instead of his usual self-aggrandizing chattiness, he's sullen and borderline uncommunicative. Which is fine, I guess, because we all have our moods."

"Right, but for most of us our moods would brighten when arriving at your door."

"And his always has. But tonight, after insisting we look at the stars from the balcony, he mentions your name."

"In what context?"

"Said he saw you at the gas station."

"He did. He didn't look good. He was edgy."

"As I said, something wasn't right."

"And you suspect he was using you to establish an alibi?"

"Maybe you really are a detective."

"What's he need cover from?"

"I don't know," she said. "But after you figure that out, maybe you'll tell me who the kid is."

CHAPTER NINE

I checked on Game when I got back. He was asleep on the couch, which he hadn't bothered to pull out. His left leg dangled off the edge, and he hugged the floral-print blanket to his bare chest. Poking out from beneath the blanket were his navy-blue-and-gold Oakville High perforated basketball shorts. His face was expressionless, and he was breathing slowly and deeply, but I couldn't convince myself the kid was peaceful, not with the cards he was dealt.

I watched him sleep for a minute, and I began to change my opinion. Maybe he was sleeping soundly, dreaming of pizza and randy cheerleaders. Maybe he realized that this involuntary exile from his difficult circumstances was the way out he couldn't admit he was looking for. I was probably rationalizing, but his actions supported my theory. He'd originally tried to escape by stealing my car, but the more I thought about how he went about it, the more I thought he'd overplayed his hand by asking about LoJack.

Why would he care that the cops could track the car if he intended to ditch it a few blocks away and disappear? When I'd given him the chance to make good on his threat to kill me, then escape, he'd done nothing. He hadn't run and hadn't shot me dead or in the foot. I'd thought he might be naïve enough to try to slip out of the house and attempt to thumb a ride. But he probably realized he'd be more likely to be picked up by a sheriff's deputy than by a Malibu local looking to help out a Black teenager in the middle of the night.

Maybe he liked his new surroundings, however temporary. Maybe, as he lay on the couch in the movie star's fancy home, he dreamed that the bleak, violent future he'd thought was inevitable didn't have to happen.

The sun wasn't far from ushering in another glorious Southern California day, so I figured I'd better try to get some rest. I thought about crashing in one of the guest rooms or on a couch or on a chaise on the balcony. However, I knew Amanda would be hurt—and would be sure to convey the depths of her hurt—if she didn't wake up next to me. Resigned to my fate, I decided to postpone it. I opened my laptop and typed in ESPN.com to see how the Yankees had done (a 10-2 pummeling of the dreaded Bosox), then perused CNN.com. After skimming a few articles, I went to *The Malibu Times* website and saw this headline: Hollywood producer is apparent suicide. I clicked the link.

MALIBU — A movie producer was found dead late Friday night in his Malibu mansion when Los Angeles County Sheriff's deputies raided the producer's home in search of narcotics.

Chris Cerveris, 49, hanged himself with a climbing rope, according to Sergeant Lon Jeffries, spokesman for the sheriff's department. Deputies found Cerveris hanging from a staircase railing in his 6,000-square-foot home in the 1100 block of Latigo Canyon.

Deputies arrived at Cerveris' home at 10:35 p.m. after receiving an anonymous tip that he had recently taken possession of a shipment of cocaine and heroin, according to Jeffries, who added: "A large quantity of narcotics were found on the premises."

Cerveris produced or co-produced more than a dozen movies in his 25 years in Hollywood, and he executive produced approximately a dozen others. In the 1990s, Cerveris co-produced a string of six movies that grossed more than $100 million each, including action-adventures and romantic comedies. Over the years, Cerveris and his producing partner, Marty Milford, helped launch the careers of some of cinema's biggest stars, including Justin Billingsley and Amanda Bigelow, who worked with Billingsley in the Milford-Cerveris blockbuster "Blue Wedding."

Cerveris is survived by three ex-wives and a brother, Keith Cerveris.

I stared at the screen until the words became smudges. Chris and I had been great friends for years. He was much less insecure than most people in the movie business—and people in general, I suppose. He possessed a confident sense of self that likely contributed to his aggressive nature and his exotic adventure travels. He and I had rock climbed together in Wyoming, rafted the Grand Canyon, and heli-skied in the Coast Mountains in British Columbia. We knew many of the same people and shared similar worldviews. We'd talked about climbing Mt. Kilimanjaro together, and we did our best to hike, bike, fish, or kayak together once a week.

My thoughts raced, and my gut felt queasy. I went upstairs. As I brushed my teeth, I tried to figure out how *The Malibu Times* could run such a horseshit story. Chris was passionate about everything he was involved in. He collected antique arms, had the largest collection of vinyl albums I'd ever seen, and half of his four-car garage was filled with outdoor gear. He kept an expensive fishing boat and an even more expensive sailboat in slips in Marina del Rey. I never heard him say anything about being depressed. He was saddened by his divorces and was disappointed when his movies didn't do well, but I knew far too much about depression, and Chris hadn't been depressed.

And he wasn't a drug dealer.

His life would have had to take a dramatic turn—a turn caused by a brain tumor, for instance—for the facts in that article to be true. I believed the dead part, but that was about it. Having formerly been a newspaper reporter, I knew when a story had been fed to the press, rather than having been reported by a member of it. This one smelled rotten, and the lack of a byline exacerbated the stench.

I gently climbed under the covers, and the warmth of the down comforter and of another human being felt nice because I hadn't fully warmed up after skin diving. I looked at Amanda and remembered how comforting it was to watch her sleep. She slept like a carefree child, never tossing or lashing out, and never talking in her sleep, as I'm told I do. She's never awakened and mentioned a nightmare to me, which I find amazing because the stresses she's under—to continue to deliver hit after hit, to live up to the myth that the PR machines have created, to prove to herself and to the world that she is more than simply a product of good genes—have certainly contributed to her substance abuse over the years. Yet somehow these pressures don't seep into her dreams. At least not that she's admitted to me.

After debating whether to check if the *LA Times* website had Chris' story yet, I decided to figure out why I was so upset by Amanda's gift. Yes, she'd broken our pact, but by honoring it for seven years weren't we acknowledging its existence daily? Wouldn't it be natural for a partner's deceased spouse to come up in conversation occasionally. Because Jami's name never did, wasn't she on the periphery of every conversation? I knew that most people wouldn't understand a couple making an agreement such as ours, not while claiming to be "life partners" or "significant others" or any other pairing that doesn't include the phrase "husband and wife."

Jami was the elephant in the room, but I'd established my terms when Amanda and I first got together, and she'd agreed to them. I wasn't willing or able to have another relationship like the one I had had with Jami, so I let Amanda know she could have what I could give, what was left, which, I was almost certain, would not be much. Although I wouldn't consciously try to hold back my feelings, I knew myself fairly well, and I knew that some parts of me would never heal.

I wouldn't lie to Amanda, belittle her, or humiliate her, and I wouldn't intentionally hurt her. These were my terms. But I made no promise to love her, and she claimed to be okay with that. It turned out we were both wrong because she obviously wasn't okay with only getting part of me, and I believed that what I felt for her approximated love. At the least, I cared for her enough not to leave her simply because she wasn't my everything, and I knew that if I walked away, she would most likely kill herself, as she'd threatened to do many times.

My love for Jami had been the "I'd die for you" kind of love. Although that kind of all-consuming love probably isn't healthy, it's the kind that Jami and I had had for each other, so it's what I knew love to be. Anything else must not be love, therefore. Or so I believed.

But I'd failed Jami, and she'd died as a result. The aftermath was so painful that I knew I couldn't live through another period even half as bad.

CHAPTER TEN

I stared at the ceiling while lying next to Amanda, mourning Jami, missing her, and speculating about what might have been. If heaven exists, then she's up there trying not to dismiss me as a failure. She would have expected me to be stronger, to have bounced back. To thrive. Otherwise, how could she have loved me as profoundly as she had? The love of her life had a backbone, ambition, but the man next to Amanda that night only existed. I don't know who I'd have been had Jami lived, but I know I would've been more than I was that night.

I slipped out of bed, got dressed, headed downstairs, and stepped barefoot into the soft dew-damp sand. Apparently, I'd been tossing, turning, and reminiscing for longer than I thought because it was only moments before first light.

I told myself I'd come down to the beach to examine the damage the spear had caused to the kayak. But as I studied the shaft protruding through the hull and debated whether I should use pliers to try to yank the spear loose, I felt a tear run down my right cheek. Then my left. I leaned over, let the tears flow, sat in the sand, and fell apart. Everything hit me at once, and I don't know how long I cried or how long Game watched me cry, but from the bottom step he said, "Couldn't get it up? I hear it happens, you get old."

"Yep, that's it. All out of Viagra. As we know, a man defines himself solely by his cock." Game walked over to where I sat and dropped down into the sand beside me.

"Ain't your problem. I heard you and Amanda Bigelow banging like all-stars. You need Viagra with her, you gay."

"Maybe that's it," I said as I put my hand on his knee. He jumped a foot sideways and yelled, "Shit, dawg. A brotha help a dude in a bad place and get felt up. Ain't right." We laughed.

I stood, wiped the sand from my pants and my hands, and said, "Come on, I'll make you breakfast."

Despite Game's protests that he didn't like fish, I sautéed the calico we'd caught in butter. I scrambled eggs well-done, the way he said he liked them, and poured him a glass of orange juice. On the assumption I'd need a couple gallons of coffee to make it through the day without having slept at all that night, I started the coffee first, then downed two mugs as I prepared breakfast. Game didn't drink coffee, he said, and I dismissed this shortcoming as the ignorance of youth.

"You gonna tell me?" he asked between bites. We were seated at the table on the balcony, overlooking the ocean, watching the sun's rays glide across the water as if being pulled across the sea. He wore basketball shorts and a black Oakville High School sweatshirt.

"Tell you what?"

"Why you crying."

"How's the fish?"

"Better than I thought. Spices make it edible."

"Cajun spices. I put them on almost everything."

"You ducking the question."

"I cried because I just lost a good friend, and I miss my wife. She died."

"How?"

"Bike accident."

"How long ago?"

"Forever ... and yesterday."

"That how I feel 'bout Lawrence and Terrell. Some days something happens to me, and I think I can tell 'em 'bout it when I get home. Crazy, right?"

"Human, I think. I've learned to block out the conversations with Jami I have in my head. Although she gives great advice, I find it too painful to listen. I have to tune her out."

He took a bite of eggs and looked at me thoughtfully. I'd dismissed Jami's whispers in my head as the workings of my overwrought mind. I didn't believe in ghosts, white light, or the ever-after. I barely believed in the here and now.

"Sometimes I kinda ask how Lawrence or Terrell woulda done things. I listen to their answers, then make my decision. But I listen first."

I nodded and finished another mug of coffee.

"Gonna get the paper," I said. I stood, walked through the house, opened the front door, walked outside, then across the driveway. The delivery driver usually hurled the *L.A. Times* to within a few feet of the front door, but that morning the paper sat in the gutter. Maybe the regular driver was out sick. I picked the paper up, pulled the plastic cover off, and scanned the front page. Nothing above the fold about Chris' death, and nothing below it. I tucked the other sections under my arm and scanned the rest of the news section. No mention of Chris' death. I opened the sports section, scanned the headlines, read the first five paragraphs of a story about collectors of rare baseball cards, then headed inside. I saw Amanda hand Game a cup of coffee.

"Good morning," I said as I approached the kitchen.

"Morning," she said. "I wanted to wake up next to you."

"Sorry. I couldn't sleep. I see you two have met." I kissed Amanda on the cheek. Game sipped his coffee.

"Yes, Game was just telling me you killed something last night. How nice. And I can still smell it."

"I saved you some."

"None for me. I'm not feeling so good."

"Doesn't surprise me."

"Don't, Jack. Not now."

I turned to Game. "Thought you don't drink coffee?"

"When Amanda Bigelow gives you something, you take it. She put cream and sugar in it. Not bad."

I sat and pretended to read the paper. Game motioned for the sports page, and I passed it to him. Amanda sipped her coffee and looked out at the ocean. She did that for two minutes. None of us said a word.

Game broke the silence. "You want me to get lost so you can fight?"

"Yes, please," Amanda said.

"No, Game, I don't intend to fight. This is between Amanda and me, and we'll deal with it later. You and I are going to head to town to see what's developed, after we talk to Big Bill." I pushed away from the table.

"Who's Big Bill?"

"The guy who invented the kayak you shot."

As Game and I approached Big Bill's house from the sand, Big Bill was sitting on a railroad tie, in the shade that the large, elevated deck created, about forty yards in front of the house he shared with his wife, Sadie. He sat about six feet from one of two upright bourbon barrels as he tossed one stick after another toward the mouth of the nearest one. Behind him, hanging from the rafter farthest from the ocean, were two Wave Skimmers, one orange two-person and a red solo kayak.

"Isn't that supposed to be a peach basket?" I asked as Game and I approached.

"I'm sure Dr. Naismith would understand," Big Bill said. "Besides, my shooting percentage is higher this way." He smiled and said, "It's good to see you, Jack. Who's your friend?"

Big Bill stood to greet us. He was seventy-two, still stood six-six and was huge, the way former offensive lineman frequently become. He had played left tackle at Santa Monica High School and tight end at Santa Monica City College. I made the introductions, and they shook hands, both saying "nice to meet you" at the same time. Game, however, added, "sir."

We chatted for a few minutes about Bill's gout and his wife's inevitable slink toward nothingness, her Lewy body dementia even causing Sadie to forget her own name, let alone Bill's.

Because I could think of nothing to add that would refute the fact that life is inherently sad, I told Big Bill why we stopped by.

"We had an accident last night with the double Wave Skimmer. I shot the boat with a spear, and I was hoping you'd know how to repair the holes. I thought I'd simply fill them with caulk but figured I better ask you first."

"Sadly, Jack, that won't do it. Well, it will temporarily, but it won't last more than a couple days, probably. The Wave Skimmer is made of a complex synthetic polymer—called Hydroglass, which is proprietary—and in order to repair an invasive breach, one must use Hydroglass in the repair process, or else the agent simply won't adhere in the long term. Sun, wind, and water will make the holes reappear. You'll have to take the Skimmer to the shop."

"Where?"

"Compton."

"How'd you choose Compton to produce kayaks? Not an obvious choice."

"The warehouse there was in such bad shape in the early eighties, the owner said I could have a year of free rent if I fixed it up enough to use it. As hand-to-mouth as I was then, that was the break I needed to launch a business and have it succeed. As the business grew, we expanded elsewhere, but I hung on to the space for nostalgic reasons, and I made sure the landlord received a large thank-you bonus for his initial kindness. Eventually, I bought the building."

"Makes sense. We're headed that way anyway. Thanks for your help."

He shook our hands and turned back toward his barrel. As we walked away, he muttered something I couldn't understand. "What was that, Big Bill?"

"Nothing. Just talking to my past." He muttered something else I didn't understand.

Game and I walked back toward the house along the deserted beach. He said, "He's a sad man, Jack. Kinda like you."

"Sad, yes, but not like me. He's been married for about forty-five years to a wonderful woman, a true partner whose side he rarely left. They were inseparable, and now he spends his days pining for a woman who no longer exists, not in a form either of them can recognize."

"Like I said—like you. Maybe Amanda's right."

I stopped walking and looked at him. "What do you mean?"

"When she fixed my coffee, she said, 'Jami has Jack's heart. I just have his cock.'"

"She didn't say that."

"For real, Jack."

"You're a stranger in her house, and within a minute of meeting you she discusses my heart and my cock?"

"Said she messed up real bad last night, then mentioned your dead ... mentioned Jami, and said she broke some agreement."

"She must really be hung over. Or still loaded. I'm not up for this now. We'll take the kayak up the stairs on the side of the house and head into town to take care of our shit before I have to wade into hers."

"Very poetic."

CHAPTER ELEVEN

Jami and I fell in love at Santa Monica High School. We met in journalism class and worked on the high school newspaper together. I'd been a shy, frightened kid until I met Jami, but after meeting her I suddenly understood why love stories resonated through the ages. I no longer wanted only to be peacefully content, to exist unnoticed—I suddenly wanted to achieve lofty goals, to conquer the world, and to satisfy her every whim. But Jami wasn't whimsical. She had a fantastic sense of humor and could goof around enthusiastically, but she was driven, dedicated, fiercely intelligent, and knew what she wanted. And what she wanted was to spend her life with me.

We attended UCLA together and collectively became known as J.D. (Jami Donohue and Jack Drake), a couple who shared everything, including initials. People either admired what we had together or hated us on sight, figuring that we had to bat each other around behind closed doors because in the world they lived in, total, immersive love only existed in fairy tales. But ours was no fable. We had a rare relationship in which a look could convey paragraphs, and a smile could make everything right. We both graduated with honors, then were married three weeks after the graduation ceremony. Mike was my best man.

My parents insisted we were too young, that I'd been with only one woman, so I couldn't possibly know what love was. I looked at their sham of a marriage and knew what love wasn't, and their disapproval cemented how right Jami and I were for each other. Jami's father had died of colon cancer when she was ten. Her mother, Denise, showed us nothing but support because she saw how happy her only daughter was with me. But it was more than that, I think.

Denise had once loved the way Jami and I loved, but her fiancé died in a car crash. She went half crazy before she pulled herself together and eventually married for circumstances—kindness, steadfastness, financial stability. She knew what going through the motions felt like, so when Jami came home and declared that after six years of being together with me, being happy with me, we were going to make it official and spend our lives together, Denise smiled and asked, "Where would you like me to send you on your honeymoon?"

We started in New Orleans, stayed at the Windsor Court, ate beignets at Café du Monde, drank Hurricanes at Pat O'Brien's, slurped down oysters at Antoine's, listened to jazz almost everywhere, laughed our asses off, then headed for the "other" Louisiana. We sampled boudin, a Cajun sausage, throughout the southern part of the state, listened to chanka-chank music in tin-roofed juke joints, fished for redfish in Calcasieu Lake and for sac-au-lait, as the Cajuns call crappie, in the Atchafalaya Basin. We had an amazing ten days, then went home to begin our lives together as husband and wife.

I was hired by the weekly *Malibu Surfside News*. I commuted from our fair-to-middling one-bedroom apartment in West L.A to the office in Malibu. Jami could only land work as a salesperson in a Westwood department store, so we hand-to-mouthed our existence, working hard during the week and enjoying Southern California's outdoor attractions on the weekends. Hiking, biking, and splashing in the surf are basically free, so we partook of these activities as much as we could. On the rare occasion that we argued, we argued about money. But our financial situation improved when I moved to a daily Santa Monica newspaper, then to the *Los Angeles Daily News*, and Jami eventually became a buyer for Nordstrom.

Money became less of a concern, but the plans we'd made for our lives required higher degrees of satisfaction and intellectual stimulation than our jobs were supplying. Frequently changing my beats wasn't enough for me to feel challenged or contented by my reporting jobs. Buying blouses for women who already had closets filled with the latest in haute couture didn't do it for Jami, either.

After reading a few of the short stories I was writing late at night to keep my synapses firing in a way I could tolerate, Jami suggested in an authoritative tone that I go back to school to earn my doctorate. "That way," she said, "on the off, off chance you don't 'make it' as a real writer—a novelist, a playwright, or perhaps a screenwriter—you'll become a professor, get to work on beautiful campuses, be surrounded by smart people, and immerse yourself in the work of the authors you love." She smiled at me. "And you'll still get to come home to wonderful me." I couldn't fault her logic, but I suggested that if we were going to go into debt, the two of us should both contribute to our indebted future. "I'll agree to apply to grad schools if you get your teaching credential, my dear." So that's what we did.

After meeting Jennifer on campus and having her confirm my suspicions about the dissertation I was foundering away on, I came home to Jami that night and explained to her the dissertation that wasn't. She pulled the box of notes and missteps from beneath the desk in the living room and told me to convert all of it into "the best damned essay ever written. To help inspire you creatively," she said, "I'm withholding my physical charms until you deliver a five-thousand-word article that meets my approval."

I knew better than to argue. The next day, Jami presented me with a present. As I opened it, she said, "It's likely symbolic because you write on a laptop, but I thought the occasion should be punctuated, so to speak, by something special."

I opened the card, which read:

My Dearest Jack,
Because I believe in you!
Love Always!
Your Biggest Fan,
J.D.

I unwrapped the present and opened the small, thin box. Inside was a Montblanc pen, black and silver, sleek, hefty, and understated.

"Thank you, my love. It's perfect. I won't let you down."

While Jami kept me fed and highly caffeinated, I wrote longhand with my new pen. For the next eleven days, I didn't work on my dissertation, concentrating my efforts instead on delivering a piece that *Esquire*, my favorite magazine, couldn't reject. I put years of aspiration into that story, which Jami had suggested I title, "Only the Winners." She read the piece and declared, "Not only will *Esquire* publish it, but you'll also be asked to expand it into a book."

Once again, she was right. The magazine piece was well received (the editors didn't like the title, changing it to "At All Costs," but they asked only for minor revisions to the copy), and I felt ecstatic for a week. Thanks to Jami and Jennifer, I could now look at all that time futzing with the *Baseball Encyclopedia* as time well spent. I bought two dozen copies of the issue when it came out a few months later, sent them to friends and relatives, added dance moves to my walk every so often, and made love to my wife frequently, the significant payday proving to be an aphrodisiac for both of us.

Two months after the issue hit newsstands, I was in the middle of a heated game of one-on-one with Mike in the Wooden Center on the UCLA campus. He was the better athlete and the better player, but my shot was falling that day, and I was four points from winning two games in a row, which would've been a first for me against Mike. He ratcheted up the smack talk to rattle me, but I'd believed myself invincible the last few months, and it appeared that belief was becoming reality. I had the ball at the top of the key when my cell phone rang. Mike told me not to answer it, but I walked to my gym bag on the sideline and picked up the phone. An editor at Simon & Schuster loved my *Esquire* story and wanted to know if I'd be interested in expanding it into a book. "We will, of course, negotiate the advance," she said. "Of course," I replied, forcing myself to finish the conversation before hanging up and shouting, "Yes!" at the top of my lungs.

"Dude, what the hell was that?"

"There's a chance I won't be teaching freshman English anymore."

"What, the book?"

"Yes, the book."

"Fuckin' A!"

"My thoughts exactly. I'm calling Jami."

"Go ahead, but don't think this game's over."

I dialed her cell and got no answer, then remembered she said she was going for a long bike ride. Neither Jami nor I answered our phones when we rode our bikes because nothing was more urgent than paying attention while riding. When we rode, we tucked our phones into a pocket in the back of our cycling jerseys and returned whichever calls we missed when we stopped riding. I left a giddy summation of the great news, told her I loved her more than words could express, and said I'd see her soon. Then I sank four shots in a row to beat Mike's sorry ass.

We headed into Westwood to celebrate. The first drinks hit our bellies at 1 p.m. By three o'clock, two bartenders had said we'd had enough and refused to serve us. At 3:12 my cell rang. It was Jami returning my call. I answered but heard an unfamiliar man's voice say, "Something very bad happened. I hit your wife with my van. An ambulance is on the way. She wants to talk to you." The stranger handed her the phone.

"I love you, Jack, you know that, right?"

"Yes, Jami, I know that, and I love you, too. Where are you? I'll be right there."

"On the coast, near the big rock we climbed that time. The pain's unbearable. I think my hips are broken. And my collarbone. My helmet shattered."

"Oh, baby. Save your energy. You'll be okay."

"Don't think I'm gonna make it."

"You'll make it, Jami, I promise. Tell that guy to tell the ambulance to call me and let me know which hospital they're taking you to."

"You know I love you, right, Jack?"

"Jami, stay positive. When I see you, I'll share some good news."

"The book?"

I could hear the ambulance's siren approaching. "Yes, and it's all because of you. Stay strong."

The siren cut into the conversation, and I heard determined voices. "I love you, Jami, and I'll see you soon. Please give the phone to someone."

"Hello?" asked another unfamiliar male voice a few seconds later.

"This is her husband. Where are you taking her?"

"Ventura County is closest. Know where it is?"

"Yes. Please take care of her."

"Do what I can," he said, without conviction.

Mike and I sprinted out of the bar toward his car, which was parked on campus about a mile away. After what seemed like forever, we reached the car, breathing hard, and he insisted that he drive because I wouldn't be able to concentrate. Had we been two drinks less drunk, we might have made a different decision. But we let panic and the alcohol decide for us, and we barely made it off campus before Mike saw the flashing red light in the rearview mirror. "Shit," he said as he pulled over. I didn't know what he was doing, so I yelled, "Go, go, go." Then I figured out what was happening, and I knew we were screwed.

The officer insisted Mike step out of the car and run though sobriety tests. "Look," I yelled at the officer, "we're drunk, we admit it. We'll serve as much time as you want when this is done, but take us to the hospital."

"Settle down, sir, or you'll be charged, too."

"My wife is dying, you prick."

He looked at me sternly and said, "I've heard them all, so save your breath."

I jumped out of the passenger-side door intending to pummel the bastard, but Mike deftly stepped around the cop and bear-hugged me.

"Jack, we'll take a hit, and Jami will recover. Settle down, or this will turn ugly." Mike had had more than a few traffic stops, so he knew how easily they could go bad.

"Okay, for you and Jami, I won't brain this asshole."

Had we hailed a cab, and had that cab managed to negotiate through traffic over the 405, then north on the 101 for fifty more miles at record speed, I probably would have been able to say goodbye to my wife while looking into her eyes. Instead, Mike was being booked, and I was being threatened again with a drunk-and-disorderly charge when Jami was pronounced dead at 6:15 p.m. on March 26.

She'd been right about the broken pelvis and collarbone. She hadn't mentioned her broken left arm and couldn't have known how severe her head injury was. I wasn't at her side to provide comfort, to let her know she was my world. Had I been there holding her hand, looking into her eyes, and reassuring her she was going to pull through, for us, for our children, could she have made it? The power of love has been known to work miracles, to deliver results that transcend the bounds of medical knowledge. If I'd looked into her eyes, could I have saved her? And how might doing so have helped me?

The driver of the van, Hugo Gonzalez, was a carpet installer, a stone-cold sober family man driving home to Oxnard. He reached to change a CD (trying to put in "Johnny Cash–Greatest Hits," he told me later), when he veered three feet right across the white line onto the shoulder and hit Jami with the right-front panel of his Dodge Ram 2500 van. He heard a thump, and, in his side mirror, saw her tumbling off the asphalt into the dirt and rocks near the road. He stopped and ran back to her.

"I knew she was bad, and so did she," he told me at his arraignment for a vehicular manslaughter charge. "She kept trying to grab me like this, but her left arm didn't work, and what she kept saying was, 'Tell Jack I love him. Tell him I love him and never give up.'" He put his hands on my shoulders and looked in my eyes.

"I'm fifty-six years old," he said. "I've been married twice. I even loved one of them very much. But never in my life have I seen anyone more sure of what she was saying."

He was trying to be supportive, to apologize, to tell me how lucky I'd been to have spent time with the incomparable Jami Donahue. But what I heard was that I'd failed to save the only woman I'd loved, and I'd now be sentenced to a life of impossible expectations. No one would ever be Jami. I wanted to hit him because I knew he was right.

CHAPTER TWELVE

After I'd replaced the rotors and distributor caps, Game and I headed to Compton in the Land Rover with the kayak secured to the rack on top. The Saturday-morning traffic along the coast was light. While Game and I talked sports, I remembered I'd forgotten to check his wound that morning. I asked him how his shoulder was, and he shrugged and said, "Awwight." Considering my complete lack of sleep and the causes thereof, the drive was more pleasant than I'd anticipated because Game's enthusiasm for sports was as intense as mine was at his age.

I pulled into the small parking lot in front of the Wave Skimmer shop in an industrial part of Compton, south of Oakville. We got out of the SUV, and I removed the straps that held the yellow kayak to the roof rack. We hoisted the kayak from the roof, carefully avoiding the protruding spear shaft, then we carried the boat to the entrance. To the left of the large, ocean-blue sign that said WAVE SKIMMER above the front door was mounted an orange one-person kayak, tilted forward, as though it was riding a wave. We set the kayak down and entered the shop.

A twenty-something, overly muscled dude with a buzz-cut and a scraggly goatee dyed bright purple nodded, dropped his cowboy boots from the counter, and swung himself upright on his stool. He wore a black sleeveless t-shirt emblazoned with the Ultimate Fighting Championship logo, and he sported a tattoo of a lime-green iguana on his left bicep. On his right was a red tattoo that read: 88. I recognized it for what it was—a symbol of hatred. It stood for the eighth letter of the alphabet, H, as in HH, as in Heil Hitler. More subtle than a swastika, but I wouldn't bet against his having one of those emblazoned somewhere out of sight on his body. His black cowboy boots appeared to be made from diamondback rattlesnakes. I bet myself that when he opened his mouth, one of his teeth would be gold.

The retail operation appeared to be minimal because the small store only had room for three kayaks, standing upright in a corner. Obviously, the customers who purchase thousands of Wave Skimmers each year bought them in big sporting goods chains such as Bass Pro Shops, Dick's Sporting Goods, and REI, or online. The floor of the shop looked as though it hadn't been swept that week, and the counter had balled-up wrappers from Carl's Jr. resting next to a stack of Wave Skimmer brochures.

"Help you?" the clerk asked in a couldn't-care-less tone. When he spoke, I lost my bet, although a front tooth did look dead.

"Yes. I stupidly put the tip of a spear through the front of my two-man, and I was told you guys could make the repair here at the factory."

"Well, yeah," he said, eyeing Game, "we can fix it, but this ain't the factory."

"No? What's that in back?" I looked through the swinging saloon-style doors at workers hunched over slabs of molded plastic in various colors. The two workers I could see wore surgical masks to keep them from inhaling the particulates kicked up by the drill and saw I heard whirring. The uninterrupted buzz forced us to speak over the top of the noise.

"We deal with handles, seats, cargo nets, hatches, fishing accessories here—and repairs—but the factory's in Mexico."

I nodded and motioned toward the door. "The boat's outside," I said. He stepped around the counter, gave Game a wide berth, and went through the door and looked at the damage to the kayak.

"No biggie," he said. He squatted, grabbed the shaft of the spear with his thick right hand, and braced his left hand against the boat, locking his left arm and taking a deep breath. He grunted loudly as he yanked and twisted the spear at the same time, his huge forearm and absurdly overdeveloped bicep noticeably straining. Nothing appeared to happen. He pulled a lighter from his pocket, lit it, and held the flame beneath the protruding shaft, letting the flame melt the plastic for ten seconds. He pocketed the lighter, grabbed the spear, grunted, and pulled again. A high-pitched squeal emanated from the boat as he pulled the shaft from the plastic.

"There you go," he said, handing me the shaft. Looking at the whole, he said, "A couple days, a few bucks, you'll be back in the water, no problem."

"Sounds good. Should we carry it through there?" I asked, gesturing toward the front door.

"Easier if you go in the side door, since it's a two-man. The turn's too tight through the front. Personally knocked a thing or two off the counter."

He and I reentered the shop. I filled out the paperwork for the repair and thanked him. I went back outside. Game picked up the front end, I picked up the back, and as we rounded the corner, Game said, "Now that a racist."

"Where do you think he hides his hood?"

"A fella can hate a guy like that on principle, but what up with that sorry-ass goatee?"

"Oh, come on, bet it works wonders with the ladies."

"Man, that dude be getting any, Stephen King think her up."

I laughed. We set the kayak down next to the side door, which was ajar. I pushed the door open and stepped inside. The power-tool din made me understand why both employees were wearing orange foam earplugs. I waved the yellow work order at a stocky Latino wearing a navy T-shirt, filthy jeans, and tan work boots. After looking at me for three seconds, he killed the power on the jigsaw he was using to cut a hatch in the front of an orange one-man Skimmer. He pulled the white mask down below his chin, got out of the crouch he'd been in while using the jigsaw, set it down, and headed toward me. He glanced at the work order, nodded, and motioned to the other employee. They walked past me, stepped outside, and quickly reappeared, carrying the kayak across the room, and leaning it upright against the wall at the end of a line of five other kayaks—two orange, two yellow, and one sky blue. I nodded my thanks to the two of them, who were oblivious to the gesture.

I walked outside. Game was gone.

My stomach jumped. I rounded the corner and looked both ways down the alley but saw nothing that hinted at which way he'd gone. And he'd likely gone at a run. Oakville is only a few miles north of Compton, and he could be back among the MLKs quickly.

"Shit," I yelled. I could pick either direction, having a fifty-fifty chance of guessing correctly but almost no chance of catching him. He was a fast, athletic teenager with a head start. I was a forty-two-year-old former athlete who'd kept himself in decent shape but who never had blazing speed. The Land Rover would increase my pace, obviously, but not my likelihood of finding him because he'd know I could follow him easily on the main streets, so he'd avoid them.

Game swaggered around the corner. I read his gait as his way of saying I'd messed up. He could've been—and maybe should've been—gone.

When he got close, he said, "Ain't much of a bodyguard, Jack."

"Are you hurt?"

"No."

"Then I've done my job."

"Say it again, maybe it be true."

"Why'd you come back?"

"Wrong question. Question is, 'Why'd you run?'"

We walked toward the car.

"If you say so. Why'd you run?"

"Saw the van."

"Which van?"

"From the other night. The white one from when we jacked the coke."

"With the white guy selling? You sure?"

"Told you the back all messed up. You step inside, that piece o' shit drive down the alley, and I saw the smashed back after it passed. Could be any van with a jacked right side, so I ran after it to see if it the same punk driver."

"And?"

"Didn't catch him. Gotta figure it him, right? I mean, you think he loan that nasty ride to people so they can tour Compton?"

"Not likely. Could've been another beaten-up white van. Gotta be others around here."

"Yeah. Here and Oakville—all the same place. Barely got police forces. Clowns couldn't find their dicks with help from a hooker and a microscope."

That he would bring up the cops surprised me because our next stop was going to be the Oakville Police Station.

Game wasn't pleased when I told him our destination, but he told me how to get to the station. When I parked in one of the spaces marked VISITOR, he didn't get out of the car. I walked to his side. He cracked the door and said, "Ain't going. Do what you gotta do."

"Game, I can't let you stay here alone."

"Didn't run when I had the chance. Ain't going nowhere now."

"Then why stay in the car?"

"Can't expect me to sit in a room full of law." It wasn't a question. I waited for him to explain. After five seconds, he did. "Cops didn't do shit to find the killers of Lawrence and Terrell. Just more Black-on-Black gang murders, so why bother, right?"

"I'm not saying you're wrong, but how does their apathy toward finding the killers have anything to do with you getting out of my car?"

"Just let me sit here. I don't know what I'd do surrounded by five-oh."

The Oakville Police Station was in an immense limestone building that impressed from the outside, at least from a distance. The architect, I'm guessing, thought that the arched entryway, above which flew the U.S., California, and Oakville flags, aptly captured the gravitas of the proceedings within the building. And it once might have, but the overflowing trash can on the limestone walkway, the weeds growing through the seams of the stairs, and the grime smeared across the heavy front door and its handle suggested that the officers inside the building had bigger concerns than the appearance of gravitas.

I flashed my P.I. license to the desk clerk, who was unimpressed. Officer Moncrief—a doughy white guy with a bald head and jowls that looked like a kielbasa necklace—sneered at me as though I'd just proffered a used Kleenex.

"I'm here to inquire about yesterday's shooting in the park," I said and slid my license into the tray that he released through the Plexiglas he sat behind.

"I'm here 'cause I didn't get into law school," Officer Moncrief said, studying my license as though it could conceal an eternal truth. He flipped the license back in the tray and pushed the tray toward me.

"To whom should I speak?"

"Grammar your thing or something?"

"Is there an officer here who could answer a few questions about yesterday's shooting?"

"Probably plenty, but not if you're asking."

Attempting to tamp down my burgeoning anger, I looked away from Moncrief. On the bench behind me and to my right sat an older Asian man whose soiled clothes suggested he hadn't slept indoors in a while. I nodded to him, and he mouthed the words "Screw 'im." I smiled, nodded again, and turned toward the officer.

"Have I offended you, Officer Moncrief?"

"No," he said. I waited for something more, but nothing came.

"I'm a taxpaying citizen, and I have a few questions I'd like to ask."

"We've established that, and now you're just taking up my time."

"Word is that the Oakville force is so corrupt that perhaps I've breached protocol by not offering you a bribe. Please forgive my impropriety." I heard laughter from behind me.

"You're trespassing," Moncrief said, "and I'm beginning to feel threatened by your aggressive behavior." I turned toward the man on the bench, as if to say, "You're my witness," but he shrugged, turned away, and put his index fingers in his ears.

"Out of curiosity," I said to Moncrief, "if someone knew why the shooting happened, and if that same someone knew who, generally, the shooters were, what should that someone do?"

Moncrief continued to stare at me.

"Guy's a moron," I said to Game when I returned.

"You think? You needed to interview a pig to find out he a pig? You call that investigating?"

"Confirming what one suspects is, in fact, a form of investigation. In this case, I'm betting the cadet I spoke with last night at the park let it be known there was a P.I. snooping around—and that could, almost by definition, make the department look bad."

Game stared at me for a few seconds, looking pensive. I waited. Nothing.

"What is it?" I asked.

"Thinking."

I nodded and waited for nearly a minute before Game said, "Ain't getting nowhere doing this your way. Cops ain't even gonna try. Buy me some Popeye's, then we do this for real."

"Meaning?"

"Meaning a five-piece with dirty rice, a biscuit, large Coke, then we worry 'bout dessert."

CHAPTER THIRTEEN

Game's plan consisted of heading to the MLK crib in downtown Oakville, asking questions until we learned something useful about the shooting, and improvising our approach from there.

"So," I said, after swallowing a forkful of dirty rice, "you have no more of a plan than I do."

"You just got ignored by a cop. Least the people I question will have answers."

"Okay, presuming I agree to interview your buddies—what information do you expect them to cough up? They're out there looking for revenge, and I'm guessing you're persona non grata with them about now."

"What's that mean?"

"It's Latin for a person who's not appreciated. I'm guessing your buddies accuse you of abandoning them in their time of need. You're likely on the outs."

"Ain't like that. They know I been kidnapped, so we cool. But I'm gonna ask questions, see if they know something they don't even know they know, then you and your license can figure out what's important. It called investigating. You should try it sometime."

"Instead, I'll try this," I said, snatching his biscuit from his tray and taking a bite out of it.

"Man, I gonna—"

"What? Buy your own?"

His face took on an odd look, and I thought he was searching for a retort, but he leaned in close and whispered, "Don't turn around. da Posse just rolled up. O.G.s Meet you at your car. I'm going out the back."

He stood and glided toward the exit farthest from the door that da Uptown Posse members had parked in front of. Thirty seconds later, two lanky men in their late-twenties—both wearing black 'do rags under red St. Louis Cardinals hats, white t-shirts, Nike basketball shoes, and baggy jeans—slipped into the booth next to mine. I knew enough about gangs to know that O.G. stands for original gangster—longtime members of high rank.

I was less subtle about my once-over than I should've been, and the two bangers stared at me. I nodded and finished the last of the biscuit. I washed the biscuit down with my Diet Coke, and I hoped I hadn't made too large an impression.

I wiped a napkin across my mouth, stood without looking at them, threw out my trash, and went out the exit through which they had just entered. I walked around the building to my car, where I found Game crouched near the rear passenger-side door. We got in, and he quickly released the seat, dropping himself below the level of the window.

"Comfortable?"

"Long as I outta sight. Those O.G. in there, not soldiers. You in the wrong league here, so we play this how we got to. Plan's changed."

"What's that mean?"

"Best you don't know, but I gotta make a phone call you can't listen to."

"Nothing illegal, Game."

"Right, you will do nothing illegal. You're a professional with a license and a rich, famous, hot girlfriend you don't even like, so you ain't gonna risk nothin'. You gonna go back inside to get a to-go order or refill your drink so I can make a call."

"Why don't we just follow them when they leave?"

"Ain't going nowhere—I let the air out their tires."

"Great. This is your plan?"

"No, my plan needs a phone call, so get out."

I hesitated but realized maybe he was right. I wasn't getting anywhere and wasn't likely to because the police wouldn't cooperate, and I didn't know anything about this world. I didn't have any leads, other than one gangbanger having told me that other gangbangers were responsible for the shooting. And as much as I promised myself I'd make a good-faith effort to solve the park shooting, my real obligation was to keep Game safe. If the shooting wasn't solved, it would be chalked up to yet another inevitable Black-on-Black killing, another casualty of the American Dream. Would the uncleared case bother the authorities? No. I was exhausted and making no progress, so I got out of the car. I headed into the restaurant to buy Mike and Rachelle lunch.

The two Posse members were still eating their dirty rice and chicken when I stepped to the counter and ordered two three-piece meals. As I waited for the food, I wondered if I'd just lost control of my life, but then I remembered the sham of a life I pretended to have control over. I hoped Game knew what he was doing because we could use all the help we could get. The two bangers finished their meals, left the trash on the table, and slowly walked out.

When I arrived at my car, I surreptitiously glanced across the parking lot at the cherried, metallic-red Impala the Posse members were standing next to. They would probably have called a low-level Posse member to change a single flat, but no one carries two spares, so they were going to be there awhile. I got into my car, and Game said from his reclined seat, "We good. Let's roll."

"Not going to tell me, right?"

"Man, you can be stupid. Why I tell you to leave so I can make a call if I tell you what I said later? Just trust me."

We pulled to the curb in front of Mike's house, a well-maintained two-bedroom with a portable basketball backboard and hoop in the driveway. Mike's 1972 convertible electric-blue Corvette Stingray—with a vanity license plate that read: LOOM—was probably in his garage.

Rachelle was at work that Saturday, so she didn't get to see that her son was okay, but as I watched Mike inhale the Popeye's (after he told me I looked like hell), Game called her. I heard him go on and on about how ridiculous Amanda's house was, and how he'd seen her naked, and how he'd gone kayaking at night, and how I was one messed up dude to be sad with everything I had in my life. Mike shouted at Game, through a mouthful of chicken, to show me some respect, but the kid was right, although not polite to impart his amateur psychological assessment within earshot of me.

I shushed Mike and said in a quiet voice, "I might've blown it. I let him make a phone call to his running mates so he could hatch a plan." Mike looked surprised but didn't say anything. He waited me out.

"I think we're going to be stymied because the gangs aren't going to go public with what happened, and the cops are less than worthless. They're stonewalling, if not covering up. Game saw an opportunity to do things his way because Oakville isn't my turf."

"When in Rome, baby," Mike said, wiping his mouth and putting his Adidas on his wooden coffee table, next to an issue of *Sports Illustrated*.

"I can't endorse vigilante justice, Mike."
"Do you know what the plan is?"
"No."
"Then you aren't endorsing shit."
"The phrase 'aiding and abetting' mean anything to you?"
"Weren't they a Ska band in the nineties?"
"I'm serious."

"No, you're kidding yourself. You're applying a moral and legal code that exists only in your head to an environment in which children die because they're wearing the wrong color clothes. Or because they're standing on a corner minding their own business and get hit by a stray. Or because a cop's having a bad day. Do you think you could stop whatever Game has put in motion?"

"No. I don't even know what it is."

"Exactly, so how can you be responsible for it? You are neither aiding and abetting nor an accessory after the fact. At least not yet. As of this minute, you are a friend of mine who's doing my female companion and me a large favor by looking after Game. Nowhere in our agreement did we say it was your duty to prevent Game from making a phone call. To that end, you allowed him to make a call. For all you know, he called his broker. Did you see him dial? No. Did you overhear his conversation? No. So, stop acting from a position of privilege, and start living the way most everyone else does. When the system doesn't work—or because the system works as it does—people do what they have to do. Ride this one out until you bump up against something that truly concerns you, something you can't overlook."

"Ain't on you, Jack," Game said from behind me. I hadn't noticed he'd stopped talking on the phone in the other room, and I didn't know how much he'd heard. "You, as they say on *Law & Order*, just a innocent bystander. And a bodyguard."

"I've kept you alive for one night, so my place in heaven is assured."

"Believe what you gotta believe," Game said.

"Time to go," I said. "Say hello to Rachelle for me, Mike, and tell her Game is safe, though a pain in the ass."

"Yeah, as if she doesn't know that."

Exhaustion overtook me on the drive home. I'd been awake for about thirty-four hours, and I was sure my lack of sleep contributed to my giving in to Game. I was so tired that I almost asked him to drive, but I set the AC to high and blasted the Rolling Stones.

Let it bleed, indeed.

When we arrived at the house, I parked in the driveway and decided not to disable the cars again because Game hadn't run when he'd had the chance. I opened the front door and saw Amanda hoisting a bottle of Crystal to her lips and chugging. My bet was she waited to hear my key hit the lock before she raised the bottle, so I'd get the full effect of her acting out.

She looked gorgeous, which was frustrating. Someone deliberately self-destructing shouldn't be able to grace the cover of a magazine. It's easier to work up the requisite concern, or loathing, depending on the circumstances, for a drunk if he or she is disheveled. But Amanda was wearing a pair of jeans that she knew created stirrings in me and a spaghetti-strap, tan silk top that I'd purchased for her. And she looked as though she'd just been touched up by a makeup artist. Knowing Amanda, she probably had been. She was provoking a confrontation, but I wouldn't give her the satisfaction. Even if I hadn't been wiped out, I think I would've ignored her attempt to start a fight. Because I was exhausted, however, I didn't even nod hello.

I turned to Game, said, "I need sleep," and headed for one of the guest rooms and locked the door behind me. It was a little after 4 p.m., and I felt as though I could sleep through the night, although I suspected I shouldn't.

Before I was fully undressed, however, Amanda pounded on the door and screamed obscenities at me. She was rich, famous, beautiful, and petulant, and she almost always got what she wanted. But she'd told me long ago that one of the things she loved about me was that I was not a pushover, that I would stand up to her and tell her the truth when no one else would, no matter the cost. So, in the name of silently speaking my truth, I stuffed earplugs in my ears, turned on the white-noise machine, put a pillow over my head, and let the din drift into the background. I don't know how long she pounded and screamed because I fell asleep within minutes—and dreamed of Jami.

I rarely did that anymore because my psyche deemed images of her too painful, pushing them from my unconscious mind the way I tried to shove her out of my waking thoughts. But in my dream that afternoon we were riding a tandem bike along the coast, a gentle breeze nudging clouds across the gorgeous sky. As we rode north on PCH toward where she'd been killed, she shouted witticisms from behind me, making me laugh. I pedaled along, a smile on my face, but then I looked over my shoulder—and she was gone, as was the back of the bike. Somehow, without benefit of a back wheel, I pulled to the shoulder, confused, then awoke in a cold sweat.

After I realized where I was, I glanced at the clock: 12:20 a.m. I'd obviously needed the sleep. I pulled on some shorts and felt refreshed. But then I looked in every room in the house and learned that Game and Amanda were gone.

CHAPTER FOURTEEN

I checked the beach but couldn't tell if there were fresh footprints leading away from the stairs. I ran to the garage, where I found only the Porsche. I guessed Amanda had taken the Land Rover because she would be driving drunk, and the large vehicle could run over pedestrians without losing momentum. And Game took the BMW because the Berretta was under the driver's seat and the Mossberg shotgun was in the trunk.

"You idiot," I shouted, hating myself for not disabling the cars again. Amanda could be wrapped around a telephone pole because I was too lazy, or too trusting, or too stupid to remove the rotors a second time, and Game could be shooting teenagers and cops with my weapons. I cursed at myself again before I ran into the house, got dressed, secured another handgun, and grabbed the keys to the Porsche.

I drove quickly toward Santa Monica on PCH, breaking the speed limit but not setting any records because I didn't know where I was going. Plus, urgency might not have been necessary—and perhaps was to be avoided—because I didn't know if I wanted to get caught up in Game's plan, whatever it was. Therefore, I drove rapidly toward a destination I hoped never to reach.

Amanda might only have crept along Broad Beach Road to a friend's house, although I didn't see the Land Rover in any of the driveways in the neighborhood, so that wasn't likely. If she hadn't been picked up for DWI and wasn't sobering up in a holding cell, she was likely ensconced in the Loews Santa Monica or in the Hotel Bel Air. I figured I'd rule out the holding-cell by stopping by the Malibu/Lost Hills Sheriff's Station on Agoura Road in Calabasas, which required a trip through Malibu Canyon. The way the last day and a half had gone, I surprised myself by remembering to remove the gun from my jacket before I entered the building.

"Well, if it isn't Jackie Drake," Billy Denton said as I approached the desk. The burly, bald sergeant and I had had more than a few run-ins over the years. He was proof the department didn't discriminate against the intellectually challenged.

"Good to see you, Billy. You doing something different with your hair?"

"No. Just my natural charm you're noticing."

"Must be, Sarge. Any DWIs tonight?"

"It's Saturday night in Malibu, Drake. What do you think?"

"Any that might be of interest to me?"

"Amanda blotto again, that it? Want me to call *The Enquirer*?"

"Actually, it's been too long since we've chatted, and I miss you, Denton."

"You always were full of shit, Drake. But all hatred aside, I'm sorry to hear about Cerveris. Musta got in too deep."

I stared at him for a few seconds. It seemed out of character for Denton to show sympathy, especially to me. A normal, healthy human would express condolences to someone who'd just lost a friend, but I'd never known Denton to be anything but broken. Was he telling me something? Did he know Chris hadn't killed himself? Or did Denton mention Chris' ostensible suicide to rub salt in my wounds while I searched for an intoxicated movie star?

"Thank you for your sympathy," I said, then asked, "Are you telling me something about Chris' death? I know he didn't kill himself, and he didn't deal drugs. What do you know, Denton? Is the department covering something up? Are you?"

Part of me hoped he'd react violently. The confrontation wouldn't end well for me, but I'd have an outlet for the emotions roiling through me, causing me to question everything. Unfortunately—and luckily—Denton didn't take the bait.

He said, "Another deputy who didn't know you're such a simpering pansy would feel threatened by you, Drake, and would kick your ass. But I know you're a moron whipped by a whore drug addict, so I'll go easy on you."

Despite almost lashing out, I didn't take his bait, either. My anger briefly turned to rage, but I rode out the emotion and calmed myself. After shaking my head at him and walking out, I decided to turn my anger into determination. I backed out of the lot and headed down Malibu Canyon, promising to make the changes I had to make to once again be the man Jami had loved.

Or maybe I could at least become a man I could learn to like.

As I drove toward Loews Santa Monica, intending to look for Amanda before I scoured Oakville for Game, I thought Denton had a point about my lack of intellectual heft. If I'd been smart enough to have LoJack installed on the BMW, I'd know where Game was. Or at least I could find my car.

I pulled in front of Loews, told the valet I'd be back in a minute, then asked the pretty, young, blond clerk at the front desk if J.T. National had checked in tonight. She flashed a brilliant smile in case I was Amanda's agent and was seeking new talent. She nodded and said, "Yes, sir. Would you like me to ring her room?"

J.T. National was the name Amanda used most frequently to

check in anonymously. It was a bastardization of Joshua Tree National Park, a fascinating outdoor wonderland in the high desert a few hours from L.A. where Amanda and I camped occasionally—a place to relax anonymously.

Had Amanda not wanted me to track her down, she could've used any other fake name. Of course, she was probably lucky to have driven PCH and made it to the hotel in one piece, so covering her tracks was not likely high on her list. In fact, knowing her as I did, I was certain she wanted me to find her, otherwise she'd have gone to another hotel, one I didn't know she loved to stay in. Running from me only to make sure I found her was the kind of bullshit I'd put up with for seven years.

"No, please don't bother her. Just checking to see that she made it here safely."

"Yes, she did, sir, and it was my great pleasure to check her in. I've always been a very big fan."

I wanted to remind her that J.T. National had no fans, but she was just another kid hoping to make the contact that would launch her career so that she, too, could one day check into an overpriced hotel under a pseudonym while inebriated and rich. I thanked her, retrieved the Porsche, and knew that finding Game could prove to be nearly impossible.

But once again I was wrong.

The last place he would be, I figured, would be at his mother's house, and at least I got that right. I slowly drove down Rachelle's street and didn't see the BMW or any lights on in her house. Of course, it was 2:20 a.m., so plenty of houses had no lights on, but Game wouldn't have stopped by the house simply to go to sleep. Game wasn't likely to be inside, and neither was anyone else.

I drove the quiet streets of Oakville slowly. Only two all-night taco stands, a diner, and a few 7-Elevens were open. In twenty minutes of driving, I saw fewer than a dozen moving vehicles, none of them owned by Amanda or me. Three of them were police cars. At a red light, an Oakville Police Department patrol car pulled alongside, and the driver stared at me. I don't know if he was worried about securing probable cause for a stop—because driving a Porsche through Oakville at nearly 3 a.m. was proof that I was either up to no good or was about to be the victim of a crime—but he decided his glare was bracing enough to scare me straight. He drove next to me until I turned into the parking lot of a 7-Eleven. The cop drove on, so I sat there for a minute, then headed in the other direction.

Just as I started to believe my search was pointless, I thought to drive by Crispus Attucks Park. I didn't know what I hoped to find, but I drove down Mallory slowly. The park was quiet—no cops or news crews, and someone had removed the crime-scene tape. I turned left at the corner and saw my BMW parked at the curb.

I parked and walked toward the driver's side. The door opened and Game said, "Where you been, man? Called you three times."

I patted my empty left pants pocket and realized that in my rush to leave the house in pursuit of Amanda and Game, I'd forgotten my phone.

"When'd you call?" I was glad to have found Game but pissed he'd stolen my car.

"I don't know, 'bout a hour and a half, then again and again. Been sitting here wondering if I gotta do everything myself." He rubbed the knuckles on his right hand with his left palm.

"You stole my car."

"Didn't steal shit, Jack. You asleep, Amanda gone, and my boys text me the plan worked. Been waiting to hear what a professional do in a case like this."

"A case like what?" I admitted that not only did I not have a right to be pissed at Game, but I also respected him. If pressed, I'd admit I liked the kid.

He said, "Follow me." The only illumination came from the nearly full moon and two streetlights—about a hundred yards from each other—that had not been shot out, as the others had. I followed him across the cracked blacktop toward the four basketball courts. As we approached a court on the left, I noticed in the limited light that there was something unusual about the stanchion nearest us. The pole that supported the backboard and rim had a dark mass at its base. When we came within forty feet of the court, the mass began to transform into definable shapes.

On either side of the pole, handcuffed to it and squatting in what appeared to be uncomfortable positions, were two young Black males. Game opened the flashlight app on his phone and quickly waved it near their faces. They looked scared and pissed off. I leaned in close enough to see their faces and noticed they'd been beaten—enough to be bloody and swollen. They both wore sagging jeans and white t-shirts. One had a red bandana tied around his right biceps, and the other wore a red 'do rag on his head. The Nike running shoes on the feet of one of them and the work boots on the feet of the other stood in a puddle of urine.

Game said, "Here the punks that shot me."

CHAPTER FIFTEEN

I walked about twenty steps away so the captives couldn't hear us. Game hesitated, then followed me but said nothing. I waited. Still nothing.

He said, "Don't ask. You know nothing and ain't even here, come down to it."

"You had the guys in Popeye's snatched, then traded them for these two, who obviously aren't worth much, just button men."

"Ain't *The Godfather*. This Oakville. But, yeah, these busters ain't shit. They called soldiers or shooters." He pushed out his chest and rubbed his knuckles, revealing he was the one who'd hit them.

I don't think I'd hit guys handcuffed to a pole, but I'd never been shot, then had the opportunity to exact revenge on the shooters. And I wasn't sixteen. I didn't mention the beating.

I asked, "The plan is we disappear, then make an anonymous call to the police?"

"Something like that."

"This scheme of yours rates a success in your mind?" A big dog barked in the distance.

"You say you gonna solve the shooting, but don't. Then I serve the bitches up in no time. Case closed. Looks like I should have a license."

"I'll admit your plan was efficient. The MLKs work quickly. If my hunch is correct, no one else was shot while enacting the plan. The two sides negotiated. Very adult. You obviously snatched the right two guys."

"Know all this. Time to grab me a shorty and get busy."

"Okay, tough guy. What your plan fails to take into consideration is that you've turned murders—which, I admit, would not likely have been solved by the local authorities—into a federal crime. Kidnapping is federal, unlike homicide. Those two punks didn't cuff themselves to that pole, and after standing in their own piss, they might be more willing to talk to authorities than you think. But I'm betting Oakville's finest, even while beating them, won't get them to sell out anyone.

"The Feds, however, may offer these guys immunity or knock their sentences way down. If they mention the hijacked drug deal, and the Feds decide to go after the higher ups, these two could get minimal time, and the MLKs could be looking at federal kidnapping charges."

Game glanced over his right shoulder at the guys squatting in the distance. I didn't like us standing in the park near bangers who'd been kidnapped, even if we were in the dark. Anyone looking our way probably wouldn't see the odd shapes at the base of the pole or see us. But I still didn't like being there.

"What you saying?" Game finally asked.

"I'm not sure. I'm just clarifying some points you may have overlooked in the Popeye's parking lot."

"They ain't gonna talk, for real. You get pinched, do your time, stand up, be strong, come out with major props. They'll be heroes. Then they ain't punks no more."

"I understand. But how silent would they be if the Feds sprung them immediately?"

"Very silent, 'cause they be dead. The only leverage they got is the set. They give up someone in da Posse, or the supplier or whatever, you think da Posse gonna wonder where that information came from? Gonna be pretty obvious, right? These busters will be dead by morning, painfully dead, and they know it. They dumb as shit 'cause they in da Posse, but they ain't that dumb."

"It's your world, so I'll take your word for it. But can the police make a case against these guys for the shooting? Because they won't confess, what evidence do the cops have on these guys? There probably aren't any prints on the guns that already came up stolen, as did the getaway car. All they have are the witnesses, who were running or ducking, trying not to get shot. Any decent defense attorney could discredit the shoe prints as being inconclusive. It's a public park, so they could have visited it anytime, and there's nothing illegal about that. Or the lawyer could say his clients weren't wearing them that day. And do you think anyone who saw them do the shooting would come forward? Not a chance."

"You starting to see how things play out in the 'Ville."

I looked at Game, confused. If I understood him, we were just spinning our wheels.

"Meaning?"

"Meaning it all one big joke. Turning these clowns over to the Oakville pigs a waste of taxpayer money. But what ain't?"

"'I can't go on. I'll go on.'"

"What's that?"

"One of my favorite quotes by a writer named Samuel Beckett. Sums up pretty much most of life."

"This from a man who lives in a beach mansion with a fine movie star."

"Let's get out of here. We'll call the cops from a burner."

I locked the Porsche, and we got into the BMW. If the cop who eyed me from his patrol car earlier saw the same Porsche still prowling Oakville in the wee hours, he'd light me up, and who knows what fresh hell he'd contrive?

I pulled away and said, "I don't understand something. Why is it okay for you to beat those guys but not to kill them? They're sworn enemies, you're a bad-ass gunslinger, and you've never avenged the deaths of your brothers. You had your chance. The cops just as easily could've found two dead guys at the base of that pole, and the park shooting would effectively be solved, without wasting taxpayer money. Because the cops weren't likely to solve the shooting, they'd be even less likely to solve these murders, if they even pretended to try."

"All white people think like you, or you dumber than most?"

We were rounding a corner when he asked the question. I considered backhanding him across the face. My frustration with all of it—Amanda's drinking, Chris' murder, and what I believed to be Jami's contempt for the man I'd become since her death—almost got the better of me. I caught myself before my hand moved two inches, but Game saw it leave the wheel.

"You gonna hit me 'cause I break your balls? That how it is? I coulda split, got a gun, and shot you when you found me, but didn't 'cause I thought we almost like friends, man. But you been wanting to hit me all this time?"

"No, I haven't. I'm sorry. And, yes, we're almost like friends. I don't know where that came from." But that was a lie. I knew exactly where it came from. We're products of our upbringings.

I drove toward the 7-Eleven I'd stopped at earlier.

"I miss Jami, my friend was murdered, Amanda's drinking, and I'm disappointed in myself. I'm not dealing with any of it well. Again, I apologize."

"We cool. Kinda know what it like. Terrell and Lawrence gone. Make you do crazy shit sometime."

I pulled into the 7-Eleven parking lot. A Latino man wearing torn, dirty, tan dress pants and what was once a gray overcoat—but no shirt or shoes—was lying to the left of the front door. When I parked the car in a space near him, he saluted us from the ground. I got out, returned his salute, and walked inside. I bought a burner phone, then went outside.

The unhoused man pulled himself nearly to a seated position, then raised his arms to protect himself as I approached.

"No, my friend. I'm not here to hurt you. You can relax."

He looked relieved, then smiled. Up close, he was much younger than I'd thought he was from a distance. Maybe twenty-eight. The last few years appeared to have been very difficult. Maybe all of them.

"What's your name?"

"Enrique Acevedo. What's yours?"

"Jack Drake."

"Like a duck."

"Yes, like a duck." My surname derives from the Old Norse word dreki, meaning dragon, but I didn't think Enrique was up for a discussion of etymology. Or maybe I wasn't.

"I'd like to do something for you, Enrique." His happy expression changed to one of apprehension. There's always a catch, a scam, a hustle. He knew at least one of them was coming.

"No, don't worry. I'm not asking you to do anything but take care of yourself, treat yourself well."

His expression changed to confusion. Had to be a catch because there's always a catch, especially when some white dude in a BMW starts telling you how to live at 4:30 in the morning.

"No drugs. If you have to buy booze, buy only as much as you usually drink every day."

"Okay. Whatever you say. I don't do drugs anymore."

"That's good. Break the large bills in a bank, not in front of other customers in here," I said, pointing with my chin to the 7-Eleven.

"Got it."

I turned away from him and the entrance, took out my wallet, folded five one-hundred-dollar bills in half, then folded a twenty around them. Before leaving the house, I had grabbed cash I'd stashed because I didn't know who I'd have to bribe—or have to tip far too much—when I found Amanda in the middle of yet another self-induced disaster.

I palmed the bills and handed them to him as I shook his hand, attempting to conceal my action from the clerk who was glaring at us from inside the store.

"This is a gift, Enrique. Open your hand after we've left and when that clerk isn't looking at you. Remember, treat yourself kindly."

I stepped back and saluted him. He transferred the money to his left hand and returned my salute.

When I got back in the car, Game said, "You know, maybe you should talk to somebody 'bout this Jami thing. I mean, she died a long time ago."

"I know. She's not usually this present. Amanda brought her up, and suddenly it's as though she never died. Or died yesterday."

I looked up the number on my phone, activated the burner, then dialed. A husky voice said, "Oakville Police Department."

A thought was rattling in my head, but I couldn't make it come together. I needed to buy time, so I told Game to follow the Porsche in the BMW until we found an open restaurant where we could talk. The business I found, a few blocks from the park, was a 24-hour taco joint that only had outdoor seating. Good enough.

We waited for our orders as dawn broke. I asked Game if he'd called his mother, and he said yes. She was glad he was safe, and she missed him. He was amped up, buoyed by his gangland success, and he rambled about the women he'd been with, although he didn't use that noun, about his proficiency as a point guard—he knew he could play college ball if he wanted to—and how rich he was going to be. I wasn't really listening but was grateful for the company.

Between bites I said, "You didn't answer my question," interrupting a story about his friend Reggie and a pair of fine twins.

"What question?"

"The one that made you ask if I was an especially dumb white person."

"What question?"

"Why didn't you off the guys cuffed to the pole? They were in the middle of a vacant park, a couple hundred yards from the nearest house, defenseless in the dark. No reason to worry about the sound of gunshots in that neighborhood, but if that was your concern, you could have slit their throats before they even had time to scream—or pistol-whipped them. You were obviously tipped they were there, so you could've picked up whichever weapon you preferred, then escaped in any direction. Of course, my car left on the scene would've blown things for you, but you could easily have driven it away and abandoned it anywhere."

"You through?"

"Yes."

"It a business transaction. Called the barter system. They had something we wanted—we had something they wanted. We ain't savages. We businessmen, just like everyone else trying to make a buck. But when we bring in the green one key at a time, it called possession with intent. When we put our heads together to seize opportunity, it called conspiracy. White folk do it, they called bankers and brokers and lawyers and politicians. You know, pillars of society. All the same green, Jack, just different ways to grab it."

I didn't acknowledge he'd spoken, just kept eating a chicken taco. In my peripheral vision I could see he was staring at me.

"What?" he finally asked.

"You've never killed anyone. Never even shot anyone. That's not a criticism, just an observation."

He didn't respond, and both of us watched as a patrol car passed slowly.

"Man, you don't know what I—"

"Don't. You say we're friends. Or almost friends, so don't lie to me."

He hesitated for about five seconds, then said, "Awwwight."

"Trading two members of da Uptown Posse for two others doesn't gain the MLKs a thing. Yes, the shooters will soon be in custody, but having justice served through legal channels isn't high on bangers' list of priorities, I'm guessing. Not much is likely to happen legally, anyway. While I was standing on the court—looking at breathing, beaten shooters—I knew something didn't wash. And then you jumped down my throat when I asked why they were alive. Don't ever take up poker, by the way."

"Dominoes my game."

"Good, keep it that way. The MLKs had to get something out of the trade, especially because you guys started this latest skirmish by ripping off the drug deal. You got the money and the drugs, so they came out blasting. They did it like idiots, but I understand why they felt things weren't square between the two gangs after the rip off."

"You asking something?"

"No. Uptown could've negotiated a truce, one that would be honored only if the shooters were allowed to live. That's a possibility. But why would the MLK's agree to a truce? Are you outmanned, outgunned? Have you been outsmarted? I don't believe either of the first two is true, and the rip-off disproves the outsmarted part.

"I understand trading two knights or bishops for two pawns, Original Gangsters for low-level shooters. That part makes sense. And for a few minutes I wondered if the ripped-off drug money or the drugs played into the trade, but again, why would the MLKs even entertain that option? It would be like handing the football back for a do-over after recovering your opponent's fumble. Makes no sense. The rip-off was a business transaction, albeit one involving weaponry, and you guys had the money and the drugs. The MLKs are the ones who got fired at and killed. You guys have no reason to negotiate."

"Maybe you really a investigator."

"Driving to Oakville tonight, I wondered if the shooters were alive because murdering people in a public park can't be good for business. Doing so would bring unwanted police attention, and, as you guys believe, you're all just businessmen pursuing the green. I thought da Posse might clean up its own mess, take care of the shooters themselves. I couldn't stop contemplating the motives, wondering."

"You wonder pretty good."

"Age has a few advantages. More wrinkles and creaking joints, true, but we've had many more years to observe human behavior."

"All those years tell you anything?"

"That da Uptown Posse and the MLKs were told to cool it."

CHAPTER SIXTEEN

Game wanted to go home so he could sleep in his own bed. Doing so seemed safe because the truce between the two gangs, if it was honored, would guarantee no retaliatory strikes. I told him that when we reached Amanda's house, he should call his mom to let her know it was safe to go home and that I would drop him off at her house later, after we got some sleep. But right then, I needed him to drive the BMW to Amanda's.

"Race ya," he said, indicating he was okay with the rest of my plan.

"Right. You have about as good a chance to blow through Malibu without getting pulled over as I have of rooting for USC."

"Not a Trojan fan, huh?"

"Rather root for Al-Qaeda."

As Game followed me toward the Coast Highway, I debated stopping by Loews to check on Amanda, but I simply wasn't up to it. The issues that she and I needed to discuss would require her to be sober, so I skipped that stop.

I drove up the incline that skirts Pepperdine University and wondered who'd told the gangs to make peace. Despite Game's belief that the MLKs and da Uptown Posse had two different suppliers, I believed the two gangs probably had two different distributors but the same supplier, and the supplier didn't like the heat that warfare would bring. So, he likely threatened to cut off their supplies, and their livelihoods, if they didn't let the drug-deal hijacking and the park shooting go. The threat wasn't necessarily idle because the supplier could likely afford to take the monetary hit more than the gangs could, or he could find others willing to sell his cocaine without shooting each other. I was only speculating, but it was easier to speculate than it was to worry about Amanda or to mourn my friend Chris.

By the time I pulled into the driveway and watched Game pull up beside me, I believed my theory about the gangs and their supplier was solid, although lacking specifics. And I was certain Chris wasn't a drug dealer and hadn't killed himself. He never even used drugs recreationally—a rarity at Hollywood parties. He and I had that in common, among many other things.

Something gnawed at me throughout the drive home. I'd tried to coax the thought out, but it wouldn't take shape. I put the key in the front door, opened it, and saw Jennifer sitting on the couch. She looked up and smiled as Game and I walked in.

"Hello," she said.

"Chris' death and the park shooting are related," I said.

"Um, okay, and it's good to see you, Jack."

She wore black sweatpants and a tight, navy-blue women's T-shirt with the word *Nothing* written in script across it. Her feet were bare. She stood, stuck out her hand, and said, "Hello, I'm Jennifer."

"I'm Game. Nice to meet you." They shook.

"What are you reading?" he asked, nodding toward the book in her hand.

"*Tender is the Night*, by Fitzgerald—one of my all-time favorites."

"One of mine, too," I said. "I'm sorry. How are you, Jen? And, yes, it's good to see you, too."

"A little distracted, are we?" she asked, stepping close and draping her arms around me, the book still in her hand. "My place was feeling very lonely, so I came over here, but no one was around. This is your copy. I'm finding it fascinating to see which passages you underlined."

"It's from college. Who knows if I underlined them or if the professor told me to?"

"I do because you wrote Prof next to some of the passages, then P thereafter. The underlined passages without a P are yours, and they're more intriguing."

"If you say so."

She went back to the couch and sat down. From beside the lamp, she hoisted a giant wine glass that sat next to a three-liter jug of wine. Jennifer knew that Amanda and I kept no alcohol in the house. She probably knocked, found no one home, decided to use her key to let herself in, then figured that because Amanda wasn't home, she could retrieve her bottle and settle into the lonely warmth of inebriation.

While Jen refilled her glass, Game got my attention and shrugged his shoulders, lifted his palms outward, and made a shocked expression that I took to mean something along the lines of, "Holy shit! She's fine!"

I nodded, smiled, and sat on the huge couch opposite the huge couch Jen sat on. Game sat next to her, at a polite distance.

The three of us made small talk until the sixteen-year-old in Game couldn't take it anymore and excused himself by saying, "It Sunday morning. Gotta be a game or something on TV."

"How's your shoulder?"

"Fine," he said, walking away.

"Let me take a look at it, please. Make sure it's not infected."

He reluctantly allowed me to peel the medical tape off and inspect the wound. It looked fine. I pressed the tape down.

"You done playin' Nurse Ratchet?"

"Uh, oh, Jen. He's making literary references. Have we ruined him?"

"I just met him, but it appears you may be rubbing off."

"Ain't neither of you. We read *Cuckoo's Nest* this year. Don't flatter yourself."

"Who would do it otherwise?" I asked.

Game shook his head and walked away, and Jen said, "I would, if I thought it would help."

"I need a lot more than flattery."

Jen stood, took my hand, and led me to the couch she'd been sitting on.

"Are you okay?" she asked. "You look awful, and you're obviously stressed."

"I took a nap after being up all night but found both Amanda and Game gone. I tracked her down—she's at Loews—though I didn't check on her. I found Game in Oakville, in the middle of some serious shit. My friend Chris Cerveris is dead, and something tells me these last two problems are related."

"Horrible. I'm sorry. How?"

"Supposedly suicide, but that's bullshit."

"Come here." She patted her left shoulder, instructing me to place my head on it. I moved closer and leaned against her. We said nothing for a while, then she asked, "Okay, which dilemma do you want, or need, to talk about first?"

"Did Jason Gilson mention Chris the other night?"

"No."

"You said he was acting oddly, as though he was trying to establish an alibi."

"Well, I may have been a bit dramatic."

"But something was different, right?"

"Right."

"It could've been unrelated or just a coincidence, but he was nervous when he saw me at the gas station, too. What if he knew something was going to happen to Chris? Or maybe he just suspected something would? Gilson's the softest, most-spineless man I know."

"Be nice, Jack."

"I'm not trying to be mean—maybe spineless is too harsh—but

soft and gentle and not overflowing with testosterone-fueled aggression. Is that accurate?"

"Fair enough. What's your point?"

"He wouldn't have anything to do with hurting Chris. He's not the type. But he could've known about the possibility of Chris getting hurt, maybe overheard something, and he wanted to distance himself somehow. He felt he needed to establish an alibi, however absurd that is."

Jennifer drained her glass and set it down.

"Well, he established he was with me, so whether he needs an alibi or not, I'm it. Aren't I lucky?"

"Spectacularly so—if only because you have me in your life."

"Yeah, that's it, you jackass." She refilled her glass. After setting the bottle down, she drained half the glass, then waited about ten seconds before downing the rest.

She scooted off the couch and settled at my feet, facing away from me, slowly twirling the stem of the glass. I gently stroked her hair.

"Are you drinking *at* something, Jen, or just drinking?"

"Just drinking."

"From my subjective point of view, you appear to be going a little hard. Or am I hypersensitive because of my living arrangement and its restrictions?"

"Probably drinking too much lately." She was quiet for a minute, then said, "Okay, there's no probably about it. I'm using a glass here only for appearances. I've been swigging straight from the bottle at home."

"Do you want me to take you to a meeting? Or give you the name of a counselor?"

"You know I see a therapist."

"What's her take on your drinking?"

"The same as mine. I'm lonely."

"I know, Jen, I know." She stood unsteadily, sat next to me, and rested her head on my chest.

"Yes, you do, but you won't discuss it or act on it—or on anything."

"I've always been there for you, and I'll always continue to be."

"Don't—"

"After I get some sleep, and after all this other stuff settles down, we can have this discussion. I give you my word we will, and you know my word is good. But now isn't the right time for a few reasons."

"Not the least of which is because you think I'm drunk."

"Not drunk. Let's say emotionally fragile, as I am. But I'm also confused as hell, trying to figure out what I should do—or if I can do anything—to help Amanda. I'm trying to keep a kid alive as a favor to a friend—and because he's a kid, and kids shouldn't get killed. And one of my best friends was just found dead, and I know he didn't kill himself. Because he was my friend, I'll find out who killed him and why, and I'll get him justice."

"Why haven't we slept together, Jack?"

I was silent for a while. Too long, apparently, because she said, "I asked you a question, the same one I've asked myself for many years, sometimes nightly. Why haven't you and I slept together, screwed, made the beast with two backs, whatever you want to call it? My therapist thinks it's a question worth contemplating, and she and I mull it over in most of my sessions. What do you think, Jack? Why haven't we slept together?"

After about ten seconds, I said, "Because I love you, Jennifer."

"Oh, great. Right. That makes total sense. I've filled far too many hours hoping you'd say those words to me and spent a fortune on therapy because you haven't. I've heard you say them in my dreams for years, yet now when you finally say, 'I love you, Jennifer,' you say it as a distancing device, a justification for not having sex with me. Unbelievable!"

"You've heard me say that phrase a thousand times because it's in my every glance at you, in the way I listen to you and dote on you and admire you and respect you. I feel your sadness and want nothing more than for you to be happy. You are indisputably my best friend, and I confide in you as I do no one else.

"We've had great rapport from the moment we met. We make each other laugh a lot, and I've tossed and turned countless nights trying to understand my feelings for you, trying to figure out how to jettison my past and allow myself to have a future."

I was tired and stressed, and I'd rehearsed various versions of this monologue many times, but it wasn't coming out as I'd planned, and I considered stopping there.

"And?"

"When Jami died, I knew there was no chance I'd ever allow myself to love that way again. I couldn't give myself completely as I had with her because her death triggered thoughts of suicide, and I even made a plan or two. Or three. Then I beat myself up for being too cowardly to follow through. Death couldn't possibly be filled with as much pain as I felt daily, hourly, and it was the loss of Jami, and my inability to help her, to be by her side when she needed me most, that caused that pain. So, how could I allow myself to love that way again, to love you that way, even if I truly want to, even if I need to, because we could—and probably will—end horribly?"

"Then don't lose me."

"How do I ensure that?"

"By loving me."

She looked into my eyes, maneuvered on the couch, and pulled me down behind her, scooting backward until we spooned. I slipped my left arm under her neck, draped my right arm over her body, and inhaled the heady combination of expensive shampoo and mediocre Cabernet. I reassured myself we'd just had the discussion we'd had. I wasn't dreaming, and a significant aspect of my life had become unstuck. The words I hadn't allowed myself for years to say out loud had just been spoken and heard.

"I love you, Jennifer."

"I love you, too, Jack."

We fell asleep entwined.

. . .

I slept for about three hours but awoke in a cold sweat, gasping for breath.

"What? What is it?" she asked.

"A nightmare. Lie back down."

Prior to the last couple nights, I hadn't dreamed of Jami's bike crash in about two years, the frequency of those nightmares having diminished slowly, then finally ceased. Jami still appeared in my dreams occasionally, but she was usually a secondary player, the woman who stood in the background and found me lacking. But that morning, I dreamed I'd pushed her in front of the van.

"I'll be okay," I said.

"Are you sure?" She settled her head on my chest.

"Not even close."

CHAPTER SEVENTEEN

Our pre-nap revelation didn't result in an awkward post-nap discussion, perhaps because the revelation revealed nothing that both of us hadn't known for years. Instead, when we awoke, we were as comfortable around each other as we normally were, meaning very. She didn't ask before using my toothbrush, and I was fine with that.

As she scrambled eggs, she asked what my plans for the day were. I told her I'd go for a run, hoping to find some clarity and, with luck, answers. She asked, "Don't you want to know what I'm going to do?"

"Yes. I'm sorry. What are your plans?"

She vamped from the kitchen to the couch, as though in a silent movie, bent down to pick up the bottle of wine she'd nearly emptied last night, grabbed her wine glass, traipsed back into the kitchen, and made a show of hoisting the bottle high, tilting it, hesitating, and pouring the remaining wine into the sink.

"I really should break the glass for effect, but you might deem that showy. I'll perhaps discuss the finer points of how one should dispose of one's alcoholic implements at my first meeting today."

"Good for you, Jen, but—"

"Don't say it. I know. Trust me: I'm doing it for me, not you. I've needed to stop for a long time, and I've known it but been too afraid or too weak or too stupid—or whatever. But I know there won't ever be a real us if I continue to drink."

I couldn't think of anything to say that wouldn't have sounded pretentious, so I went to her and wrapped myself around her. We embraced for a minute, and I knew I had to pull away before the embrace turned into more than I was ready to handle. But I couldn't pull away. I wanted to, but when she tilted her head back and stared up at me with her gorgeous brown eyes—eyes that didn't just invite but beckoned—I did what felt right, and our kiss was the first real one I'd experienced in nine years.

We allowed our pent-up desire for each other to express itself, and I felt a sensation I hadn't felt in a very long time. It took me a few seconds to recognize what it was, but eventually it became clear: I was in the moment, there with Jennifer, kissing her, embracing her, allowing myself to feel. For an instant, I was not living in the past, burdened by guilt, or worried about the future. But as soon as those thoughts filled my head, I was out of the moment.

"Jen," I said, disengaging from her. "We should go slowly. I've wanted to do this for years, even though I wouldn't admit it to you, but I think we should hold off. You're vulnerable, and I may be in the middle of a nervous breakdown."

"Shut up. Just kiss me."

"I can't."

"Stop thinking so damned much. You're a man. Let yourself be one."

"I obviously want you, but this isn't right, not here and now. Not on the day you declare yourself to be sober—and while you're still hungover."

"I sure know how to pick 'em, don't I? You're a true romantic, and the wait was well worth it." But she smiled, and her tone was teasing.

"I promise you—I want this to work, and I think it can if we start from a position of strength, not weakness or desperation."

"If you say so."

"Trust me. Amanda hit on me when I was about to disappear, when I wanted not to exist, and I allowed her to be my lifeline. She kept me alive, and I've done the same for her, but it's not enough. From the outside, she and I have everything, but I resent her and hate myself for my inability to leave her or to truly love her."

"I'm not Amanda, and I'm not Jami. You're afraid. I am, too. Love is hard, relationships are hard. And the most real of loves ended in a devastating loss for you. I understand. Or I think I do. I've never experienced anything like what you and Jami had, so I haven't felt the depths of despair you have. But I understand trauma and abuse, and they've contributed to why I've spent all these years alone, without a real connection, without true love. I've dated. I've thought I've been in love, but I've always really been alone, even when I was with someone. We both need to change our lives, and we've just taken the first step."

"We have, and I'm happy about it. Kissing you felt far better than I imagined, and I have a great imagination. But our first step should be followed by a second step, not a sprint."

"Then I take it back. I don't love you." She smiled, stepped back into my arms, and kissed me on the neck.

"I definitely don't love you either."

"You two gonna get busy, or what?" Game asked from the other side of the kitchen.

Jen and I both stepped back.

"Did you sleep?" I asked him.

"I was taught not to answer a question with a question."

"I was taught to mind my own business," I said, then asked, "Who's up for a run?"

"I'm in," Game said, but Jen hesitated.

"Not sure my head's up for it, and I want to find a meeting."

"We'll walk briskly if you prefer, and I'll take you to a meeting when we're done."

"Okay. Give me a couple minutes."

"You want me to let you two go alone?" Game asked.

"No, it's a beautiful morning. No June gloom today, so let's all enjoy the sun together."

The three of us walked briskly down the beach toward Trancas Canyon, with the piecemeal rocky seawall protecting expensive houses on our left from the ocean on our right. I felt far more comfortable than I should have. Nothing about my life at that moment made sense. The movie star I'd lived with for seven years was hiding in a hotel, most likely as a whistle-stop before checking into another high-end rehab. The teenager walking to my right was nursing a shoulder wound sustained during a gang shooting, and he and his gang had sworn vengeance. It was my job to prevent him from exacting revenge and to keep him alive. But the gangs involved had declared a truce. The woman walking on my left had loved me for years, and she'd told me a decade ago that she'd wondered the day we met if the two of us would have been a couple if I hadn't been married.

But then my wife left this world, and I essentially did, too. I'd breathed and worked and ate and slept and traveled and attended premieres and received gifts, but I hadn't loved.

About four years ago, when Jen and I were jogging on the beach, I'd admitted to myself that my feelings for her had become more significant than friendship. I'd wondered how the two of us would be as a couple. I didn't tell her I'd had those thoughts, but not long afterward, she'd seen those thoughts in my eyes and in my actions.

As we walked down the beach, Game expressed his amazement as we passed the mansions.

"You living with a movie star, loving a hotter sista, gotta choose between a Land Rover, a BMW, or a Porsche, got more than one Jacuzzi in your beach mansion, and this your front yard, but you sad and angry." He sat down on the soft sand, out of reach of the waves that rolled in. We sat next to him.

"Do you want to tell him, or should I?" I asked.

"I will," Jen said. "Depression can affect anyone, no matter how wealthy, successful, popular, or attractive. From the outside, a depressed person may seem to have everything anyone could want. But a depressed person can't look at herself or himself from the outside, and the inside is filled mostly with darkness."

Game asked, "How'd you know what he was asking?"

"We've been best friends for years," Jen said. "It's accurate to say we're, what, simpatico?"

"At the least," I said. "We truly understand each other."

"Even if one of us doesn't understand the other's sudden celibacy," she said.

Game said, "You more than depressed, you don't wanna get with Jen."

"What a wonderful view," I said. "I can see a change of subject on the horizon."

"Coward," Jen said.

"Chicken," Game said.

We talked about Game's summer plans (play basketball, hookup with girls) and his career goals (be an NBA point guard or the CEO of a corporation). He asked Jennifer how long she'd lived at the beach.

"About fifteen years. I was extremely fortunate to have had a successful modeling career that enabled me to purchase the house, and I invested well, but modeling rendered my Ph.D. meaningless.

"Because I'm much older now, and the modeling opportunities at my age are few and far between compared to what they were when I was twenty-one, I'm toying with the idea of looking into a professorship. I'd obviously have to refamiliarize myself with all the material, and it would be a longshot to land a job at my age, but—"

"But 'Life is a gamble, at terrible odds—if it was a bet you wouldn't take it,'" I said.

"As you know, that's my favorite play," Jen said. She looked at Game and said, "*Rosencrantz and Guildenstern Are Dead* by Tom Stoppard."

I looked down the beach and saw a group of people, including two EMTs, gathered in front of Big Bill Watson's house and under his deck. I became nauseated instantly, and I knew the universe had just compensated for the magic of Jen's kiss. I didn't want to go closer, even though I knew the three of us would. I stood and steeled myself to the horror that awaited us. Jen and Game looked at me, but before either could say anything, I started to walk toward the group. They stood and followed.

Seven of the people who were gathered—four of whom had their dogs at the end of leashes—were neighbors, and they nodded as we approached. The other five people in the ragged arc around the EMTs were strangers who'd likely strolled along the sand from Zuma Beach. The two EMTs weren't doing anything but waiting because their job was to tend to the living. Big Bill hung dead at the end of a rope, below the deck and above the sand.

Could Big Bill have stepped off one of the two bourbon barrels that he liked to throw driftwood into, his neck then breaking when the line stopped his fall, with his bare, size-fourteen feet just inches above the sand? Could Sadie's incremental disappearance as Lewy body dementia ravaged her brain and body have led him to take that fatal step?

Not if I knew anything about human nature. Yes, suicide can happen almost spontaneously. A high percentage of people who fail at their first attempt to kill themselves never make another attempt, meaning they eventually overcome the momentary impulse that led them to their first attempts. Using a gun rarely allows for such a change of heart.

Big Bill could've felt overwhelmed by despair, then untied the anchor from one end of the line he used to secure his orange two-man kayak while he fished. He could've tied that end to the beam that was farthest from the water and calculated the length of rope he'd need to ensure he would dangle after he'd tied a noose in the other end. He would have had to fashion a noose, overturn one of the bourbon barrels so he could stand on it before he jumped, convince himself he never wanted to see Sadie alive again and was comfortable letting her suffer alone, climb atop the barrel, slip the line over his head, tighten it, make peace with whomever or whatever he needed to make peace with, then jump.

Or someone could've wrapped a line around Big Bill's head while someone else held him at gunpoint and threw the other end over a beam. Then they could've pulled hard until Big Bill's toes lifted off the sand, then knotted the line at that length. His neck wouldn't likely have broken because he wouldn't have dropped from a height, but the blood flow in his carotid arteries would've been cut off, causing him to black out quickly, followed soon after by death.

Would the murderers have gagged him first so he couldn't scream? Probably, although the crashing waves and the distance to neighboring houses would likely have greatly diminished the likelihood that neighbors could've heard screams, if Big Bill could've screamed with a rope crushing his trachea. After removing the gag when he stopped twitching, the killers likely walked through the sand to the public accessway, then disappeared.

I felt confident my supposition was accurate. I stepped between two neighbors to take a closer look. Both bourbon barrels were upright, with the openings at the top. Now I was certain he hadn't jumped. No one would try to balance on the edge of the barrel in bare feet before placing the noose around his neck, risking a fall that could injure him but not kill him.

Big Bill was seventy-two and weighed at least 260, so the likelihood of him committing suicide in that manner was near zero. Because he was as large as he was, I suspected that three men were probably involved because hoisting him up while he struggled to stay on the ground would've been nearly impossible for only two.

Depending on how effectively the bastards who did this managed to surprise him, and depending on whether they used a gun as I suspected they had to subdue him, the medical examiner would likely find defensive wounds on Big Bill. Even at his age, he would've put up a serious fight, although a gun pointed at him would've limited his options.

I stood there seething, certain these murderers had also killed Chris Cerveris. Two hangings of people I knew in Malibu on the same weekend? Not a coincidence.

High tide had washed away the footsteps under the deck, except for the ones made by the group gathered around Big Bill, so any clues the killers might have left were gone. Except for those upright barrels.

I didn't look at Big Bill's face, preferring to remember him as he'd looked while alive. I glanced at Jen, who'd turned away and was wiping a tear from her eye. Game wasn't next to her. I looked toward the water and saw him leaning over, his hands on his knees as a wave receded. He was breathing heavily, and I suspected he'd thrown up into the preceding wave.

I looked toward the public-access entrance about two hundred yards down the beach and saw two sheriff's deputies and what appeared to be a member of the coroner's office stepping around the end of the chain-link fence onto the beach. Part of me wanted to examine the scene more closely before they arrived and forced everyone to step back, but I knew I'd be wasting my time. The ocean had guaranteed that, so I gently took Jen by the elbow, motioned to Game, and started to head to the house. I stopped and said, "Give me a sec." I jogged about twenty yards toward the three approaching officials assigned to investigate Big Bill's death.

"Excuse me, gentlemen." The three of them, all in their thirties and muscle-bound, looked at me but didn't speak. "I was a friend of Big Bill Watson, the man hanging under his deck over there. He didn't kill himself. I know no one wants to believe that members of their family or friends were despondent enough to kill themselves, but this is different. Look at the barrels, then ask yourself how a guy his age and size could've stood on the rim of one of them while putting a noose around his neck. That, plus, his neck may not be broken, which it almost certainly would be if he jumped. And I'd bet he has defensive wounds."

The two deputies stared at me, but the guy wearing the dark-blue jumpsuit with Los Angeles County Department of Medical Examiner-Coroner embroidered on the left breast said, "Thank you. I'll look into it."

"Thanks," I said and walked back to Jen and Game.

The three of us didn't speak until we approached the steps that led to the house. Jen started to walk up the steps, and I asked Game, "You okay?"

"Yeah. You the one just lost another friend. You awwright?"

"No. In my experience, every positive is countered by at least two negatives. That's depression. But the way I feel now is more than depression. I'm dangerously angry."

We walked up the steps and washed the sand off our feet in the outdoor shower. We toweled off and went inside. I asked, "You still want to go home, right?"

"Yeah." He launched himself onto one of the couches.

Jen gave me a hug. "You okay?"

"Processing," I said. "Thanks for asking. You okay?"

"Despite two of your friends being murdered, I'm doing better than I can remember doing. Sorry, but I feel hopeful for maybe the first time ever. Does that make me selfish?"

"I don't think so. Not that I'm speaking from experience, but it probably makes you healthy. Want me to find a meeting?"

"No, I should do it. Part of the process, right?"

"Taking initiative and owning your behavior certainly are."

"You'll go with me, right?"

"Of course."

She pulled out her phone and found an 11:30 meeting a few miles away on Morning View.

"We can make that, right?"

"Sure."

I grabbed the keys from the counter and walked out front to unlock the mailbox. Sitting on top of it was a blood-red envelope with Drake scrawled across it, almost illegibly—as though someone had written it with his off hand.

I tore the envelope open, and the yellow index card inside read, in the same scrawl: BACK THE FUCK OFF!

"No!" I shouted. A couple seconds later, Jennifer stepped outside and asked, "What's wrong?"

"Someone just threatened me, and he showed me he knows where I live."

"Seriously? What do we do now?"

CHAPTER EIGHTEEN

"Go get ready," I said, "and I'll convince Game to attend the meeting with us."

"We're still going? Shouldn't you deal with this?"

"I *am* dealing with it. If they wanted to kill me, they wouldn't have warned me to back off. We go to the meeting and appear as though we've backed off."

"We've? You get threatened, and now we're a 'we' all of a sudden? How romantic, Jack." She smiled and walked up the road to her house, two doors away.

I spent five minutes in the office rewinding the security-camera footage, then replaying it. The only thing I discerned was that the guy wasn't an idiot. He'd walked into frame from the left, wearing all black, including a baggy work shirt, baggy cargo pants, a wide-brimmed sunhat, combat boots, gloves, and ski mask, which he'd probably pulled down out of frame before slipping his big sunglasses back on. He didn't rush in, set the envelope down, and run away, leaving as little footage as possible. Instead, his gait was slow, and his movements were contrived—limping, shaking his head, shooting his arms up straight, dragging a leg while feigning a hunchback, and waving his arms frantically. He looked down when he got close to the mailbox, keeping the top of his hat facing the camera, then moved out of frame to the left, using the same herky-jerky movements. The only possible clue I noticed was that when he lifted his arms above his head, I saw a flash of yellow on his right wrist. Possibly a watchband. If it was a watchband, did his wearing it on his right wrist mean he was left-handed?

He looked about five-nine, with a thin build. His unusual movements had prevented me from identifying the familiar gait and mannerisms of someone I knew, which meant he was trying to hide them. Or maybe he knew I'd come to that conclusion, and he wanted me to think he was someone I knew.

I rewound the feed and fast-forwarded to see if he'd made the mistake of driving past the house before parking farther along Broad Beach Road, then walking into frame from the left. But the only vehicle that passed in the twenty minutes prior to him walking into frame was the white Grand Caravan driven by our neighbor Jess Gant, who lived a few houses beyond Jennifer's house. I figured I wouldn't find clues because anyone who knew where Amanda and I lived would likely know that Broad Beach Road accesses the Coast Highway in two locations. Of course, any navigation app would show that to be true, and most of the Maps to the Stars that are available to stalkers include Amanda's address, although I've seen three versions that had us living elsewhere, including in Cher's house.

In other words, practically anyone could've threatened me.

We'd have to hurry to get to Jennifer's first AA meeting, but I had time to wonder: Back off from what?

I knew Chris hadn't committed suicide, but I hadn't been investigating his murder, unless mentioning it to that jackass Sergeant Denton counted. And I'd just told the deputies and the coroner that Big Bill hadn't killed himself, so no one would've had time to communicate my concerns to the guy who wrote the threat, then dressed head-to-toe in black.

I was trying to keep Game alive, but how had I investigated the shooting at the park? I'd poked around the crime scene and spoken to the Oakville PD officer on post, but Game and the other MLKs had delivered the shooters without involving me. So, the murder at the park seemed closed, although I wouldn't bet the shooters would be convicted.

What was I supposed to BACK THE FUCK OFF from?

It was 11:15. We'd still be on-time if we hustled.

I found Game sprawled on the couch in the guest room flipping channels.

"Ain't no sports on but soccer in Europe and fishing in Georgia or some other nowhere state. Then NASCAR coming on, like that a sport."

"I feel your pain. I'll give you something else to complain about. I just received a hand-delivered threat, so I can't leave you alone when Jen and I go to the AA meeting."

He stared at me.

"It's not a matter of trust. I promised to keep you safe. The bastard who threatened me isn't likely to attack, or he would have without issuing the threat, but I can't take that chance. You have to experience your first AA meeting with us."

"Food?"

"Coffee and cookies. Maybe donuts."

"That'll do." He got up and walked to the bathroom.

I pulled out my cell and called Amanda. Straight to voicemail. Instead of leaving a message, I texted her: *Please let me know you're ok.*

In a few minutes, Jen, Game, and I were driving along PCH in the BMW. I heard the chime indicating I'd received a text. I pulled into the parking lot and checked my phone. The text from Amanda read: *I faked my orgasms with you!*

America's Sweetheart was alive, and her adoring fans would be glad to know she hadn't lost her charm.

"How long you been alcoholic, Jack?" Game asked as we walked toward the entrance to the school where the meeting was held. The parking lot had about fifteen cars in it. Jason Gilson's gray Mercedes, featuring his A WRAP license plate, was one of them.

"I'm not alcoholic."

"Thought you said you don't drink, dawg. You just a health nut?"

"I was drunk when Jami was killed," I said as we approached the door, which had a man on the left and a woman on the right side of it, verbally greeting and shaking hands with arrivals. "So, I don't drink."

"To punish yourself," Game said and shook the woman's hand, as I shook the man's.

"Welcome," said the man, whose name I didn't remember, although I'd seen him at most of the meetings I'd attended with Amanda.

"Yes," I said to Game as Jen shook the man's hand. The three of us entered the room. A circle of twenty-five chairs filled the center of the large room. A table against the wall had a silver fifty-cup coffee urn, an open package of vanilla sandwich cookies, and a chocolate cake on it. The room smelled of coffee and cigarette smoke, even though none of the fifteen people seated around the circle was smoking. I didn't know if smoking was a co-addiction for recovering alcoholics or a replacement one, but I did know that they smoked at a far higher rate than the average Californian.

Gilson had his back to us, but when I approached the circle and asked if two of the attendees would mind scooting to their left one seat so the three of us could sit together, I saw Gilson look at me. He started to turn away but saw Jennifer beside me. I thought I saw surprise in his eyes. Gilson nodded, I returned his nod, but Jennifer hesitated. After three seconds, she lifted her hand in a half-hearted wave. Game pointed to the table, and I said, "Hurry." He hustled to the table, grabbed three cookies, and hustled back to his seat.

"It's 11:30, folks, so let's get started," said the fifty-ish, bearded man who'd greeted us at the door. "Welcome to the 11:30 Sunday Topic & Discussion Meeting of Alcoholics Anonymous. I'm Derek, and I'm an alcoholic."

"Hi, Derek," said everyone but Jennifer and Game.

Derek proceeded to run an efficient but not a militant meeting. When he asked, "Is anyone here in their first thirty days of sobriety?" Jen raised her hand. Nearly everyone applauded, and a few people said words of encouragement: "Good for you." "Keep coming back." "Great job."

"What's your name?" Derek asked Jen.

"Jennifer."

"And?" Derek asked.

"And I'm an alcoholic," Jen said, then smiled.

"Hi, Jennifer," everyone responded.

"How many days?" Derek asked.

"Not even one. I drank last night, so I'm not sure how it works."

"If you haven't had a drink since the sun came up, then this is Day One," Derek said. "This is your sobriety date. Congratulations. I hope you feel great about yourself because we feel great you're here. We've all been exactly where you are, so we know how hard taking that first step can be. Some of us have taken it many times. So, congratulations. This is by far the most important day in your sobriety. Until tomorrow."

Gilson collected a chip and took a birthday cake for five consecutive years of sobriety. We sang "Happy Birthday," ending the song with "Keep coming back." He blew out the candles, then said, after Derek asked how he did it: "I couldn't have made 1,826 consecutive days, counting the extra day in this leap year—and, as we know, every day counts—but I couldn't have done it without my unshakeable faith, my absolute and total belief in our lord and savior, Jesus Christ. Without him, I never would've managed day one. Thank you all for celebrating my real birthday, the one that matters to me, here today. I love you all."

We applauded.

Game fidgeted through most of the hour, but he managed to endure the meeting without irritating or embarrassing me. Jen seemed deep in thought throughout, her expression vacillating between relief that she had finally admitted she had a problem and fear. She probably had no confidence that she'd be able to make it through the day without drinking. When Derek asked her if she wanted to share, she asked, "Do I have to?"

"You don't have to do anything but not drink," Derek said. "And, to be honest, you can even do that, if you're not ready to be here."

"No, I'm ready," she said. "To be here, I mean, not to talk about why I'm here. Not yet."

After we all joined hands and recited the Serenity Prayer, I approached Gilson as he poured coffee from the urn into an insulated paper cup. The woman who'd greeted us at the door, whose name turned out to be Sally, was slicing the cake and handing slices out on small paper plates. Game had been second to receive a slice. He walked over to the open door, stood beside it, and ate his slice quickly. Jen didn't have cake, and she appeared to be uncomfortable as she stood next to Game.

"Hey, Jason. How are you?" I asked, as he sipped his coffee.

"Okay, I guess. Another year sober, so things could be worse."

"Yes, they could. I haven't heard anything about Chris' funeral. Have you?"

"Shit, Jack. That's my fault. Chris' brother, Keith, contacted me and asked me to help him put together a memorial. He's in Illinois, so he doesn't know who should be invited out here. I said I'd help. I've been racking my brain because I didn't want to leave anyone out, but, obviously, I did. Sorry. The service will be on Tuesday at 3 at Holy Cross, with a reception at my place afterward."

"Okay, I'll be there."

"Bring Amanda," he said, then glanced at Jen, who was waiting by the door with Game, ready to leave. "Or who you want."

I said, "I'm glad you're doing this for Chris and his brother. It's good of you. See you on Tuesday." I shook Jason's hand and left.

Why hadn't Jen said hello to Jason? On Friday night, they'd hung out at her place. She didn't say anything about them arguing or not getting along, only that she had a weird feeling he was using her as an alibi.

On the drive home, Jen said, "I have a problem, and I don't know what the protocols are about those meetings. They're supposed to be anonymous, but what if I know something about someone. Should I say something?"

"The anonymous part means, what happens in those rooms stays in those rooms. Obviously, if everyone's sitting in the rooms with famous people, the celebrities aren't anonymous in the rooms. You're just not supposed to blow their cover outside of them. The problem you have is that Gilson took a chip and a cake but isn't sober."

"How'd you know?"

"I can't think of any other reason you wouldn't have said hello to him. You're friends but didn't greet each other. He looked as surprised to see you as you were to see him. Did you drink together the other night?"

"Yes. We didn't get drunk, but we downed two bottles of wine. So, when I saw him in the meeting, I ... I don't know ... I didn't know how to behave."

"Neither did he. You behaved fine. It's not your job to keep him honest, keep me honest, or keep Game from eating all the desserts." Game laughed. "It's only your job to convince yourself you've made the correct decision to become sober. Then your job is to remain sober one day at a time. No one can remain sober for a week at a time, so don't try to be the first."

We turned onto Broad Beach Road, and Game said, "How you know if someone got a drinking problem?"

"It's not easy," I said. "A lot of the time, maybe most of the time, the drinker is the last person to know he or she has a problem. No matter how troublesome the drinking has become to everyone else—unless the drinker reaches the same conclusion—no one will be able to get him or her into an AA meeting. Except a judge, of course."

I pulled into the left side of the driveway, in line with the slot in which I parked the BMW. I saw shards of an amber fog light at the base of the yellow fire hydrant that sat just off the curb near the right side of the driveway. My blood pressure rose instantly. "Amanda's home," I said.

"How you know?" Game asked.

I didn't answer him. I walked over to the hydrant. A short streak of forest-green paint had transferred from the Land Rover to the hydrant.

"I'll get out of here," Jen said. I nodded and gestured toward the hydrant. I said, "This stuff means nothing. This is Day One, the start of your new life."

"I thought you'd say, 'our new life.'"

"Of course. But there's something I have to tell you: AA strongly recommends that newbies don't enter into new relationships during their first year."

"Year? You're kidding, right?"

"Nothing is hard-and-fast, but the recommendation exists because new relationships frequently collapse, leaving newbies sad, vulnerable, and prone to drink."

"But ..." Her eyes started to tear up. She stepped close and gave me a tight hug.

"We'll discuss this, and we'll get through it. But right now I have unrelated garbage to deal with. Go home, pour out all the alcohol, and treat yourself well. Give yourself credit. Maybe call Inga for a massage. I'll call you as soon as I can."

"Okay, but I'm not sure I should be alone. I don't know if I can do this. I stopped because you were with me."

"I *am* with you, I promise. But I have to take Game home and figure out how to deal with Amanda. Based on that hydrant, she's still drunk."

Jen let go of me, looked at Game, turned back to me, and said, "I'm afraid you'll go back to her."

"I haven't even let her know I've left her, although she's known since she and I got together I haven't really been hers. Please trust me. Let me extricate myself so we can start being a couple." She stepped close again, gave me a kiss on the cheek, and silently mouthed the words, "I love you."

"I love you, too."

Glass shattered loudly behind the three of us, causing us to flinch. I turned toward the street in time to see the tattered bottom of a dark-green wine bottle skid across the asphalt onto the far shoulder. The other shards and the small amount of wine that had been in the bottle were strewn across the street. Just after we turned toward the source of the noise, we heard from behind and above us: "Fuck you, Jack!"

We turned toward the house. Amanda leaned over the railing of the deck on the top level, about twenty feet above us, where she'd been eavesdropping. She was wearing a white Loews robe that she'd likely stolen. She'd taken at least three others home with her after previous stays in the hotel. She was probably wearing nothing else. If Amanda had bothered to check out, the hotel clerk had probably been too embarrassed to bring up the robe. I hoped the clerk charged her for it. Not a single bill ever arrived through the mail or electronically. Amanda didn't want to be bothered, so she had all of them sent to her accountant, who paid them out of Amanda's seemingly bottomless accounts.

I'd never seen her look so awful. Even as I'd driven her to various rehabs, she'd managed to be incredibly attractive. But, apparently, between the last time I saw her and that moment, she'd surrendered. She looked as though she hadn't slept or eaten in a week, and she seemed to have taken styling tips from Shrek and Medusa.

"You love her?" she screamed. "Thought you could only love Jami, you hypocrite!"

CHAPTER NINETEEN

I didn't respond. I looked at Game and said quietly, "If you want, I can pack your stuff, or you can do it. I'm not sure which is more likely to turn ugly."

Jennifer kissed me on the cheek—provoking Amanda, I thought—and said, "See you later. Be careful."

"I'll get my stuff," Game said, loud enough for Amanda to hear because she responded: "This is my house, every inch of it, and I'll call the cops if you—"

"Go," I said, and Game ran to the front door. Amanda hadn't locked it. I hoped she wasn't drunk enough to think she could physically confront Game. Unless she had a gun, a confrontation with Game would end badly for her. I'd never told her the combination to the gun safe in my closet. She'd probably tried my birthday, forward and backwards, but I'd used my father's birthday, and I'd never told her anything about him, other than "he's a bad bad guy—a horrible husband and father." I'd instantly regretted telling her that much, because she'd asked how he'd treated us badly and who I meant by "us." "Never mind," I'd said.

Amanda stepped out of view. I ran inside, suspecting she could be drunk enough to confront Game. I ran upstairs in time to see her grab her cell phone from the bedside table, then wobble toward the bathroom. I got to the bathroom door before she could slam it on me. She was fumbling with her phone, trying to dial 911 while trying to keep me out of the bathroom. I wrapped my right hand over hers and her phone, then looked at the counter next to the sink.

I thought about letting her make the 911 call and pushing her out of the bathroom because on the counter were an Amex Platinum Card with white residue on one edge, remnants of white lines next to the card, and a large, open Baggie of cocaine. She had enough coke to kill her many times over if she chose to go out that way.

Was that her plan, to make good on her suicide threats, the ones she'd made many times over the last seven years when she thought I was going to leave her? Was that why she'd purchased so much coke?

"Let go of me! Let go of me, you asshole!" she shouted while sitting on the closed toilet seat. She tried to free her hand, but I had a firm grip on it and her phone with my right hand. She swung at my face with her clawed left hand, hoping to scratch me or take out an eye with her expensively manicured nails. But I was out of range, so she started to dig her nails into my right wrist, trying to break my grip. Her pupils were so large that their blackness almost eliminated her green irises.

"This is kidnapping!" she screamed. "And this is my house!"

"Calm down, Amanda. If you call the cops you'll go straight to jail, not rehab. You own the house, but I legally live here, and Game is my guest, so he's not breaking any laws. They've gone easy on you in the past, but this time there are witnesses. That's a hell of a lot of blow, and you seem to have snorted far too much of it, so you'll probably get charged."

"After everything I've done for you? Are you serious? You're nothing! A loser! Just a pathetic empty sack of sad pathetic memories."

She tried to wrench her right hand out of mine again but failed, so she tried to backhand me with her left fist, missing me but knocking the bag of coke into the sink with the sleeve of her robe, spilling a lot of it.

I didn't think shouting to Game would work because he was two floors below me and on the other side of the house, so I decided to count slowly to twenty, trust he'd finished packing his duffel, and hope Amanda would calm down, although the coke she'd snorted didn't make the last part likely.

"You think you've done a lot for me?" I asked. "I've been your butler, your chauffeur, your chaperone, your chef, your caretaker, your sober companion, and your gigolo. Every time you've derailed, I've picked up the pieces and put you back together." I hadn't loosened my grip on her right hand. My left hand shook.

"You've been a pathetic leech since we met," she said. "You'd be homeless if you had to live off the pennies you make, and almost all your business comes from you fucking me. And not well, by the way, not as well as all the others."

Arguing was pointless. By demeaning my sexual prowess, she was trying to get me to hit her, I thought, so she could build a case against me when the police arrived. Maybe a bruised cheek or a bloody lip would distract them from her dilated pupils. Or maybe she could bribe them with coke, cash, or sexual favors. The last was least likely, but I knew there had been many others. Whether she was telling the truth about their relative carnal performances, only she knew.

The words I wanted to say would've been cruel, and she didn't need more reasons to drink and use. Being cruel would've lowered me to her level. She hated herself without my piling on. I didn't hate her. I resented her. I said, "Goodbye, Amanda. I'll come by to get my stuff." I suddenly liked myself more.

I let go of her right hand, and she slugged me with it and her phone, but she hit me in the gut, so I barely felt it. I turned away, pulled my phone from my pants pocket, took one step away, opened the camera app, and carefully captured Amanda, the Baggie of cocaine in the sink, the rolled-up bill, and the AMEX in the frame.

Then I took a closeup of just the card and the coke. She saw me take the photos but didn't seem to care. I left the bathroom and heard three tones from her iPhone, indicating she'd dialed 911, or at least wanted me to think she had. She would've hidden the cocaine by the time the cops arrived. I couldn't imagine even the very wealthy Amanda Bigelow would flush that much blow, although that's what she should've done.

After I'd gotten Game into the BMW, I left it running in the driveway and ran inside to grab the mementos I'd kept from my life with Jami, in case Amanda became vindictive and decided to hurt me as deeply as she could. I grabbed the photo album, the birthday cards, the love letters, the congratulatory pen, and the inexpensive Casio watch Jami'd given me, all of which I kept in a locked desk drawer in my study. I placed all of these in a backpack and put it on.

I needed clothes, so I had to go back upstairs. I braced myself for another confrontation with Amanda, but she wasn't in the bedroom. I stuffed a few T-shirts, a light jacket, two pairs of jeans, some shorts, socks, and underwear into a duffel. I put two suits and dress shirts, along with a black tie and a pair of dress shoes and socks into a garment bag. I left the collection of watches Amanda had given me. I opened the gun safe, grabbed my passport, birth certificate, the title to the BMW, and various other documents and stuffed them in the duffel. I grabbed the eight straps of $100 bills, two handguns, and two boxes of ammunition, then stuffed them in the backpack. I closed the safe, stepped out of the closet, and looked around the bedroom. I grabbed my laptop, its charger, and my phone charger and stuffed those in the duffel. Then I looked in the bathroom.

Amanda was still sitting on the closed toilet, but she was now leaning over, snorting a line of coke through a bill. If I left her alone with the coke, her heart would explode, although she could find time to write a suicide note that absolved her of any responsibility for her demise. But that would've required her to be aware that acts have consequences, and in the state she was in, I didn't expect her to develop new levels of self-awareness.

I stepped into the bathroom, yelled "Ahhhhh," and charged at her as though I meant to hit her. She spun away from me on the toilet, leaned against the wall, and covered her face. I expected my plan to work but not so well. I thought she'd at least scratch me while I disposed of the rest of her coke, but I'd forgotten that Amanda became extremely paranoid when loaded, so she recoiled not just from the fear of potentially being attacked, as most people would, but also from cocaine-induced paranoia. She hid her face and closed her eyes, awaiting the beating she thought I'd administer to her, although I'd never done more than raise my voice to her, and only a few times at that.

"Don't kill me, don't kill me, don't kill me," she shouted as I blocked her from the coke with my body and proceeded to wash it down the sink a little at a time. "Don't kill me, don't kill me, don't kill me," she said, as the last of the coke disappeared down the drain.

I rinsed off the Amex card, wiped the counter with a washcloth, rinsed out the Baggie, and checked to see if I'd forgotten anything. I let the water run from the faucet a little more as I looked at her. She'd dropped her hands from her face and was looking at the counter where her coke had been. As I turned off the water, she jumped up, grabbed my left arm, pulled it toward her, and sank her teeth into it.

Instead of hitting her to free myself, I rotated my body into her, forcing her to fall back onto the toilet, which caused her to release my arm, but not before she drew blood. I looked at her, slumped on the toilet, with dilated pupils and her face bunched up in a snarl, and I wondered if I'd looked that wounded and defeated when she'd let her bathrobe drop in the presence of her bodyguard that first time seven years ago. She couldn't have seen strength and confidence in the shell of a man standing in front of her. Had she been deceived by my physical presence, or had she preyed upon my vulnerability?

"Goodbye, Amanda." I grabbed the Baggie and washcloth. I left the bathroom, grabbed my bags, and went downstairs to the kitchen. I dropped my possessions, ran downstairs to the laundry room, threw the washcloth into the washer, added a few clean towels, and started the washer. I grabbed the small metal trashcan from the office, ran back upstairs, lighted a paper towel on the gas stovetop, dropped the towel into the trash can, and set the Baggie on top of the flaming paper towel. I watched for about eight seconds as the towel disintegrated the plastic. I picked up the trashcan and carried it back downstairs.

My left arm was bleeding, and my right arm was scratched. I went to the bathroom and extinguished the last of the burning paper towel, then daubed the blood off my arm with toilet paper. I applied pressure with another fistful of paper, grabbed the first-aid kit, went upstairs, picked up my bags, and left the house.

I dropped my bags in the trunk of the BMW and went to the passenger's side. Through the open window, Game asked, "Where you been, dawg?"

I said, "I need you to put tape on my arm while I hold the gauze. It's a circus act to do it alone."

"Awwwight," he said. "She got you, huh? Not too bad, just some blood." While I kept pressure on the wad of toilet paper and the gauze, he applied one strip of cloth first-aid tape to either side of the gauze.

I moved his duffel from the back seat to the trunk, got in the car, and looked up to see if Amanda had any parting words or gestures that she wanted to deliver. I couldn't see her, but the sight of her not being there reminded me I hadn't cleaned up the glass in the street. I opened a garage door, grabbed a broom and dustpan, swept up the shards and smaller pieces, and carried them around the house. I unlocked the gate and dumped the glass in a trash bin.

"You okay?" I asked after getting in the car.

"Yeah," Game said. "You got a fine house and all, but, man, you got one messed up life!"

CHAPTER TWENTY

We headed to town, and Game said he was hungry. I was, too, but I refused to enter a fast-food drive-thru, as he requested each time we approached one. Instead, I insisted we go to Campos Famous Burritos on Pico in Santa Monica. After taking a few bites of his chicken burrito smothered in Spanish sauce, he said, "Old folk do sometimes know things." He smiled and wiped sauce from his chin with a napkin.

I wasn't in a talkative mood as I drove Game to his mother's house. Thinking about schemes and scams, hatching suppositions, and contemplating resolutions were how I worked every case. I should've been able to use the same thought processes to arrive at a conclusion that resolved the various aspects of this case: How were the murders at the park related to the killing of Chris Cerveris and Big Bill Watson? And how did those developments lead to someone threatening me.

Considering that I'd just been released from the loveless relationship that had been holding me back, and considering that Jennifer and I had expressed our love for each other, I should've been clear-headed and full of insights.

Instead, my mind mulled over a psychological abstraction. I speculated that personality is the accumulation of scars a person has—character being how slights, wounds, and disappointments manifest themselves in our words and actions. A nice, kind person has not yet been hurt, or is too dense to know how deeply. Children smile until life teaches them to frown, their frowns later turning to anger, cynicism, and possibly hatred. Few of us are defined or influenced as much by our successes as by our failures—our triumphs transitory, our tragedies forever.

The fact that these thoughts filled my head as we drove south on the 710 was disturbing, so I tried to shake them as I pulled to the curb in front of Rachelle's house.

"Give me a few minutes, Game. I'll meet you inside." I popped the trunk, he got out, grabbed his duffel, closed the trunk, and walked to the house. He gave a perfunctory knock on the door before using his key and entering. I set my Calm meditation app on my phone for five minutes, then concentrated on my breathing. But every few seconds extraneous thoughts intruded. However, when the timer chimed, I knew what I had to do next.

"Hello, Jack," Rachelle said as she gave me a lengthy hug. "I owe you big-time." She finally let go.

"You owe me nothing." I closed the door and set the backpack filled with cash and guns on the floor. "I would refuse to take anything you insisted on giving me because hanging out with Game and getting to know him were a pleasure."

Game, Rachelle, and I sat in her living room, and I explained how dramatically my life had changed since I last sat in that room. Game told his mom how ridiculous Amanda's behavior was and how fine Jennifer was, and how lucky I was to dump Amanda so I could be with Jennifer.

"Good genes," I said, then shrugged. Rachelle and Game laughed, but she said, "You have a lot more going on than looks, that's for sure, but you sure have them."

When I asked how Mike was doing, Rachelle said, "He's fine.

Golfed at Chester Washington yesterday and had an early tee time in Bel Air today."

"Good for him. Do you golf?"

"No," she said. "Don't understand the appeal. He took me to a driving range on our second date, but it seems like a waste of time. Maybe someday, after I spend years practicing, I could be okay, but what would I have accomplished?"

"That's how I feel about algebra," Game said.

Eventually, after Rachelle suggested I have a second Diet Coke and tell her about Jennifer and how our relationship had progressed over the years, she asked, "What do you think will happen to Amanda?"

"I wish I could tell you she'll be fine, but I can't guarantee that. For years, she's threatened to kill herself if I left her, and now I've left her."

"Ain't on you, dawg, that happens. She's an adult with free will."

"He's right," Rachelle said. "She's been emotionally blackmailing you for years. No one should lay a trip like that on someone. I mean, I hope she doesn't harm herself. I wish no one ever did. But this world proves too much for a lot of people."

"They don't generally live in $30 million homes and have millions of adoring fans, but I get your point. Having been truly depressed, I don't think she is. She's needy and seeks constant approval, but she's not depressed. She gets far too happy over a new purse or bingeing the latest Netflix series to be deeply depressed. When I've been at my darkest, I wouldn't have been able to muster anything more than 'Oh,' if I'd won the lottery. Drawing breath sometimes required more effort than it was worth, it seemed. If she kills herself, I don't think she'll do it directly—make a plan, leave a note, execute the plan. She'll wrap the Porsche around a tree or snort coke until her heart explodes. Her fans could then mourn her sad, tragic death, saying she lost control of the wheel or misjudged her tolerance because the other option is unthinkable. Anyone can become depressed enough to consider suicide. Social standing and popularity have nothing to do with someone making that decision. But she's obviously troubled and out of control, so who knows?"

I became overwhelmed with guilt after saying the last sentence. Was there anything I could do to save her from herself? I couldn't have her involuntarily committed because she'd have to publicly display suicidal or homicidal behavior, and I'd just gotten rid of the coke that I could've used to have deputies show up at her door. I could ask the sheriff's department to do a welfare check, but, at best, Amanda would convince them she was fine, if she even answered the door. And the deputies would probably pose for selfies with her and maybe take home a signed eight-by-ten headshot.

In the middle of running through these options, I realized I was feeling guilty about not being able to save Jami. Then I had a thought that my guilt-ridden brain had not allowed me to have until then: I had nothing to do with Jami's death and couldn't have done anything to prevent it.

Had Mike and I not been drunk and been pulled over, we would likely have made it to the hospital so I could've said goodbye to her, perhaps while looking into her eyes and telling her I loved her. But no matter how strong love is, it can't stop internal bleeding or fix a cracked skull. Love can dramatically diminish someone's depression, but it can't perform surgery or stop a van before it runs into a cyclist.

After stepping back into the present, I said, "I'm going to take off. Game's in one piece, so my work here is done."

"True, but you still got a mess out there," Game said.

"Thanks for that." I stepped close to Rachelle and gave her a hug.

"You're my hero, Jack. I owe you big time."

"My pleasure. Anytime. Take care of yourself, Rachelle, and let's stay in touch." I gestured toward the front door and said to Game, "Got a sec?" I slung the backpack over my left shoulder.

"Yeah." He followed me onto the porch and closed the door. He sat on the blue two-seat glider, above three pairs of Adidas.

I said, "I know this isn't my world, but I think I know this much—

when someone enters a gang he buys into the concept of blood-in, blood-out, right?"

"Kinda. Not as simple as that, but I know what you mean."

"I should've asked the logical follow-up question the other day when you admitted you'd never killed anyone. As I meditated a few minutes ago, I realized you've been lying to me. You're not in a gang."

Game turned away from me and stared into space. He crossed his arms on his chest and said nothing.

"I'll take your silence as confirmation. You must've found yourself in a no-win situation Friday night: If you ran out to retaliate against da Posse, pretending to be with a gang you didn't belong to, you would've been spinning your wheels, walking around the neighborhood, trying not to be found by us."

From the corner of my eye, I saw Rachelle pull the window curtain aside to look at us. She let go of the curtain when she saw me turn toward her.

"But if you didn't go with me, you would've had to explain to your mom and Mike that you'd been lying to them, that you were in no danger because you weren't in the MLKs."

He shifted in the glider, turned toward me, started to say something, stopped, then looked down at my shoes.

"Is this really how you want to play this?" I asked. "You say I've been straight with you, but you can't show me respect?" I waited him out.

Eventually he said, "They wouldn't let me in."

He was still looking at my shoes, but he continued. "They said because my mama lost Lawrence and Terrell, they ain't letting her lose her last son."

He hesitated for about fifteen seconds. "Told them I gotta do something 'bout my brothers. Only a buster do nothing after his brothers get killed. But they say it ain't gonna happen, not with them, and I ain't joining no other set. But I can't let Mama think I okay with losing Lawrence and Terrell, so I did what she figured I'd do—joined the set—but I didn't. And all gangs ain't blood-in, blood-out, with killing someone. Some just jump you in by giving you a beating."

"Thank you. I know that wasn't easy, and I'm glad you're not in it. You're obviously close with guys in the MLKs"—he nodded—"because you got them to take action at Popeye's, and they told you specifics about the drug hijacking and the messed-up white van, which means you weren't there when it went down." He nodded again. "Just said you were because you thought it would make me believe you were in the gang." Another nod.

"Look, I know you think it's none of my business, and maybe it's not, but you should come clean with your mom. I know how difficult it is to live a lie, how debilitating. Living a lie can make us hate ourselves. Trust me." Another nod. "Your mom has twice lived through what no parent should ever live through once. Worrying about losing you could cause her to have a stroke, or at least is making her daily life miserable, so you should man-up and tell her the truth. She may be upset you've been lying to her all this time, but she'll be very happy to hear the news."

"How you know?"

"She'll be happy, trust me."

"No, 'bout me lying?"

"You were on the couch when I got here Friday. If I'd been shot superficially but could still walk, I'd have walked until I found the shooters. And then you asked about LoJack. If I needed a car to make an escape, I'd have taken the car, then dumped it before the owner knew it was gone. LoJack would be irrelevant."

"Why'd you stay quiet?" He stood up slowly.

"Didn't put the pieces together initially. I just knew things weren't adding up. I should've figured out earlier you weren't in the gang, but sometimes things take a while to coalesce. You should tell your mother, now that you're back home, so I mentioned it."

"Awwight. Coach Sherwood right. You a good man. Messed up, but a good man."

"Thanks, Game. You're a good man, too. I'll be in touch soon."

He put his hand out to shake, but I gave him a hug. He returned it, stepped away, and nodded.

I walked to the car and heard him ask, "What now?"

"Have to find someplace to stay." I intended to drive to the westside, find an extended-stay hotel, and crash there while I solved the case I'd given to myself—to catch the murderers of Chris and Big Bill and to prove those killings were connected to the park shooting.

My thoughts raced, so I drove the freeways randomly for about two hours, thinking about the murders and Jennifer and Amanda and Jami. I wasn't sure I'd reached any conclusions by the time I took the Bundy exit from the 10 West, intending to pull over to Google extended-stay locations. My phone rang as I reached the bottom of the offramp. I hit the answer button and turned left onto Pico.

"Hello, Darling," Jennifer said.

"Hello, Gorgeous."

"Guess where I just came from?"

"Disneyland?"

"Better. My second meeting of the day. The 1:30 in the Palisades."

"That's great. Proud of you." I crossed Centinela.

"Gonna do at least thirty in thirty," she said. "Maybe ninety in ninety."

"Great, but please remember you only have the present. You only have to get through the day you're in."

"Of course. Thank you, Jack. I feel great and hopeful and happy."

"So do I."

"Guess who took another cake?" she asked.

"The un-sober Jason Gilson. But that's not surprising. Guys like him are all about appearances, impressing people, showing off. Look at his clothes. He's shaped like an inflated pear but thinks bespoke Savile Row suits and monogrammed dress shirts will convince us he's sexy and muscular." I zig-zagged to Olympic, intending to pull over at Memorial Park, but Jen said, "Are you coming over?"

"I want to. I've had to fight the urge many times to knock on your door late at night, but—"

"Now you can, but not late at night. I'm inviting you over now. You're finished with Amanda, right?"

"Yes, but you're in your first day of sobriety. It would be unfair to you and unethical of me because you're extremely vulnerable."

"You told me this morning you loved me. We've wanted each other for, what, about forever, but now you play hard to get? Come on, Jack."

"I'm not playing." I pulled into a parking space next to Memorial Park. "I don't think I could want us to work more than I do. I've felt more alive today than I have since ... since Jami died. Sorry."

"I understand. It's okay. I know she's still with you. I'm fine with that. She was also my friend, remember, and I think I hear her voice sometimes, too. I understand she's with us. Are you saying you don't think she'd want us to be together?"

"No. She'd want us both to be happy. She'd have mocked us for waiting so long."

"So, why won't you come over?"

I hesitated, then said, "There's no way we're going to be able to keep our hands off each other. We both know that. And we'll be amazing together when we get there, but now's not the time. You're too vulnerable, and I'm in total flux. I'm about to start looking for a place to stay."

"You're infuriating. Sexy as hell but infuriating. My house is enormous. You can have two floors to yourself, if you want them."

I watched a father and son playing catch on one of the diamonds. The kid, about twelve, had a canon for an arm.

"Jack?"

"Yes. You win. I'm on my way."

"Fantastic. See you soon, Darling."

"See you soon, Gorgeous."

I pulled away from the curb, filled with anticipation and self-loathing. Most of the time, we know we've taken a misstep only in hindsight. But I knew that Jen shouldn't enter into a relationship immediately after getting sober. She'd probably argue that we'd loved each other for years, so only the sex aspect of our relationship would be new, but she'd be rationalizing. I'd lived in suspended animation for nearly a decade, so why couldn't I wait the recommended year so Jen could learn who she was sober—and learn whether the sober Jen still wanted me? We wouldn't likely hold off for a year, but Day One was a horrible idea. I continued to drive toward Jen, and I was pretty sure I wouldn't be able to turn down her advances when I arrived.

As I approached Trancas Canyon, my cell rang. The caller I.D. said Amanda. I didn't want to talk to her, especially not as I was on my way to start my new life with Jennifer. Amanda and I had a dozen topics to discuss, and we would talk about them soon, but I wasn't in the mood to accuse each other, shout at each other, and catalogue our failings. I listened to Amanda's voicemail, which said: "Jason Gilson's dead. Thought you'd want to know. Pick up your stuff whenever. No hard feelings. And you were right to get rid of the blow."

CHAPTER TWENTY-ONE

Amanda could be gracious and generous and charismatic and kind, but she'd always been horrible during every crisis she and I had lived through, especially those she'd created. Therefore, I found her calm demeanor more unsettling than the news about Gilson's death. She hadn't said how he'd died, and it wouldn't have surprised me if he'd succumbed to his many unhealthy indulgences. His spheroid physique and fondness for the bottle indicated that fitness and health weren't among his highest priorities.

I drove past Zuma Beach, then did something I'd only done two or three times in about seven years of living with Amanda. Instead of turning onto Broad Beach Road at the Malibu West Beach Club, I went up the coast and turned onto Broad Beach Road at the other entrance. I wouldn't pass Amanda's house by going this way, in case she was outside or was looking out a window. I wasn't ready to deal with whatever bullshit she'd spew at me.

I pulled into Jennifer's driveway, two doors away from Amanda's house. Over the years, I'd entered Jennifer's house from the sand or walked from Amanda's front door to hers, so it felt weird to pull into her driveway for the first time. I anticipated her enthusiastic greeting and looked forward to re-starting my life.

But I still had plenty of work to do to extricate myself from my old one, and I hadn't figured out who'd killed Chris and Big Bill. Amanda's calm demeanor after I'd dumped her and after I'd gotten rid of her coke bothered me, so I did what I did when I felt overwhelmed: I tried to meditate.

As occasionally happened while I meditated, an epiphany hit me. I'd taken the long way, entering Broad Beach farther up the Coast Highway, rather than taking the first entrance and driving past Amanda's house and its surveillance cameras. I could gain an advantage if the guy who'd threatened me didn't know I had moved out of Amanda's house into Jennifer's. If my car was on the video driving past Amanda's, then it would be obvious I didn't live there anymore.

And that led me to the conclusion I'd done my best not to reach: Amanda could be involved. Only she could access the surveillance footage shot by her cameras, or she could grant access to them to someone else—either way, she would be involved. As a conspirator or a patsy, I didn't know.

I got out of the car, grabbed the backpack and duffel from the trunk, walked to Jennifer's front door, and knocked. She opened the door, and I took a few seconds to take in the wonder of the moment. She looked tremendous. She'd had time to prepare for my arrival. She didn't need makeup or haute couture to make herself gorgeous, so when she took the time to put makeup on, slither into skin-tight jeans, and slip into the white Chloé ruffled ramie wrap blouse I'd admired in the past, she became almost too beautiful to touch, as though my physically interacting with her would ruin a work of art. But she didn't give me the option to stand back to admire her. She jumped into my arms and kissed me again as she'd kissed me that morning—as though she'd been dreaming about that kiss for years. When our greeting finally ended, and before it progressed into more, I asked, "You have room for my car, right?"

"Of course. Why?"

"I think it makes sense, and could be safer, if nobody knows I'm here."

"Okay, but Amanda has to know you're here, right?"

"She could suspect it, but she won't know for sure."

"Yeah. Give me a sec." She went through the house as I walked back to the car. By the time I started the engine, the far-left garage door was rising. She had a three-car garage. I pulled in beside her black Tesla Model S, which sat next to her black Range Rover with a surfboard rack on top. I got out of the car, hit the button to close the garage door, and entered her house.

I didn't know how Jen's wealth compared to Amanda's, although I thought her taste was far better. Jen had been the face of L'Oréal for more than a decade when she was younger, then she'd started her own cosmetics line that sported her initials, JP, for Jennifer Pearson. Her high-end products were worn and endorsed by celebrities, including Amanda, whose signature Flourish line was one of JP Cosmetics' biggest sellers. Jennifer had also purchased a huge quantity of Apple stock with the money she made from modeling while she was an undergrad, back when Apple stock was just above nothing per share. So, she'd done very well.

Nearly every item in Jen's house was expensive, but her décor didn't scream "Look at me—I'm successful and very deserving of your love and admiration," as Amanda's did. Instead of the Steuben crystal and Venetian masterpieces in Amanda's house that made visitors feel as though they were only as welcome to touch the objects as they would be in a museum, Jen's house was filled with huge abstract oil paintings that she'd created, mostly in earth tones. If she'd marketed them, I'm sure she would've earned another bundle because they were very good, and because she was Jennifer Pearson, supermodel and cosmetics icon. But she painted because doing so made her feel good while doing it. The completed paintings were a bonus.

Jen's artwork and the earth-toned furnishings that complemented them made her house feel homey, similar to the way a well-appointed ski lodge induces guests to make themselves comfortable. The books in nearly every room, many thousands of them throughout the house, made Jennifer's home inviting. Every time I visited, I wanted to pull a book from one of the many shelves, then sit in a well-lighted place as I learned something or lost myself in another world. And I'd done so many times.

As comfortable and inviting as her home was, it was also very high-tech, being outfitted from top to bottom with Apple Homekit, which allowed her to manipulate nearly every piece of electronic equipment remotely, including the deadbolts, lights, cameras, motion sensors, and outlets. Her house had eight security cameras, as opposed to Amanda's four. Jennifer spent on practicality, while Amanda spent on vanity.

Jen was understated and down-to-earth, as I considered myself to be, despite her many millions. Long ago, she'd established a foundation in Los Angeles that helped children of color who suffer from cystic fibrosis. Called Michael's Breath, the foundation honored her younger brother who'd died of the disease at age twenty. She gave fifteen percent of everything she earned to the foundation.

Jennifer prepared an amazing Lebanese meal, the same multi-dish feast she'd served the year before to Jason Gilson, Mike, the woman he was dating at the time, Charlene, the guy Jen was dating, Ethan Hoffman, and Amanda and me. We had all been impressed by the meal, especially the hummus, which was far better than the packaged hummus any of us had eaten. During our first real evening together as a couple, Jennifer and I devoured delicious fattoush, tabbouleh, manakish, and hummus.

After we ate, I debated how to let Jen know I was serious about us not having sex, at least not that night. I didn't want to start this new phase of our relationship by arguing, but I understood that we had to put Jen's sobriety first. If that required us to argue, then that's what we'd do. She was smart and intuitive, so I was hoping she'd understand.

The stressfulness of my thoughts must have shown on my face because she said, "You're right, Jack. Stop worrying. They told me at the Pali meeting I absolutely should not leap into a relationship now. I'm choosing to take that limitation to mean I shouldn't have sex right away. They can't ask me not to love you because if that's what they mean, they can kick rocks." I laughed and hugged her.

We enjoyed our first evening together—snuggling, reading, watching Netflix, then reading and snuggling some more. The only hiccup was when Mike called to tell me about Jason's death.

"Have you heard about Jason?" Mike asked.

"Amanda left me a message saying he'd died. Heart attack?"

"Hell no. His housekeeper found him hanging from his bedroom door. This is bullshit. Chris and Bill and now Jason, dead within a few days. Truly awful. How are you holding up?"

I took a few seconds to process the news. I hadn't wanted to connect Jason's death to Chris' and Big Bill's when I'd heard Amanda's message. Natural causes seemed more likely than another murder of someone I knew, especially back to back to back. Even though I didn't like Jason, I took this news hard because his death meant the killers were getting desperate, and no one should die in his late forties, let alone the way he had. It was possible the coroner wouldn't connect the three murders because each ostensible suicide could believably have occurred on its own, although Big Bill standing on the edge of that barrel before jumping strained credulity.

Why wouldn't the murderers have varied the M.O.s? People kill themselves in numerous ways, so the perpetrators could've made all three killings look like suicides if they'd given their plan more thought. Didn't they care if the three suicides by hanging bunched together made the deaths suspicious to anyone who knew the victims? Why take the trouble to set up suicides, rather than just shooting the victims, if the killers didn't care about being cautious? The answer I came up with was: They're desperate, which made them unfocused. And bullets can be matched to guns, which could lead law enforcement to identify the murderers. The killers probably used ropes they'd found at Chris' and Jason's homes, just as they'd used the line they'd found under Big Bill's deck.

To Mike I said, "I knew Jason was dead, but I didn't know how he died, so I'm holding up less well than I was before you called. This is a tough stretch. But, despite all the garbage, I have good news."

"What?"

"I've left Amanda."

"Hot damn. That's fantastic, dude. About time, if you ask me. But we arrive where we have to be whenever we get there."

"Or we don't. I could've been stuck in my rut forever, but she came home from Milan loaded, then did something else she shouldn't have. The combination was enough to make me take action."

"That's great. I'm truly happy for you. Rachelle will be upset because she was hoping to meet Amanda, but—"

"Maybe that's still possible. She's taking it well. Disconcertingly well."

"Maybe she's relieved. Maybe she knew using again would kick your ass enough for you to finally leave."

"The tantrum she threw seemed genuine, and we both know she's not a good actress."

"You gotta let that go. She's not nearly as bad as you think she is. Be glad you're out. No reason to look back. You've been doing that for what, nine years? Just be grateful. I take it you moved out."

"Yes."

"Great. Where're you staying?"

"The Wilshire Motel, at least for now." I looked at Jennifer, who raised an eyebrow.

"Cool. I'm guessing it's not the Ritz."

"It's fine. Just a place to crash until I land somewhere."

"Great. Gotta go. Congratulations again. Take care of yourself."

"You, too. See ya."

Jen hadn't known about Jason's death, so she was shaken after I told her, especially after she'd seen him at two AA meetings that day. For a second, I thought about not telling her how he'd died, but I didn't want to begin our relationship by withholding information, so I told her how he died.

"That's awful. I can't believe it. He didn't seem sad at the second meeting. He was just as full of it at that one. He took another cake, bragged about how he managed to make it another year. Do you think he was distraught over living a lie, claiming to be sober but still drinking?"

"A week ago, I'd have said that was possible. No one ever knows why people kill themselves, and suicide notes can be riddled with obfuscation, deflection, and delusional accusations. But Jason didn't leave a suicide note, I'm guessing, and he didn't kill himself."

She set the copy of *The Sun Also Rises* she was reading in her lap and said, "Why not? You just said nobody ever knows why people do it."

"Chris, Big Bill, and Jason didn't hang themselves within days of each other. It defies probability for three people I knew to kill themselves in such a tight cluster by the same method. Had there been the tiniest possibility that Chris or Big Bill had killed himself, that possibility just disappeared. They were all murdered."

She set the novel on the coffee table and asked as she walked to the kitchen, "Herbal tea?"

"Please."

While she made tea, I checked the websites of the *Los Angeles Times* and *The Malibu Times*. Neither had an update on Chris' death. It would be classified as a suicide until I could prove it wasn't one. Middle-aged people who live alone kill themselves in large numbers. Chris had produced two consecutive box-office disasters, movies so bad that the studios wouldn't give advance screeners for the last one to reviewers in the hope that moviegoers would fill theaters on opening day, recouping some of their investments, before the reviews eviscerated the movie and kept audiences away.

Someone accustomed to success, as Chris had been for decades, could've become distraught over his ego-crushing failures, so his suicide wouldn't likely raise red flags the way the suicide of a producer who had the Midas touch would have. I didn't know what

Chris' financials were like, but his having three ex-wives probably didn't help his bottom line or his sense of self.

Los Angeles County requires autopsies on homicides and suicides, and the resulting reports are generally made public. But my search for Chris Cerveris' autopsy report on the County website came up empty. The *Times* didn't run a story about Big Bill's death because he'd only been a retired businessman who'd kept a low-profile, and suicides of old people who have terminally ill spouses aren't newsworthy. Big Bill's obituary would probably run soon in the *Times*, and the local paper would almost certainly include at least a blurb about his death, then would run his obituary.

Had the coroner who arrived at the scene under Big Bill's deck agreed with my assessment that Big Bill wouldn't have been able to get on top of the barrel to stand on its rim? If so, had the coroner classified Big Bill's death as a homicide? Or would the sheriff's deputies suggest that the coroner classify the death as a suicide so Big Bill's killers would think they'd gotten away with the murder?

Jen returned from the kitchen and handed me chamomile tea in a white mug, on which was written World's Greatest Nothing in black script. When I'd seen her drinking from it in the past, I'd told her the slogan was downbeat and self-negating. She'd told me she interpreted the phrase as an expression of Buddhist detachment, as a reminder to stay humble and grounded in an ever-changing world filled with people whose lives are brief.

She sat next to me on one of the two enormous dark-chocolate couches and sipped from a white mug with Michael's Breath scripted in royal blue on it. She asked, "Why didn't you tell Mike you're here?"

"He said something odd, and my gut told me to mislead him."

"To lie, you mean."

"Sure, if you insist words have meanings. And it's only a lie tonight. Tomorrow, it will be true."

"Wait, you're not going to stay here?"

"Okay, it will be kind of true. I'll stay here, but I'll check into the motel, then leave my car there. See what happens."

"What could happen? What did he say that was odd?"

"It could be nothing, and it probably is. Mike worked as a model long ago and booked a few commercials before getting his teaching credential. He could've heard about Chris' death and Jason's death from someone in the business. Word travels fast. But how'd he know about Big Bill? He was a retired businessman, not a Hollywood player. Mike could've heard about Big Bill in a hundred ways, but I went on alert when he mentioned him. It just didn't feel right, so I misled him."

"Lied, you mean." She smiled, scooted closer, and leaned her head on my shoulder. Even amid turmoil, I felt comfortable in a way I hadn't felt in years.

We talked about sobriety and relationships before we started to read again. At about 11:30, Jen led me to her bedroom, said, "I promise to behave myself," then quickly fell asleep with her head on my chest.

Waking up next to Jen felt perfect, and the morning went smoothly until I went out front to pick up the *L.A. Times*. After grabbing the paper, I turned toward the house, then saw a red envelope sitting on the mailbox attached to the house. Instead of being addressed to Drake, as the one on Amanda's mailbox had been, this one said: MORON. I opened the envelope. On the yellow index card, written in the same off-hand scrawl used to write the other threat, were the words: NO MORE WARNINGS!

Someone was watching me, or at least following me. If Amanda was involved, as I thought she could be, she could've guessed I was at Jen's, then walked over to drop off the threat. Or maybe she happened to walk onto her driveway when my car had been parked on Jen's driveway. Amanda could've seen my car if she'd looked up the street.

Jen's brand-new sobriety didn't need more drama, but I wasn't going to lie to her. I went inside and handed her the index card and the envelope. She sat at the kitchen table, wearing her favorite brown sweatpants and a navy-blue New York Yankees T-shirt.

She looked at the index card and said, "Oh, no." With fear in her eyes, she asked, "Shouldn't we have them checked for prints?" She dropped the index card and the envelope onto the table.

"There won't be prints. I want to see your surveillance footage."

In her office, she found the relevant footage and hit play. Within two seconds, what looked like the same figure, wearing black from head to toe, including gloves, a hat, and a ski mask, entered the frame from the left, making the same herky-jerky movements that Amanda's surveillance camera had captured. I could barely distinguish the whacky gestures on this footage from the ones on the other tape. The light was different, and Jennifer's camera was mounted about two feet lower than Amanda's front-door camera was, which changed the angle. But we learned nothing new of significance from the tape. The perpetrator tilted the top of his black hat toward the camera, as he'd done at Amanda's, then limped, traipsed, and Quasimodo-ed out of frame to the left. If there had been a flash of yellow on his right wrist, we didn't see it. We watched the arrival and departure four times.

"Thank you," I said. "I'd say it's the same person, but I can't tell if it's a man or a woman. That he was a man was my default position on the first tape—just assumed someone who delivered a threat would be male, but I don't rule out it could be Amanda. They're the same height and general size. What do you think?"

"I'm not leaning either way. Too hard to tell." She hesitated, then looked at me and said, "This is awful. We're supposed to be celebrating getting together after all this time. We're supposed to be making love. Instead, we're being threatened, soon to be what—hunted, gunned down?"

"You're right. But this is where we are. The only way out is to deal with it. I'm not letting Chris and Big Bill get killed without doing everything I can to catch their murderers. Would I bother if only Jason had been killed? Probably not, not if pursuing justice for him interfered with the two of us becoming a couple. We don't have to like this, but we have to deal with it. If we run, we can lose them because I know how to be evasive and cover my tracks, so at least they'd no longer have the advantage of knowing where we are. Or we could make good on what I told Mike—that I'm staying at the Wilshire Motel, then see if my paranoia was justified or was just paranoia. Or we can hunker down. We're well armed. I don't think their threats are idle anymore, and they're not going to be able to sell another suicide by hanging. They won't have to be subtle while killing us."

"Jack!"

"I'm sorry. I really am."

"I need a drink," she said. My heart jumped, but before I could respond, she said, "Kidding. I'm sorry. Couldn't resist." She kissed me and said, "You're all I need right now."

"I feel the same way about you, but we could also use some answers."

CHAPTER TWENTY-TWO

My plan involved driving two cars into Santa Monica, checking into the Wilshire Motel, and leaving my car there. I was betting we weren't being watched nonstop. They were probably just checking on us occasionally. Of course, the extent of their surveillance depended on the size of their crew, and I had no idea how big their operation was. The killers obviously knew where Jen and I were, but that wouldn't be enough, not if we executed my plan well.

On a hunch, I told Jen I had to check on something and would be about twenty minutes.

"Check on what?"

"Who's taking care of Sadie, Big Bill's wife, and who's writing his obituary."

"Good luck. I'll get ready"

I went out the back door and walked down the flight of stairs made of weather-resistant pressurized wood. Jen's house had two fewer floors than Amanda's did. Jen's didn't have the additional top floor above the main floor, and she didn't have the bottom floor that had required the builders of Amanda's house to cut deeply into the bluff. As a result, Jen's house didn't flood, as Amanda's had twice during storms in the years I lived there.

I walked along the packed, wet sand until I reached the house that Big Bill and Sadie had shared. The bluff that Jennifer's and Amanda's houses were on was smaller at the Watson's house. Jennifer's house was only a few houses away from the pinnacle of Broad Beach Road, and the bluff sloped downward before flattening out as the arc of beach swept toward Trancas Canyon, Westward Beach, and Point Dume. The beach in front of Big Bill's house was significantly deeper than it was in front of Amanda's and Jennifer's houses.

The area under Big Bill's free-standing deck gave no clue that its co-owner, a Malibu resident for more than fifty years, had been murdered there. Sheriff's deputies had removed the yellow tape they would have put up to keep people out of the scene, even if they didn't consider Big Bill's death a homicide. The two whiskey barrels sat where they had when Bill had been found, and only the line that he had been hanging from appeared to have been removed. I started to walk up the few steps on the left side of the deck, then stopped. Something else was missing.

I walked back under the deck and looked around. It took me a few seconds to determine what wasn't there: The red kayak that had been hanging under the deck when Game and I had visited Big Bill on Saturday was gone. The orange two-person craft still hung from the rafters, but the red one-seater wasn't there. The aluminum hooks the boat usually hung from were still tied to the ends of the yellow lines wrapped around the dark, wooden rafter. Was I certain I'd seen a red kayak while I was doing my best not to look at Big Bill hanging there? No, I wasn't. But I wasn't certain of anything.

My plan had been to stop by the Watson home to try to solidify the theory I'd been mulling over. The missing kayak didn't confirm my theory, but its absence suggested my theory could have merit.

I walked up the steps and along the path on the left side of the property leading to the house. The house was among the oldest on

Broad Beach. Most of the other "beach shacks" that had been built more than fifty years ago had been torn down so gazillionaires could buy adjacent lots and construct elaborate temples to their greatness, as though immortality could be achieved through architectural gaudiness. One concrete abomination a few doors down recently listed for $100 million.

Big Bill and Sadie Watson, conversely, had made a life for themselves in a modest two-bedroom home, albeit one sitting along a stunning, exclusive stretch of sand. I'd been in their house two dozen times to play chess with Big Bill, and Amanda and I had attended birthday parties every year there for Big Bill and Sadie. Big Bill and I never played chess in Amanda's house because he felt uncomfortable among the art pieces, and he said he couldn't find a single piece of furniture he could sit on or in without squirming. He claimed his extreme height caused his discomfort, but I suspected that Amanda did. I never asked him what he disliked about her, but I guessed her "always on" persona had something to do with his coolness toward her. He'd had the grace never to say anything to me about his feelings toward her, but one day I asked him why he didn't want to play chess at our place, and his response was: "I like Big Macs," then he shrugged.

I walked onto the patio at the back of the house and approached the sliding glass door. I knocked gently. In a few seconds, I saw Frank Watson, the only offspring of Big Bill and Sadie, approach. He slid the door open, stepped out quickly so the yellow Lab, Kayak, didn't get out, and threw his arms around me as he said, "Jack! It's great to see you! How've you been, my friend?"

Frank was two inches shorter than his father, but that still made him six-four, so he had two inches on me and probably forty pounds.

"I'm fine, but the question is: How are you holding up?"

He let go of me and gestured to a pair of sun-tattered, rainbow-colored, fabric beach chairs, the ones Big Bill and I had sat in while we'd played chess. We sat, and I adjusted my chair so I faced Frank.

"You know me," he said. "I'm not a philosophical guy. I don't pretend to have answers to the big questions, but deep down, children know their parents are going to die sometime."

"Some of us are more aware of that than others."

"Of course. Even though it's a total surprise Dad died before Mom, I'm trying to be strong and put the best spin on losing him. He was seventy-two. Not old, obviously, but it's not like I lost him when I was a kid."

"I think being able to see the positive is essential, although that's not my strength, that's for sure."

"In your job, you're probably served by believing the worst of people."

"Probably, but it doesn't make for exceptional mental health or excellent sleep."

He nodded and said, "I know you're genuinely here to express your sympathies. And I appreciate them. I do. But, knowing you for forever and knowing what you do, I'm sure you're also here to ask about his manner of death. Am I right?"

"Yes."

"Not a chance Dad killed himself. After Mom dies, I could believe it. Absolutely. But now? No way."

"I saw the scene. It confirmed murder. The killers made a mistake. They should've inverted a barrel. I pointed out the near impossibility of it being a suicide to a member of the coroner's office. He said he'd look into it. Don't know if he did."

We heard a sound behind us in the house, and he turned to look and listen. I knew that his mom was in there. I guessed her primary caretaker, Maria, was, too.

"How is she?" I asked.

"Going downhill fast. It's awful. But not fast enough, if you know what I mean. I know that must sound bad."

"No, it doesn't. It sounds loving. She's suffering, and everyone else around her feels helpless and stressed. Because her dying is inevitable, dying with less suffering and more dignity is what everyone should be hoping for."

"Right. But I can only be here so often. With Leslie and the kids, and the practice, I've got my hands full. Maria is great, really great, but ..."

"I understand. Try to hang in there. One day at a time, brother."

"It feels more like second-by-second, but I hear you."

"If you'll forgive my directness, who's writing the obituary?"

"We're two friends talking. You can't be too direct. I plan to write it today. Why?"

"I know this is an absurd suggestion, and I know people only get one obituary in their local papers, but what if you let the guys who did this know someone's onto them?"

"Say he was murdered?"

"Yes."

"If you think that will work, great. Mom's not able to read it, and everyone who knew Dad knows he didn't kill himself, so, yeah, I can do that. But why? What happened to the element of surprise?"

"In most cases, surprise works to your advantage, but when perps are desperate and getting sloppy, letting them know you're breathing down their necks can cause them to make more mistakes"

"Ones that could get them caught."

"That's what I'm hoping. Which leads me to my last question, but then I have to go. I left Jennifer waiting."

"Pearson? What happened to Amanda?"

"Let's just say we're no longer co-stars"

"I wish I could say that surprised me."

"Why can't you?"

"Because I've heard things." He paused, then said, "Look, I'm sorry I said anything. I should've just said, 'That's too bad.'"

"No, what did you hear?"

"That she's been using."

"Really? Who said that, and how long ago?"

"Probably six months, maybe a little more. Heard it at a party down the beach, at the Prabhu's. Gilson, the twerp, was holding court, or thinking he was. Most of the time people just laugh at him, not at his stories. He was bragging about having seen a certain big-time actress on her knees. 'But not the way you're thinking,' he said. Then he delivered what he thought was the punchline: 'She was snorting a line off a toilet seat. America's Sweetheart, my ass!'"

"The guy was a zilch. You know he's dead, right?" He shook his head but didn't look as surprised as I would've guessed he would look. "Housekeeper found him hanging from his bedroom door. He probably had reasons to kill himself, but I'd bet everything I have that Chris Cerveris, your dad, and Gilson were killed by the same people. And that's one of the reasons why I'm here: Did your dad ever mention Marty Milford, Chris' producing partner?"

"No, why?"

"No casual references or unwarranted, vicious criticisms of his movies or—?"

"Not that I can remember. Why?"

"I think he's behind the killings. He's an arrogant blowhard, but he's made some good movies. He and Chris produced probably a dozen together. Gilson, Marty, and Chris ran in the same circles, worked together. Family members and business partners are always the first suspects. I don't know much yet, including how Gilson was involved, but your dad's murder makes me believe he must have been in Milford's orbit somehow. But I don't know what that connection is, and without it, my theory falls apart."

"What theory?"

"If it didn't involve your father, I'd hesitate to tell you because I have zero proof, and I'm not doing much more than spit-balling."

"What's your theory, Jack?"

"I think Milford is smuggling cocaine in Wave Skimmers."

"Jesus, dude. What's gotten into you? You're obviously under a ton of stress. I've personally watched the entire process, from the barrels of resin powder arriving in the factory in San Felipe, to the kayaks being shipped north, to them being inspected by drug-sniffing dogs at the border, to being fitted with handles, seats, and hatches at the shop in Compton. Trust me. There is nothing being smuggled in the kayaks."

"I believe every word you just said, except the last sentence. I'm not saying I understand how it's being done, and I'm not saying your dad had anything to do with it. I'm saying that Chris, your dad, and Gilson were all murdered within days of each other, all by hanging. The universe throws out all kinds of coincidences, some far outside the realm of probability, but these murders can't be coincidental. I have no idea how the pieces fit together. Don't know if Chris was in on the smuggling, don't know how Milford managed the smuggling, don't know how Gilson was involved, don't know if your dad was involved, don't know how the MLKs and da Uptown Posse are involved, but those are the pieces I have, and I need to solve the puzzle."

"Look, I'm going to tell you something that's going to hurt you a lot. Something I haven't told you all these years because I'm your friend, but only a friend could tell you this. It's something I suspect you already know, so it may not hurt as much as it would if you were delusional or stupid. You aren't very good at your job."

I stared at him. I'd known that being an investigator was not my dream profession. I'd known that I'd fallen into the work because I needed something to keep my mind occupied so I could try to decrease my thoughts about losing Jami. I'd known that I lacked the passion for my law-enforcement mission to be a great investigator. But I didn't think those realities made me bad at my job.

When I continued to stare at him, Frank said: "It's kind of a running joke in this town. I don't take pleasure in saying it, but it's true. Other PIs are more ruthless, less principled, more corrupt, meaner, more willing to admit there are no rules. I'm sure you're smarter than all of them, but intelligence is only part of what a person needs to do your job well. They're brutal bullies, and you're not."

"You think that makes me bad at my job?"

"Obviously, or I wouldn't have said it. But I said not very good."

"You could be right. Regardless of whether you are, thank you for your honesty. I'm about to prove you wrong, though, but I'll need your help, if you're willing to help me."

"Sure. I'm not saying I don't like and respect you, Jack."

"We're cool. I swear. But I need you to write an obituary stating outright that your dad was murdered and connecting his murder to the murders by hanging of Chris Cerveris and Jason Gilson. Can you do that?"

"Of course."

"Great. Then I need you to go through your father's paperwork, all of it, sheet by sheet, looking carefully for any mention of Marty Milford, or Martin Milford. I don't care if it's a dinner receipt from the Holiday House in 1982. I need you to find a connection. I'm not saying to invent one, but I'm telling you a connection between the two exists. You know how I know?"

"No."

"Because I'm a good detective." I smiled and stood. "Maybe not great but good enough."

"Trust me, Jack, I'm not rooting against you. If you're able to figure out who killed Dad and put these assholes away, I'll tell everyone I know you're better than Sherlock Holmes."

"Thank you. Take care of yourself. During one of your mom's lucid spells, tell her she makes the best lemon bars in the world."

"Will do." We shook hands, and I started to walk away. But I remembered something, so I turned and asked, "What did you do with the red kayak under the deck?"

He looked at me as though he was confused, but he didn't appear to overreact. Frank had filled in about ten times when the monthly floating hold'em game I played in was down enough players to threaten the integrity of the game. He'd been good company and a good sport, but he was a lousy poker player and a terrible bluffer. I'd surprised him with the question about the red kayak to test his reaction, to see if everything I'd just told him would ensure he would go inside to destroy documents, then call Marty to tell him to suspend all smuggling operations immediately. If Frank had been involved in the smuggling scheme, especially without his father's knowledge, could his father have found out about it, then been such a liability—threatening to expose the operation, perhaps—that Frank and the others had to eliminate him so he wouldn't talk? As I'd sat there and told him my theory, I realized I could be tipping him off, causing the operation to shut down and destroy all traces of its existence, but I had to take that risk.

"I didn't know it was missing," he said. He didn't repeat the question, as people trying to think of a believable response frequently do, and he didn't lift his chin as he'd done when he was trying to bluff me off my pair of queens with his pair of treys. But he might have become a better liar.

I had to believe him because if I didn't, and he really had removed the red kayak, then he'd helped commit the murders, which meant I'd be dead soon. Because I had many more reasons to want to live than I had a few days before, I believed him.

CHAPTER TWENTY-THREE

"I'm sorry," I said to Jen when I returned to her house. "I didn't intend to stay that long."

She was at the kitchen table reading, with a coffee mug and an empty cereal bowl in front of her. She put down *The Sun Also Rises*, stood, and said, "That's okay. Learn anything?" She gave me a hug and sat down.

"I either learned that my theory is idiotic or that Frank Watson has learned to lie." She raised an eyebrow. I told her my theory about Marty Milford importing cocaine in Wave Skimmers. To her credit, she didn't suggest I take antipsychotics. However, she said, "You've given this a lot of thought, and solving crimes and catching criminals are not within my field of expertise, so I'll buy your theory because you've espoused it. However, you didn't supply any evidence for your theory."

"I don't have any yet."

"Your honor," she said, in a pompous, authoritative tone, "I propose an unsubstantiated theory, bolstered by supposition and my staunchest hunch. Based on this theory, which is accurate because I'd like it to be, I suggest you sentence Marty Milford to the maximum sentence allowed by law. And if you could eviscerate him publicly, that would suit me even better."

"Thank you for believing in me."

"That's my job now, right? I support your theories, and in my spare time I continue my fight to prove that Earth is flat."

"It's important to have goals. Joking aside, I have a question, and I need you to be honest."

"Unless I'm obviously joking—which I'll never do regarding the flatness of the Earth—you can assume I'm being honest with you. I'm not going to remain sober otherwise."

"Okay. Do people think I'm a bad investigator?"

She finished her coffee and said, "I wouldn't say that. I'd put it differently, but I'm not sure how best to put it. Okay, I'll give you a parallel example. Initially, I made my living with my looks, making gobs of money primarily from my genes. Because I look the way I do, people assume I can't also be smart. I worked my ass off finishing my Ph.D., then I worked at least twice that hard launching JP and building its market share, battling the recession, then regaining market share. But almost everyone thinks I was blessed with good looks, so I didn't really accomplish the rest of it. Of course, I launched JP because I was a model, but you understand.

"I think this town perceives you in a similar way. You possessed enough talents or traits, physical and otherwise, to attract Amanda, one of the world's biggest movie stars, and you've been riding her coattails since—or that's the perception. You don't have to be a great P.I. because people like to associate with fame, and if they hire you, they're only one degree of separation from Amanda."

I sat down in the chair next to her but didn't say anything for a few seconds.

"People settle for someone they believe to be a lesser investigator because they hope to meet Amanda?"

"That's my theory, anyway. I'm not saying I think of you that way. I've known you since grad school. I know you. They don't."

"Frank said the perception is that not only am I not good, but it's also widely known that I'm not ruthless."

"Listen to yourself. You're a good person. Why in the world would you want to be ruthless? In sports and frequently in business, people talk about winning at all costs as though that's the ultimate goal. Sacrifice your principles, cheat at every opportunity, thumb your nose at laws, trample on your friends and competitors, and ignore you family, all to raise a trophy or your company's stock price. It's warped. Making sacrifices to achieve goals? Sure, that's fine. We've all done that. But abandoning your humanity so others think you do your job well? That's not you." I nodded.

"Frank's right," she said. "You're not ruthless. I know in this town being an asshole is considered to be an asset, but in life it generally means you're so miserable and unself-aware that you consider destroying people to be admirable."

She gestured for me to stand as she stood, then gave me a hug. "For the record," she said, "I'm sure you can do whatever you need to do when push comes to shove."

"We'll see."

Twenty minutes later, we were in her garage, finalizing our plan. We'd packed overnight bags, and I set them in the trunk of the BMW and in the backseat of the Range Rover. Jen made six sandwiches and put them in a picnic basket, along with many pieces of fruit and a box of apricot Clif Bars. She filled the reusable water bottles I kept in the trunk, filled four of her own, and put them all in a large, silver Coleman cooler. I put my backpack and duffel into the Range Rover. I hung one black suit and one of Jen's many black dresses on the hook behind the BMW's driver's seat, then hung one of each behind the driver's seat in the Range Rover. I removed the Beretta and the Mossberg from the BMW and put the handgun in my bag in the Range Rover. I removed the camera equipment and the night-vision goggles and put them next to my bag, followed by the empty, stakeout pee bottle. I stood the shotgun in the right-rear corner of the garage and asked Jen to choose one of the six hats in a box in the trunk, next to the one with a few changes of clothes in it. She chose the navy New York Yankees cap, tied her hair in a bun at the top of her neck, and put on the cap, followed by her sunglasses. I chose the blue UCLA Bruins cap and put my sunglasses on. We both wore black hoodies, which we pulled up over our caps. She wore black yoga pants, a blue T-shirt, and gray Adidas running shoes, and I wore jeans, a black T-shirt, and Brooks running shoes. I reminded myself to slump a little and hoped Jen would remember to sit tall.

"You're certain of the plan, right?"

"It's possible you're a good P.I., but you're lousy with trust."

"It's just that you're too good looking also to be intelligent."

"Good luck, pansy."

"You, too, airhead."

I backed the Range Rover out, followed by Jen in the BMW. I closed the garage doors, checked for oncoming cars, and swung the tail downhill across the road into the far lane. She backed out but faced the opposite direction, downhill. We nodded to each other and pulled away. Jen passed Amanda's house and her street-facing security camera, and I went out the other way. Amanda's camera had no chance to capture an image of who was driving the BMW because the passenger's side was closest to the house, and the camera was mounted high above ground level. I went up the hill, checked for any people sitting in cars by the side of the road, didn't notice any, then made a U-turn. I went back down Broad Beach Road, passing Jen's and Amanda's houses on my right, certain that Amanda's camera could only identify our vehicles, not their drivers.

We each made three circuits of Broad Beach Road, turning left onto PCH at Trancas Canyon Road, then back onto Broad Beach Road, varying our speed significantly each time. During my three laps, I didn't notice any suspicious cars. I took PCH all the way to Santa Monica, checking for a tail frequently. In Santa Monica, I took Montana to Bundy, pulling to the curb before I reached the Ralphs, accessible from Bundy and Wilshire. The supermarket was only a few doors away from the motel, but not within view. I had a while to wait because Jen was taking the long way around: North on PCH, through the San Fernando Valley on the 101, over the hill on the 405, then off on the Wilshire exit. Traffic could have allowed her to arrive an hour and change later or caused her to arrive four hours after I did. While waiting, I listened to Stevie Wonder's *Songs in the Key of Life*, then meditated.

Eventually, I received a text from Jen: *On Wilshire. Finally. Great*, I texted. She'd be there in five minutes. While waiting, I realized I might be a lousy P.I. because if I'd been trying to follow Jen and me, and I knew where we said we'd end up, why would I try to follow us from her house? Why not just set up on the Wilshire Motel, then wait? Of course, I could have only said I intended to stay at the Wilshire Motel, then gone anywhere else. If I'd lied, then someone would have had to follow us from the house. In other words, I couldn't determine whether I was good at my job based solely on how we'd executed this evasive action. But at least I was sure no one had followed us.

I heard a tap on the passenger's-side front window and opened my eyes. Jen smiled, and I unlocked the door.

"Hello, Lover," she said.

"Well, not quite."

"You really are a jackass. But you know that, don't you? Even take pride in it."

"Thanks for noticing." I leaned over to kiss her. I intended to give her a peck, but she had other ideas. After a few seconds, I pulled away. "How'd it go?"

"Fine. Some traffic but no followers I could see."

"Great. Are you ready?"

"Yes."

We got out of the Range Rover. I locked it, walked back to the BMW, and got in. I drove to the corner of Bundy and Wilshire, made a left on Wilshire, and turned left into the motel entrance. The Wilshire Motel consists of a small courtyard lined with green rooms, some free-standing, some connected to the unit next door. The doors for a few of the rooms were recessed, and guests parked their cars in front of these doors, within the alcoves made by the adjacent rooms. Other guests parked their cars in front of their rooms, in full view of the street. I hoped to check into one of these rooms. If we weren't being watched as we checked in, the people looking for us would be able to see my BMW parked at the motel, in front of the room we were supposed to be staying in. Ideally, I'd have wanted to stay in room twenty-one or twenty-two, nearest to Wilshire. The clerk, a goateed, long-haired, twenty-something probably hoping to be discovered while working this dead-end job, told us that those rooms were rented.

"Check-in's not 'til three, but we got room twelve available now," he said, "so I don't see a problem. Twelve's right at the back, near the alley. Has a nice table out front with a awning." He smiled broadly, not the seductive smirk that was probably featured on his headshots. He was one of a hundred-thousand others like him who arrived from across the country so they could "make it" in Tinseltown. He was good-looking and had as good a chance as any, which meant he had very little chance at all.

"We'll take it," I said.

After filling out the paperwork, I asked, "Has anyone asked whether Jack Drake has checked in?"

"We're not allowed to disclose that information, sir. It's policy. Certain people would rather not let the world know they're here, if you know what I mean."

"Sure, I understand. But I'm willing to bet that if someone bribed you, let's say with a hundred bucks, you'd tell him if I'd checked in."

"Sir, this is making me uncomfortable."

"Sorry. That's not my intention. Here's the thing: What if I were to give you two hundred bucks to allow yourself to be bribed by anyone who asks if I'm in my room? You can employ Stanislavski or Meisner, whichever enhances your process. Play it however feels right."

"Sir ... Mr. Drake, there's a camera pointed at this desk, right there. I couldn't be seen accepting a bribe. I'd lose my job."

"But if you found two hundreds just outside the door in the planter to the left—it's a money tree, by the way—you'd probably manage to keep your job while communicating our whereabouts."

"I believe I'd manage, Mr. Drake."

I nodded.

Looking at Jen, he said, "Hey, aren't you—?"

"Yes, Jennifer Pearson. You can let them know I'm here, too."

I dropped the hundreds in the planter, then parked the car in the space in front of number twelve as Jen walked through the courtyard to our room. I popped the trunk and grabbed the two overnight bags. They contained nothing we needed. They were decoys, meant to sell the perception that we were staying in the motel, in case anyone was watching us. Our supplies for the next couple of days were in the other bags in the Range Rover. Jen grabbed the suit and the dress from behind the seat. I locked the car, walked to the other side, and fumbled the car key. I bent down to pick it up but instead hid it behind the rear tire on the passenger's side. Then we entered the room.

I'd stayed in the motel once before, for one night about a month after Jami died. I was considering suicide, and I'd thought that a stranger who found what was left of me would be far less traumatized than our landlord or a neighbor would have been upon finding me. I'd planned to tape a note to the door, written in English, followed by Spanish, saying that the housekeeper shouldn't enter the room but should call the police because there was a dead body inside. If the housekeeper didn't believe the note or felt compelled to verify its message before calling the police, he or she might have looked inside. What was inside would be shocking but not traumatizing, I hoped, because I would have been just another nameless nobody who'd decided to leave this world early, not a friend or neighbor.

During that night nine years earlier, I'd stayed awake hour after hour, weighing the benefits of oblivion against the torturous pain and emptiness I'd have to endure for the rest of my life. Because the rest of my life could've amounted only to minutes that night, it would've been logical to have gone through with the plan: to put the Beretta I'd purchased three days before in my mouth and pull the trigger.

Logic and suicide, however, rarely work in concert. In fact, they're usually antithetical. But logic didn't play a role that night. What kept me from pulling the trigger were guilt and blame and self-loathing. If I'd killed myself, I wouldn't have felt the overwhelming pain, loss, and anguish I thought I deserved to feel.

Jen looked around the small, clean room, hung the suit and dress in the closet, turned to me and said, "As flophouses go, this is the most recent one I've checked into."

"Nothing but first class when you're with me, Gorgeous."

She sat on the bed and patted the space next to her, encouraging me to sit down. I did, and she said, "I understand that this spy-craft is necessary because of the threats, but you said no one who intends to kill you warns you first. He just kills you."

"That's generally true. And you're right: All of this could be unnecessary. Maybe no one's following us. They could simply surprise us at your house. But if someone shows up here looking for us, then we know Mike's involved. He's the only one I mentioned the motel to, and we certainly lost any tail we might have had."

"But that's where I start to worry about you. Mike's your oldest friend. He was the best man at your wedding, forchristsake. Because he made what could be a slip of the tongue, or because he knows information you don't know the source of, you're accusing him of threatening us, of murdering three people? He's your best friend."

"First, you've been my best friend for years. Mike and I have been very close, but we've been guy close. We talk about sports and politics, and women in inappropriate ways, but he and I have never confided in each other as you and I have. After his sister died, I told him I'd be there for him, but all he'd ever said to me about what he was going through was, 'This sucks. I really miss her.' There's nothing wrong with that, but it's not the kind of self-disclosure you and I have. For example, he knows I don't get along with my father, but I've never told him why."

"Don't guys tell each other stuff like that? You told me all the awful details."

"Exactly. Not only have you shown empathy because that's who you are, but, sadly, you also understand abuse because you've lived it. If I'd mentioned the belittling and the beatings to Mike, he'd either have said something like 'Welcome to the club" or would've changed the subject. During poker games or on golf courses or basketball courts, men don't explore their feelings and mull over the effects of childhood traumas."

"But you do, and that's one of the reasons I love you, and have for a long time. Amanda said something to me a few years ago that made me respect her for saying it and envy her for being with you. She said, 'Jack's a man in all the right ways, if you know what I mean, but he's also one of the girls when he needs to be.'"

"I won't wear your clothes, if that's what's worrying you."

"Jackass." She leaned her head against my shoulder.

"But I'm your jackass, and you wouldn't want it any other way."

"You're right, I wouldn't. But are we gonna to do this or not?"

"Let's go."

We stood, I unlocked the back window, and slid it horizontally. I pushed out the screen, tearing it in the process. Had I been too thick to fit through the window, I'd come prepared to remove the air-conditioner in the adjacent window, which would've given us plenty of room. Jen easily stepped through the window, careful not to step on the gas line outside. She looked down the alley to her right, studying the roof lines, looking for motion or an unexpected reflection. After she was satisfied no one was watching us from that direction, she turned to her left, and searched until she was satisfied no one was watching us from that direction, either.

She started to climb the black wrought-iron fence with spikes at the top. Because the fence was meant to keep people out, it was not easy to climb. She struggled to get very far. Just as I was about to advise her to use the wall of the motel room behind her and the roof to climb the fence—with one hand and one foot on the wall and the other hand and foot on the fence, the way rock climbers climb rock chimneys—she figured it out. She stepped on the flat crossbar and held onto the thick support column as she rotated her body, stepping between the spiked rods, causing her to face me. Instead of dealing with the tricky downclimb, she simply jumped backward, letting out a grunt when she landed, allowing her flexed knees to absorb the shock.

"Ugh. That hurt."

"Excellent job," I said, grateful I hadn't man-splained how to climb the fence. I squeezed through the window, closed it, and climbed up and over.

"Show off," she said as I downclimbed by using a rock-climbing layback move to descend the support column.

We walked down the alley to the Ralphs parking lot, then to her Range Rover parked on Bundy. She got behind the wheel.

"First stop's the bank," she said as she pulled out, adding, "I feel a little like Bonnie."

"You realize Bonnie and Clyde *robbed* banks, right?"

"I meant Bonnie Raitt," she said, then sang, "Let's give them something to talk about."

She pulled into the parking lot at 26th and San Vicente. I went into the bank, carrying my backpack. I placed it on the counter in front of a fifty-something female teller and pulled out the eight stacks of hundred-dollar bills. I didn't look at her, so I didn't know how she reacted as I set eighty grand in cash on the counter. I tore off the mustard-colored band on one of the stacks and counted out fifty bills. I folded those, then stuffed them in the right-front pocket of my jeans, next to my wallet.

"I'd like to deposit the rest, please. Should be seventy-five thousand." I looked at her. Her face was devoid of expression. I was glad she didn't play in our floating hold 'em game.

"Let's go, partner," I said when I returned. Jen pulled out of the lot onto San Vicente and worked her way to the 405 South. I transferred a thousand dollars from my pocket to my wallet and put a thousand dollars in each of our four bags, which I retrieved, one after the other from the back seat, before returning each of them.

While I'd been in the bank, Jen must've set up her phone to play the album she wanted because after she got up to speed, heading south on the 405, she hit just one button, and "So What" began to play through the Bose speakers. I smiled.

"You're the best."

"True, but you don't know that yet. You could soon, though, if you play your cards right. Or if you play them wrong. Or if you've never heard of card playing."

We teased each other and sat in comfortable silence as I directed her to the kayak shop. I repeatedly checked the side mirror to see if I noticed a tail. When we arrived and entered the shop, the same white supremacist sat behind the counter. His purple goatee and lime-green iguana tattoo looked just as ridiculous that day as it did when Game and I had left off the kayak.

"Got your boat ready. Was just gonna call ya," he said. His response to Jennifer, whose skin was a shade lighter than Game's, seemed far more accepting than it had been on Saturday.

"Hey, uh, you, uh, ain't you that model?"

"I am that model, yes."

"Hey, would you mind if I got a selfie with you?"

"Yes."

"Cool." He pulled his phone out of his pocket and took a step toward the edge of the counter.

"Yes, I would mind."

"What? ... Oh." His expression changed. "Thought you meant ... shit, really?"

"Yes, really. Your eighty-eight tattoo indicates you shouldn't want a selfie with me, so why do you?"

"I don't." He turned to me. "That's eighty-four, ninety-four, including Uncle Sam's cut. Mostly labor. Them greasers make more than I do. Can you imagine?"

"Easily," I said. "Don't let it be said that the world is always unjust." He looked confused, which I assumed was his default look. I handed him a hundred. He hesitated before starting to make change, and I guessed he was hoping I'd wave off the difference. Or maybe he wouldn't have wrung in the sale at all and pocketed the hundred. But I made sure he understood my intentions by putting my hand out. Eventually, he gave me the change and handed me the receipt.

"They'll bring it out for you."

The two Latino workers I'd seen on Saturday came out carrying the kayak about three minutes later. They easily hoisted it above their heads and set it on the surfboard rack on top of the Range Rover. They centered it, and I gave them the fifteen dollars I'd just received in change.

"Muchas gracias," they said simultaneously.

"De nada."

After I'd used ropes and Bungee cords to secure the kayak, trying to compensate for the fact that a surfboard rack is not as stable as a kayak carrier, Jen pulled out of the parking lot, and asked, "Where to now?"

"A meeting. I checked. There's one in fifteen minutes off Imperial Highway."

"Great," she said.

As I waited in the car while Jen was in the meeting, my cell rang.

"Hello, Frank."

"I apologize, Jack. I—and everyone else, come to think of it—was probably just jealous you bagged Amanda, and now Jennifer. I had no real reason to think you're a bad P.I. Just being a dick."

"Thank you for the apology, but I could truly be bad. Time will tell."

"Time has already told. That's what I'm saying. I have no idea how you knew. I obviously knew Dad my whole life, and I was there in the garage when he was pouring this into that and that into this while practically wearing a HAZMAT suit, hoping to turn an idea into a product. Eventually, that product put me through college and med school, but I never had any idea, even after a thousand conversations with Dad, that Marty was a silent partner.

"Dad must've been embarrassed he needed a cash infusion during the recession, so he never mentioned it. I don't know which of them approached the other, but somehow Marty ended up owning forty-nine percent of Wave Skimmer. Dad kept control, obviously, and the company has bounced back and is doing well now, but it would've gone under if Marty hadn't stepped in in 2009. It was probably Marty's idea to sell kayaks directly to the cruise lines so they could keep dozens of boats on their private islands and have the boats pay for themselves within weeks as they overcharged cruisers to rent them. But that's just a guess. The timing seems right."

"That's great news because it means my theory hasn't evaporated. Yet."

"I don't believe your theory is more valid than it was before I found the Marty connection, because, as I told you, I've seen the whole process, from powder to boats, and there's—"

"How long ago did you watch the process?"

"Don't remember. Fifteen, twenty years, when the San Felipe factory opened. Probably closer to twenty."

"A lot can change in that much time, including bringing aboard a new partner."

"Obviously. And because you were right about Marty being connected to Dad, I'm not going to jump up and down telling you you're wrong about the coke."

"I don't need you to believe me. I just need to find proof. I may need your help again, though."

"Whatever you need. I'll email you the scanned documents, if you want."

"Great, but put the documents in a safe-deposit box."

"Sure. Thank you for looking into this. I still have a funeral to plan, but every time I try to concentrate on who I should call, I see images of Dad hanging there. And I didn't even see him. Man, I'm really glad I didn't. The nightmares are already horrible."

"Unfortunately, I know what those are like. When's the funeral?"

"Friday at 4 at Holy Cross."

"Good luck making the arrangements. Jen and I will see you there."

"Good. You two be safe, okay?"

"We'll try, but I anticipate a rough week."

CHAPTER TWENTY-FOUR

We had a long drive ahead of us, and we weren't getting an early start. We ate burritos at Tacos El Unico on Atlantic, then Jen filled the tank. She drove to the 405 and headed south through the urban sprawl of Southern California, one city's fast-food joints, auto shops, and strip-malls indistinguishable from those in the next one. The 405 became the 5, and Jen continued to drive south until she made the transition to Interstate 8, heading east from San Diego.

During the drive, I remembered an article I'd read in college by a man who argued that we can only succeed in proportion to how willing we are to fail. The potential for—and the flirtation with—disaster validates our possible successes. If this was true, most of us are far too afraid ever to become complete failures because our sense of self-preservation and our desire for comfort prevent us from risking everything, shielding us from both heroic greatness and abject defeat. I had lived too long in the nebulous middle. I'd avoided the ultimate failure of suicide and avoided the ultimate success of love. As we drove, I felt the long-dormant euphoria and hope that love engenders, but I also knew that happiness could evaporate in an instant.

I called Game.

"Whatup, dawg?"

"Chasing bad guys, fighting injustice, and perfecting my brioche recipe."

"What's brioche?"

"Not sure."

"You still think you funny, I see. How's it going with Jennifer?"

"We're building our relationship one crisis at a time. It's important to establish a strong foundation."

"What's going on with the murders?"

"We're on our way to Mexico. I think Chris, Big Bill, and Gilson were murdered because they knew something about the drug-smuggling that Marty Milford, Chris' producing partner, was doing. I'm pretty sure he's importing cocaine in Big Bill's kayaks."

"For real? Can you prove something like that?"

"We're heading to the factory. We'll see what we find. I feel lousy about missing Chris' funeral, but San Felipe is too far away for us to make it back in time. We could be waiting for days to learn anything. I want to know if you're willing to do a big favor for me, although if you look at it as you unofficially working as a private investigator you might find that more exciting."

"Sure. What you got?"

"Don't agree yet, because if you agree to do this, you'll have to fly the dreaded color red."

"Stop playing."

"I'm serious. This is your decision. I'm not putting pressure on you, and I can probably make the plan work without your help, but I'm hoping you can approach Milford at the funeral when he's got people near him—even if the other elements don't fall into place, he'll at least be rattled."

"What should I say?"

"Something like, 'Didn't get our delivery. White boy didn't show. Amanda lost her blow and needs more. But we can't supply her with no supply.'"

"I can do that. What reaction you looking for?"

"If you say that, it means his hierarchy has broken down. No Posse member should know who he is because he should have buffers. So, one or more of those buffers betrayed him. This will be the first he's heard about another delivery being hijacked, which of course will make him suspicious of the white guy who got hijacked, what, a week ago? With luck, Milford will become suspicious of everyone. A star of Amanda's visibility should not be getting her drugs from street dealers. Even if he doesn't believe you, he'll know he's in trouble. He's desperate enough to have killed three people and threatened to kill me, or at least I think he did.

"Your statement won't prove anyone knows that Chris didn't commit suicide, but Milford knows he didn't, and the goons who killed him know he didn't. Whenever more than one person is involved in a crime, at least one of them can turn on the others to save his skin. But the plan could easily go wrong. I'm worried about you getting out of there in one piece."

"Don't worry. We'll be at a funeral. People ain't gonna draw down on me there."

"Okay, if you're sure, this is how I think you should proceed. I left the BMW at the Wilshire Motel, at 12023 Wilshire Boulevard. The key is on the ground behind the rear wheel on the passenger's side. Dress as though you were going to a job interview at a bank—a dress shirt, nice slacks, dress shoes, not Adidas. Take buses if you can, or get someone to drop you a few blocks away. Do the same thing if you take a taxi. Of course, I'll reimburse your expenses and give you plenty more. When you're at the cemetery, change into the gang attire you think will be convincing, but remember that in acting, less is more. Don't overdue the garb or the attitude. You're just a businessman trying to stay in business by keeping the supply line operational."

"Got it."

"I suggest you arrive about a half hour after the service is scheduled—it's at three—and wait in the car near the entrance. When everyone exits, ease into the procession. It won't wind through city streets. They'll follow the hearse to the gravesite."

"Okay. What's he look like?"

"Long red hair, blue eyes that are almost always hidden behind tacky Elton John glasses. About five-ten, a paunch, but not fat. Just soft. Probably dressed expensively."

"Cool," Game said. "How will we know if it works?"

"One of the pieces I'm hoping falls into place is that the white dude who got jacked is there. He probably works for Milford, but I don't know how many layers of insulation are between them. Maybe Milford has fired him for getting hijacked. That part's not essential. What is, though, is that you give the message to Milford, and you aren't seen by Mike. I don't know if he'll be there, but he could be, and he obviously knows you. But as I say this, I realize it wouldn't be a disaster if Mike sees you. He knows you're not in da Posse, so he'll know something's up. He'll conclude I'm the only one who would put you up to this. So, now that I've said it out loud, it could even work to our advantage if Mike sees you."

"Can't believe Coach is involved. He's the only teacher I liked."

"I hope I'm wrong."

"How do we know if it works?"

"After you give the message to Milford, take five steps, then turn and watch what he does. If I'm right, he'll turn to the white dude, if he's there, or to Mike, if he's there, or at least make a phone call. If I were a movie producer who had nothing to do with gangs, drugs, and murders, I'd just say, 'What the hell?' I wouldn't get angry or frightened, and I wouldn't feel compelled to call someone immediately."

"Got you. But ain't you making yourself a target?"

"Yes, but I can't think of another way. If everything goes perfectly in Mexico—but when does everything go perfectly?—I could call you to cancel the plan. We'll see."

"You want me to leave the keys in the same place?"

"Yes. But I can't emphasize this enough: This isn't a joy ride. You're to drive as slowly and carefully as you can. If you get pulled over in a car that isn't registered to you, with gang clothes in the car—"

"Got it. We cool. Won't let you down."

"Thank you, Game. I owe you one."

"More like two or three."

I texted him the address of Holy Cross Cemetery and hoped I didn't just make an irreversible mistake.

When Jen and I arrived in Calexico, we filled the tank, used the restroom, and drove to the storage business I'd found online, Self Stor-It. I filled out the paperwork to rent the smallest unit available, and Jen drove until we found 104 B. I put the bag that contained the Beretta, ammo, and a thousand dollars in the unit, then locked it. Although I could need the gun in Mexico, I couldn't risk being caught with it there. A car problem, a fender-bender, or just some Federales demanding a bribe could not only put an end to the plan but could also land us in a Mexican jail.

The frenetic pace of the daily commerce in Mexicali, the town on the Mexico side of the border from Calexico, was winding down. I'd taken the wheel before entering Mexico. I parked near a taco stand, then Jen ate two fish tacos while I ate five. We purchased supplies at nearby stands and shops, including bread from a bakery.

We had a two-hour drive to San Felipe on Mexico 5, the major route that had been nearly deserted the five times I'd previously been to San Felipe. On those trips I'd driven the route in daylight.

"Do you mind if I nap?" Jen asked after about twenty minutes.

"Of course not. Get some rest."

She balled her jacket up, put it against the window, and leaned her head against it. After about three minutes, she asked, "Why do you think Mike's involved?"

"I think he could be involved because I can't figure out why people who were willing to kill to protect their operation would warn me twice. I've batted around possibilities since this garbage started, and I really hope Mike isn't involved. I have no evidence he is, except I was warned twice, and he seems to have more money than he should as a teacher in Oakville School District. His residual checks from the acting he did long ago are sometimes only a few dollars. He showed one to me. He has expensive tastes, though."

"I really hope you're wrong."

"So do I."

Within a few minutes, she breathed the deep breaths of sleep.

The drive south was disconcerting, despite my having made it before. On a previous trip, four black-clad members of the Mexican Army had brandished automatic weapons at a checkpoint that sat in the middle of nowhere. They didn't find anything that troubled them as they searched my truck, then waved me through. On another trip, two cars had passed me on the right shoulder of the road while a truck approached from the opposite direction in the other lane. The trip south that night, however, went smoothly, except for the armadillo that tried to double-back, after reaching the middle of the road. I knew not to swerve, so I tried to avoid a collision by stomping the brake pedal. But that wasn't enough to prevent the armadillo from thudding under both tires on Jen's side of the car. She woke up.

"What was that?"

"An armadillo. Hoping that's the worst luck we have down here."

I put on the hazard lights, pulled over, centered the kayak, retied the knots, then turned off the hazards and continued.

I hadn't been able to find an address online for the Wave Skimmer factory in San Felipe. I drove through what had long ago been a sleepy fishing village but had turned into a thriving tourist destination. At least that's what it had been when Jami and I had visited about fifteen years before. I noticed that many basic cinder block buildings had been built since my last visit, and many of them appeared to have been abandoned, unfinished. The Great Recession probably caused funding to dry up, and no one had deemed the projects worthwhile since.

At a Pemex station, I said to a man in his fifties, "Perdón, señor." He looked at me and smiled. Pointing to the kayak on the roof, I said, "¿Tu usted sabe adónde es la fábrica de kayac, por favor?"

"Sí. Dos kilómetros de esa manera, cerca del mercado. A la derecha."

"Muchas gracias, señor. Tenga una buena noche."

We found the factory a few minutes later, and I drove around it on dirt roads that were parallel to the edges of the buildings but were not near it. One road was nearly half a mile away, so we couldn't see anything on that side, but the other roads were closer, so at least we could tell the factory didn't have any roads that ran from a rear entrance.

The building was a large cinderblock structure built in a perfect square. It only had one inadequate light shining down from the top of each corner, so the factory was mostly dark. Each of the four sides had two thirty-six-inch pedestrian doors about fifteen feet from the edges. The side that faced the dirt parking lot and was closest to the market—a hundred and twenty yards away—had an additional large, metal door that opened upward. It appeared to be large enough for a van to pull into, but not large enough for a semi. We didn't see a sign advertising which product the factory produced. The lights affixed above either side of the large door weren't on.

I pulled into the market's small lot and parked in the space farthest from the market and closest to the factory. The lot only had one car parked in it, an ancient red Pinto. Jen and I went inside and bought far more snacks than we could eat, hoping our extravagance would buy us some goodwill if we were still loitering in the parking lot in the morning, as seemed likely. I stuffed a twenty into the tip jar and winked at the sixty-ish woman behind the counter. She winked back.

The factory seemed to be closed for the night, but one of us always had to be on watch. I told Jen I'd take the first shift, so she could get sleep. Three customers pulled into the lot in the next hour, spent a few minutes inside, and drove away. At 10:55 p.m., the woman who'd sold us the snacks locked the front door and waved to us before driving away. I didn't see or hear any signs of life for nearly eight hours, except for Jen's deep breathing, the growling in my stomach, and the seven vehicles that passed the market on the nearby road.

Jen woke up at about seven, waited a few minutes for the same woman who closed the market the night before to get the coffee going, then bought herself a cup and left another nice tip. I told Jen I didn't want coffee because it was my turn to sleep. I'd reclined the driver's seat and was in the middle of a dream when Jen shook me awake. I looked at the clock on the dash. 8:01. We watched as an eighteen-wheeler slowly backed up to the large metal door. The parking lot now had fifteen other vehicles in it—nine trucks and six passenger cars. Two men from inside the building flung the sliding metal door upward.

"How many did you see go in?"

"Twenty."

We couldn't see the back of the trailer, but it was obvious the driver had opened the door and dropped the lift because soon two men on the side we could see were rolling black fifty-five-gallon drums through the open door. They used the lift to lower the upright barrels, tipped them over, and rolled them through the door. The trailer blocked the right side of the door from our view, so we could only guess what was happening on that side. We counted four barrels being rolled in. Then the same men started loading kayaks into the hold, not using the lift but handing the kayaks to men inside the trailer. We counted twelve kayaks handed up on the left side—three orange, three yellow, three sky blue, and three purple. The trailer probably had racks to hold the kayaks, so they didn't get jostled and scratched. Because the driver would want a balanced load, it was safe to assume that another twelve kayaks had been loaded on the right side.

"We're going to follow him, right?" Jen asked as the driver closed the back of the trailer and headed to his cab.

"No. We saw four different colors but no red. It's possible any red ones were loaded on the other side, but segregating them that way would bring attention. Too many employees are involved in this transaction for it to be illicit. I know I'm going all-in on the red kayaks, but the only red Wave Skimmer I've ever seen, was stolen the night Big Bill was murdered."

"He's leaving. Are you sure?"

"To bet my life on it, no. But I have to play my hunch. We just watched the powder arriving to be processed, and the legitimate kayaks leaving. If we follow that truck, it will head to Bass Pro Shops in Cucamonga or to any of a half dozen Dick's Sporting Goods or REIs in Southern California. I think we wait for something more clandestine."

"If you say so. I'm just here eating Red Vines, Corn Nuts, and Hostess Donettes for breakfast. What do I know?"

"We'll wait. If I'm wrong, it will be the first time in ... about ten minutes."

CHAPTER TWENTY-FIVE

Over the next sixteen hours, we spent about a hundred dollars in the market, buying access to its parking lot and restroom. The owner of the market knocked on the driver's window at five asking why we were still there. I asked him if we could rent his parking space for a hundred per day. He asked for two hundred. I shook my head and handed him a hundred. He smiled and accepted my offer. Within an hour, a Federale pulled up next to us. He knocked on Jennifer's window. She gave him the two hundred he asked for, but only after she acted as though that sum would severely cut into our cash supplies. I thought she'd acted her part well, but he either wanted to see her again or just knew he could extort more from two people sitting in a Range Rover. He demanded another two hundred at midnight. Presumably, his shift ended because we made it through the rest of the night without another shakedown.

I felt awful about not attending Chris' funeral. He was a good friend, and I really respected him, but the situation was what it was, so we were where we were. At about 5 p.m. on Tuesday, I wondered how Game had done at the gravesite. Had he spoken to Milford and gotten out of there safely? Did he see Milford's response, and was that response useful to us? I looked at my phone but had no reception. If Game had called, I'd have to leave the dead zone we were parked in to find out how his mission had gone. Leaving the factory wasn't an option then, so we continued to wait.

At 3:55 a.m. on Wednesday, a black Ford F-150 pulled into the lot and parked to the left of the large door. I nudged Jennifer, and she woke up slowly. The lighting on the building was inadequate—probably by design—and even after I pulled on the night-vision goggles, I didn't learn much about the two men who got out of the truck, each carrying a backpack. They entered through the pedestrian entrance on the left. Both wore cowboy hats, cowboy boots, jeans, and long-sleeved shirts. I never saw their faces. Even $3,200 night-vision goggles can't bend light or see around corners, so I couldn't identify anything else about them except that they were both about five-six. They entered the door but didn't turn on a light, at least not one I could see. They probably turned off an alarm after they entered.

At 4:10, a black Ford Transit Connect Wagon with tinted windows passed the market and pulled into the factory parking lot in front of the large door. As the driver turned the van around so he could back it into the door, he killed the headlights, and the door opened but the lights above it didn't go on.

Jen couldn't see anything in the moonlight but the hint of a black van, with its lights off, pulling into the black hole in the wall. The night-vision goggles didn't deliver much more information because the cowboys were cautious enough not to face in our direction, keeping their backs to the outside while they opened the door and closing it behind the van after the driver backed in. Their vigilance concerned me because it could indicate they'd made us. We weren't stupid enough to sit inside the SUV with the light on so they could see us, but we did stick out, sitting in a dirt parking lot outside a tiny market in a Range Rover with a kayak strapped to the surfboard rack on the roof. I was hoping the kayak on top of a vehicle sitting outside a kayak factory would make us less conspicuous. But, as we waited for them to load the van with red kayaks, I realized that once it became light, I was going to have to get rid of the kayak. If we spooked the driver after all this, the two of us not only wouldn't be able to prove that Milford was transporting cocaine in kayaks, but we would also likely be dead, as the written threats suggested.

While Jen and I waited, I revised the plan. I'd originally hoped to tail whichever vehicle left the building carrying red kayaks, staying as close as possible without getting made. Then, when the vehicle approached the border checkpoint, I'd maneuver right behind it so I could see what was happening at the border. Would the vehicle go through a specific lane that was manned by a corrupt Customs and Border Protection agent who was willing to let the vehicle through because he'd already received a bribe? Would he only receive his bribe after the vehicle carrying the contraband had been admitted without incident? Or was something else going on?

I'd crossed the border at Tijuana or Mexicali more than twenty times, and I'd always seen agents search large vehicles, either in front of their booths or at the secondary station. It seemed reasonable to assume that CBP would search the van. However, my original plan suddenly seemed impractical. The driver would spot us when it got light, and I didn't know what he'd do after he knew he was being followed. Could he manage to shake us on the way to L.A.? Would he find somewhere to dump the kayaks if he thought he was being followed?

"New plan," I said as I turned the key.

"Why?"

"The first pickup was too in-the-open to be illegal, and this pickup is being done in darkness. I think it's safe to assume this isn't a legal transaction. If I'm right, there's no need to tail the van. We know it's going to the Compton shop. I'd like you to drive."

We switched positions, and after we'd gotten back on Mexico 5, heading to Mexicali, I said, "We would've been made following the van. We could've dumped the kayak to give the driver a different look, but this vehicle is going to stand out. I should've rented something inconspicuous. The kayak could still be useful to us, so we shouldn't dump it. Even though Game overturned the apple cart, we can't tip Milford off that we know how he's importing the coke."

"But we don't know."

"Not yet, but that's why you're driving. When I get service, I have research to do."

"I've practically got bed sores from sitting so long. We haven't eaten a real meal in days, I've hardly slept, and I missed a meeting on my third day of sobriety."

"I'm sorry. We'll get you back on track for thirty-in-thirty or ninety-in-ninety, I promise. But I can only keep that promise if we survive, so we have to catch these guys. We have nothing to take to law enforcement, so we'll watch until watching proves to be ineffective, then we'll poke the bear in the eye."

"Okay, but I'm scared."

"I know. We just need to get to the shop before the van does. Because we have to swing by the storage unit to get the gun, you need to drive quickly. Don't break any records but go a little faster than the speed limit. I'm sure he'll drive cautiously, considering his cargo."

"You mean, considering his theoretical cargo. He may only have a van full of kayaks. Or it could be full of papayas."

"The middle-of-the-night, illicit papaya trade doesn't receive the media coverage it deserves."

"Something's wrong with me. How else can I explain why I love you?"

It took a long time to get through the border checkpoint because the morning commuter traffic slogged. We eventually made it through without being hassled. As the agent handed our passports back to Jen, he said, "Nice ride."

A few minutes later, I punched in the gate code at Self Stor-It, retrieved the bag from the unit, and locked it. I heard a chime from my phone, meaning I had service. I had eight missed calls, four voicemails, and four texts. Jen made good time heading west on Interstate 8, and I read the texts. From Amanda: *I'm at Malibu Serenity. Thought you should know.* From Game: *Left a message. Hope you're good.* From Mike: *Sorry I couldn't make the funeral. How was it?* And another from Game: *Should I do more James Bond shit to find you?*

The first voicemail was from Frank Watson: "Hey, Jack. Hope you're doing okay. Letting you know the obituary is up on the website of *The Malibu Times*. They said it will run in the paper, too. Basically, it says Dad didn't commit suicide, and everyone knows it. Take care of yourself. See you at the funeral."

The second voicemail was from Amanda: "Jack, I'm not sure why this doesn't hurt more than it does. Probably because we were both going through the motions for a long time. I mean, I'm not saying I don't care for you. I do, and I probably always will, but when I tracked down the baseball card for you, I really thought I was doing it because I want you to be happy. I didn't have an ulterior motive. Or I didn't think I did. Subconsciously, who knows? That's between me and my blow. Ha-ha. That's probably not funny. But, seriously, I'm letting you know I'm going to check into Malibu Serenity. Haven't tried that one yet, and someday I might write a book: *How Not to Get Sober on $60,000 a Month*. Sorry. I shouldn't joke. But maybe I should. Anyway, thought I'd let you know. Get your stuff whenever you need to. Bye."

The third and fourth voicemails were from Game: "Shoulda seen me, brotha. I was smooth as silk, dropping lines like Denzel. The whole place was filled with white folk. I'm the only brother 'cept the security guard outside the chapel. Didn't see anyone coulda been the van driver, don't think. But I strolled up to Milford, after Chris in the ground and people are hanging 'round. Four dudes standing in a group, soft and middle-age. One of them is Milford, with his stupid red ponytail. I walk up from the side, so he don't see me 'til I'm right next to him, and say, 'Dude got jacked again, or he stealing from you, cuz he never show up. How we gonna get Amanda her blow if we ain't got none? We doing business or what?' His eyes go scared like he 'bout to get hit for the first time in his life. He finally says, 'Do I know you?' The other three stepped back by then. Just him and me, but they can still hear. I say, 'Been slinging for you for years, but you busy what, sampling the product, instead a learning who the players be?' I walked away. I know it ain't what we agreed on, but it just came out. I looked back, and he's on his phone, not looking happy. Hope that's what you wanted. Car's back where it was. Hope you and Jennifer staying safe."

His second voicemail said: "I want another assignment, Jack. Holler back."

Game's call reminded me that I needed to call Rachelle. I called her, and after we exchanged hellos, I said, "You mentioned that Mike had an early tee time in Bel Air. There's only one course there, the country club. Do you know who he was playing with?"

"No, sorry. He didn't say. He only said he had an early tee time, and it was safe to go home."

"Wait. You didn't stay with him Saturday night?"

"No. Just Friday. He guaranteed I'd be safe at home."

"Okay, thank you. Please take care of yourself."

"I will. You, too."

Jen turned north onto the 5, and we hit gridlock immediately, plodding along with the tens of thousands of work commuters. I felt confident we'd make it to the Wave Skimmer shop before the van did, but it's difficult to feel confident about much when stuck in bumper-to-bumper traffic, mile after mile. During the drive, I watched videos on YouTube about how kayaks are made.

Based on the videos and Frank Watson's comment about having watched powder enter the factory and kayaks leave it, I determined that Wave Skimmers are made through a process called rotomolding. It involves pouring linear polyethylene, also known as high-density polyethylene, which can be any color, into a mold, sealing the mold, then melting the polyethylene at a temperature of 550-degrees Fahrenheit in a large, sophisticated oven for about nineteen minutes. The mold is rotated in numerous directions to ensure even distribution of the polyethylene. The mold is moved to a cooling chamber, which decreases the temperature slowly, so the plastic holds its shape and doesn't shrink. After the plastic has cooled, workers open the mold and remove the kayak. According to the video, workers outfit the kayaks with handles, seats, cargo nets, hatches, or fishing accessories, according to which model they're creating.

In other words, the workspace attached to the shop in Compton technically had a reason to exist—I'd had my kayak repaired there—but was it really a front for illegal activity? If employees of other kayak manufacturers outfitted the kayaks in their factories, then shipped them directly to retailers, why did Wave Skimmer add another step? According to the videos, Pelican, Hobie, Wilderness Systems, and Ocean Kayak didn't require a second factory visit. I was betting that was because those companies only made watercrafts and related accessories and didn't smuggle coke.

I pulled up the UCLA faculty directory online and scrolled until I found the chemistry professors. I called three of them but got voicemails. I didn't leave messages. I called a fourth.

"Hello," said Paul Katz, a tenured professor of chemistry. He didn't recognize my number, so his greeting was tentative.

"Hello, Dr. Katz. My name is Jack Drake. You don't know me, but I graduated from UCLA a long time ago. I'm a private investigator, and I know I'm coming at you from left field."

"Yes, you are."

"I apologize. I know this is weird, but I'm not asking for anything but your opinion. I'm working on a case that involves kayaks. My question is, do you think it would be possible to add cocaine to the polyethylene powder that is melted around molds to create kayaks, bring those kayaks into the country, then extract the cocaine, probably by melting the plastic again?"

"Mr. Drake, I'm not in the habit of helping facilitate criminal enterprises."

"Dr. Katz, I can show you my P.I. license when I get to L.A. Or I can take a picture of it and text it to you. My girlfriend and I are driving to L.A. now. I'm almost certain we've uncovered a cocaine distribution ring, and we know the big picture of how they're doing it, but not the nitty-gritty."

"First, my specialty is atmospheric chem, so petrochemicals are outside my field of expertise. But, second, based on my decades of experience, I feel comfortable speculating that what you've proposed sounds possible. How possible, I can't say with any degree of certainty, but nothing about what you said sounds beyond the realm of possibility. After all, companies are turning recycled soda bottles into jackets and sneakers. I won't testify as an expert witness, certainly, but I wish you luck in your investigation, and I hope you catch the dealers. My son died of a heroin overdose seven years ago. The bastards who sell those poisons are the worst kind of evil."

"I'm sorry for your loss, sir. And I wish you all the best. You've been very helpful. Thank you."

"You're welcome. Catch the bastards."

"I promise to do my best."

CHAPTER TWENTY-SIX

Listening to *Rubber Soul* and *Revolver* helped ease the traffic frustration a little, but I wasn't paying much attention because my thoughts were bouncing around: Chris, Big Bill, Gilson, Amanda, Game, Mike, Jennifer, kayaks, cocaine, and burdens of proof.

And Jami. Once again, Jami.

She was in my head more than she had been in years. All my thoughts about her weren't sad or guilt-filled, as they used to be, but she was present again because I was letting myself feel for the first time in nearly a decade, and bits of happiness were emerging like wildflowers repopulating a field in the spring.

Was she giving me permission to love again, or was I rationalizing, hoping she wasn't judging me, condemning me? As the Serenity Prayer states, I needed to find the wisdom to know the difference between what I could change and what I couldn't. I couldn't change the fact she was gone, so I hoped I had the courage to change the part of me that felt guilty about her death, the part that clung to the past, the part that expected nothing more from the future than bleakness.

When we were two blocks from the Wave Skimmer shop, I said to Jen, "Let's see how far we can stay from the shop and still see who enters. I probably missed another entrance at the back that would be big enough for the van to pull into."

She drove down East Oaks Street and passed the front entrance to the shop. A yellow Camaro was parked in the space to the far left of the front door. She made a right on North Santa Fe Avenue, passing the side of the shop and workspace, but I didn't see a large door. Just past the shop in the adjacent alley that Game had given chase in, I saw a white, beaten-up van that was probably the one he'd chased. It was facing away from us, so I could see the badly dented rear-end.

"Don't stop, but I saw the van the dealer was driving the other day. The door we're looking for is probably on that side, but I couldn't see it because it's flush. I think I saw a camera above it."

"What should I do?" She kept driving, taking three lefts around Cesar Chavez Park, eventually putting us back on East Oaks, heading west.

"The van with the kayaks isn't likely far behind because we stopped at the storage unit. We don't know how long he was in the factory, but loading the van shouldn't have taken long. How many could it fit, six, eight? To be safe, we have to assume he's right behind us. Why don't I get out and find a place that allows me to see the entrance to the alley?"

"Okay. I should just keep driving around?"

"No. Find a parking space a couple blocks from here."

"Got it."

"I don't think they'll wait until dark to pull the van inside because the alley provides cover. It's a legitimate business, or part of it is, so a delivery van shouldn't raise suspicions."

"Okay, but what if he doesn't show up?"

"Then I've totally blown it. He could've gone anywhere. We'll have to tail him again, probably with rental cars. But let's stay positive."

"Okay. See you soon."

I grabbed the camera bag, got out, and closed the door. Jen drove away, and I walked down the east side of Santa Fe to a large oak on the western edge of Cesar Chavez Park. I leaned against the trunk, took out the Canon, swapped the 50mm lens for a 100-400, slung the strap over my right shoulder, and set the bag at my feet. I took out my phone and held it in front of me as though I was looking at it, but I kept my eyes on the alley. From that angle, I couldn't see both ends of the alley, but I could see past the large door and the white van, so if the black van entered from the other end, I'd still see it arrive and enter the shop. Every once in a while, I scrolled through my newsfeed, in case someone was watching me.

Thirty minutes later, the van hadn't arrived. I texted Jen: *He could've stayed longer than we thought he would, or he could've stopped for lunch because he hadn't purchased one hundred dollars of junk food.* She responded: *It's only junk food if you buy into the misinformation being disseminated by doctors, nutritionists, and the media.* I responded: *That assumes I was using the word junk as a pejorative.* She responded: *Keep waiting. But you owe me lunch at Versailles.* I responded: *Sure, but I owe you a lot more than that.*

Fifteen minutes later, the black van stopped in front of me, waiting in the middle lane to turn left from North Santa Fe into the alley. I took multiple photos as the van turned, capturing the license plate in all of them. The van pulled up to the door. Within a minute, the door opened, and the van pulled in. Two minutes later, the white dude I expected turned the corner into the alley. He was wearing dirty tan work boots, torn jeans, and a brown, long-sleeved shirt. I took shots of him as he turned the corner and walked down the alley toward the white panel van. I grabbed my camera bag, looked left, waited for a pickup truck to pass, and stepped into the middle lane.

He'd been driving a long time, so he stretched, rotating his trunk left then right, and throwing his hands high over his head, tilting his torso back to increase the stretch. I photographed his actions in bursts. He got in the van, started it, and let it idle. It sounded awful and was probably hitting on only seven cylinders. A cloud of exhaust billowed as he hit the gas and pulled away.

He'd just emptied the other van of what I believed were cocaine-infused kayaks. If I asked Jen to follow him, and we confronted him, the only leverage we'd have was that some MLKs, posing as da Uptown Posse, said he intended to sell them cocaine—before they robbed him. Because I suspected that da Uptown Posse and the MLKs were receiving their cocaine from the same source, no one in either gang would testify. So, we didn't have enough leverage on him to get him to turn on his bosses.

Even if law enforcement had stopped him with a van full of loaded kayaks, drug-sniffing dogs wouldn't have responded to the drugs. CBP agents must've used dogs to explore the van on numerous trips north without triggering an arrest. I decided not to have Jen follow him. I texted her my location. She pulled up five minutes later.

"How'd it go?"

"The guy driving the black van was the guy who drives the white van, his personal vehicle. We don't have anything on him that will stand up in court. Gang members won't rat because if they do, they'll be killed."

"Damned if they do ... I'm hungry, and you owe me a meal at Versailles."

"We can't, not now. Everything depends on our next move, or else we'll have to start the process again." I pulled out my phone and looked up nearby car-rental companies.

"What's our next move?"

"After we eat more of these delicious, non-nutritious snacks, we have to continue to watch the shop. The kayaks have been delivered, so if we're right, they'll be chemically taken apart. Someone has to arrive, grab the coke, and leave with it to start the distribution process. I don't know how many levels the organization has or how many times the coke gets stepped on before the white guy I just saw sells it to da Uptown Posse."

"You don't know much, do you?"

"I know that 'if' is the middle word in life," I said.

"Proving my point."

"The guy I just saw was the one who delivered the threats."

"Why?" she asked.

"He's the right height and build, and look at this." I pulled up the best shot of him on the camera with his arms overhead and showed it to her. The sleeves of his shirt had slid down his arms far enough for a yellow watchband on his right wrist to show.

"You did it," she said. "How many lefties could commit the same crime against fashion?"

"Probably a lot. Remember the Livestrong bracelets? Yikes. If you want to donate to charity, feel free, but broadcasting your generosity by wearing a ghastly yellow plastic band that celebrates a cheater is self-congratulatory and ridiculous."

"How do you really feel, Jack? You're waffling."

"You're right. I should learn to form definitive opinions. I'm sorry about lunch. We'll eat there as often as you like when this is over. Take a right at the light."

"Where're we going?"

"To rent two cars so we can surveille the shop properly."

"I love it when you talk spy."

I rented a tan Ford Taurus, and Jen rented a white Nissan Versa. We transferred gear and snacks into each rental car, with the binoculars going with Jen and the camera and night-vision goggles going with me. We left the Range Rover in the parking spot next to the rental-car office.

I said, "I'll cover the alley, and you take the front entrance. Any questions?"

"Plenty regarding big-picture stuff, but not about this."

"You probably have enough time to go to a meeting before anything happens here. I can't imagine that liquifying kayaks and extracting coke will happen quickly, but I took one chemistry class to fulfill my science requirements, so what do I know?"

"I give you my word—and you know my word is golden—I'll get my ninety-in-ninety. I'll go to a couple a day to make up for missing a few."

"Good, let's go." I parked on North Santa Fe, near the oak tree I'd leaned against, and Jen parked within view of the front entrance on East Oaks Street.

Four hours later, Jen sent her sixth text to me: *The skinhead closed the shop and pulled away in his spiffy Camaro. And I really need to pee.* I responded: *I'll head to you, pull into your spot while you find a restroom, then you pull into my spot.* She responded: *Sounds good, but this could take days.* I responded: *Welcome to the world of a private eye.*

At eleven, I saw two men exit the front door. They looked like the two who'd taken my kayak inside the shop to be repaired. They walked down Oaks in different directions. At midnight, Jen texted: *Want to switch again?* We did, and I parked across from the alley. For five hours, I'd been alternating between wearing the goggles until my head hurt because the strap was too tight and looking through the telephoto until my head stopped hurting.

Just past three o'clock, while wearing the goggles, I saw a 1972 electric-blue, convertible Corvette Stingray make a left off Santa Fe into the alley. I'd never been so unhappy to have a theory pan out. As the car turned, I read the vanity plate: LOOM.

Mike Sherwood—the best man at my wedding, the one who'd kept me out of jail and comforted me as well as he could after Jami died—pulled up to the door, got out, and punched a code into the box mounted on the wall. The large metal door slowly opened. He got in his car and pulled into the building. The door closed.

I texted Jen: *Now.* She responded: *OK.* The plan was for her to pull into the alley and park perpendicularly across it, blocking a vehicle trying to leave. She was then supposed to turn off the engine, get out of the car, and walk away in case he decided to ram it. By forcing him to leave the alley on Santa Fe, I'd be the one to tail him. Had he arrived before we'd switched positions again, Jen would've blocked the Santa Fe side of the alley.

Mike pulled out, closed the large door, re-armed the alarm, and drove toward me. He turned left onto Santa Fe, heading north. I let him get a half-block ahead before I followed. I tailed him to North Mayo, where a young Black man approached the Vette. If they spoke, they did so quickly because within seconds, the man took a large backpack and headed back inside. I followed Mike without my headlights on until he made a left on Long Beach Boulevard and transitioned to the 105 West, where I turned on my lights.

On the 105, then the 110 N, I alternated my speed and the lane I was in. I was one lane farther left than I should've been when he got off without signaling on West Adams Boulevard. I slowed, let a car pass, then veered aggressively to the right.

He'd turned right on Adams by the time I reached the bottom of the ramp. I accelerated quickly, kept his taillights in sight, and watched him turn left on Grand. I let him gain distance, then crept through the intersection, without turning on Grand. He slowed and turned right on 25th. I continued until I hit Hill, turned left, and made a left onto 25th, parking in the first space I saw.

He'd stopped on the south side of the street across from an apartment building on the north side, the side I was parked on about sixty yards away. He killed his lights, despite being in a traffic lane. I opened my door, put my left foot on the ground, and stood to get a better view. A minute later, the white driver who'd delivered the kayaks from Mexico approached the Vette. Mike handed him a large backpack. I got in the car and pulled the door closed. The guy walked away, and Mike drove toward me. I leaned over to my right, out of sight. I counted to twenty, then sat up. They were both gone. I got out of the car and walked down 25th for half a block. I spotted the beaten-up white van on the same side of the street the Taurus was on. I went back to the car and called Jen.

"Are you okay?" she asked before I'd said hello.

"I'm fine. Sorry I didn't let you know what was going on, but I was following him."

"Was it Mike?"

"Yes."

"Shit."

"Wish I'd been wrong."

"I'm sorry."

"It was a tough tail. If he'd made me, I would've screwed up everything, and if I'd lost him, we would've had to start again at the shop."

"Good job. Where are you?"

"On 25th. I found the van driver. He's our leverage. He took the coke from Mike, so now we have to convince him of the error of his ways."

"I don't want to know how we're going to do that, do I?"

"Probably not."

"I'm exhausted and dirty and need a real meal."

"You can sleep in the comfort of my terrific Taurus or your voluminous Versa."

"You know this is why people drink, right?"

"Still not funny. I have a question."

"What?"

"How's your aim?"

CHAPTER TWENTY-SEVEN

I sat in the dark, thinking. Jen arrived thirty minutes later. She found a parking space half a block away on the other side of 25th and walked to the Taurus. She kissed me and asked, "Is it accurate to say your plans seem seat-of-the-pants?"

"Not inaccurate, but I prefer to call my plans improvisational."

"If you say so. I just walked past the notorious white van you're looking for, so I should find other aspects of you to mock."

"Have at it. But everything can still go wrong. Up until now, if I screwed up, we could start the tail again. I could've come up with a way to prove the kayaks contained cocaine—break into the factory or stop the black van at gunpoint to steal a kayak. But neither of those is necessary now. I don't need more proof than Mike handing over a backpack at 3:30 in the morning, after having left the shop in which I'm certain the cocaine was extracted. But now we need to finish the play."

"Which requires?"

"You to get a few hours of sleep while I make sure this guy doesn't take off. He'll probably get a late start. He's not likely to make a drug delivery at 9 a.m., but I have to watch the van just in case.

Right now, I need to find a tree, empty my pee bottle, and heed nature's call. Then look at his van."

"Let me know if you find a good tree."

About thirty yards from the Taurus was a Coast live oak at the side of a front yard. I kept the tree between me and the house, did what I had to do, and walked to the back of the van. I looked at the damaged right side and felt it in the dark. The streetlight nearest the van was out. A large vehicle had rammed the van because the point of impact was high on the right door, high enough to affect how the door closed, or didn't quite. Because the middle of the right door and the right side of it were smashed inward, the lock didn't work. I pulled gently on the misaligned handle. The door opened partially, and I could see a Bungee cord holding it closed.

I went back to the Taurus.

"That tree works. But because I can use coffee, and because you'd probably be more comfortable using a restroom, I have a favor to ask."

Twenty minutes later, she pulled the Versa into the same spot she'd pulled out of, then handed me a large cup of the finest brew available from the nearest gas station. I told her my latest plan.

"If you think that'll work, fine, but I have to sleep."

"Sweet dreams. I'll wake you when it's time."

At 10:30, long after the neighborhood had come to life, with residents having walked their dogs or left for work, and amid the sounds of the city—trucks rumbling on South Grand and West Adams, and sirens blaring—I got nervous about how late it was, so I shook Jen awake.

"Good morning, Sunshine."

"Morning." She shook her head and dragged her hands across her face. "Is it time?" She popped a green Tic-Tac in her mouth.

"Yes. Good luck, but you'll be fine."

I grabbed the duffel bag of gear I'd organized while Jen slept. I took my Ka-Bar law-enforcement knife out of the bag and set it next to me on the seat. I pulled out the Gould & Goodrich pancake holster, undid my belt, slid it through the loops on the holster that allowed me to use the forward FBI cant, rethreaded the belt, and adjusted the holster behind my right hip. I slipped the Beretta into the holster and put on a navy-blue windbreaker. I grabbed the duffel, opened the door, and picked up the closed knife. I got out of the car, walked to the van, and opened the knife. I pulled on the misaligned handle and slipped the knife through the opening, sawing through the Bungee cord in three seconds. I closed the knife and slipped it into the right back pocket of my jeans. I stepped into the van and pulled the door toward me. I cut an eighteen-inch length of paracord and tied the door closed. If the back door hadn't been broken, I had a Pro-Lok slim-jim in my duffel.

The back of the van wasn't crammed with stuff. It contained a large white drop-cloth, four gallons of paint, an aluminum painting tray, a roller, two large paintbrushes, a flathead screwdriver, a folding, wooden step stool, some rags, and an old pair of work boots, dappled with paint. A black hat, shirt, pair of pants, gloves, ski mask, and pair of boots sat in a pile near the backdoor. The painting supplies were meant to provide him cover, not to be used in his profession, because all legitimate house painters would have a full-sized ladder affixed to their vehicle.

I slid through the opening at the front, opened the glove compartment, and retrieved the van's registration. The vehicle was registered to Mildred Slattery, who lived at 1649 Colby Avenue in Los Angeles. Mildred was probably his mother or sister because something told me this guy didn't have a wife. I climbed into the back.

Jen was supposed to watch the entrance to the apartment building. She knew what the guy we were waiting for looked like because I'd shown her his pictures. When she saw him exit the building, she was to intercept him on the way to his van. I'd told her, "If you don't feel compromised or objectified by doing so, you may consider undoing a button or two on your blouse to secure his interest."

"First, I've been in three *SI* swimsuit issues, so modesty isn't high on my list. Second, do you think I'll need tawdry theatrics to lure this low-rent drug runner into my sphere? I mean, look at me." She made the funniest face she could make, but she still looked like a world-class beauty making a funny face.

I was getting hot, and I'd forgotten to bring a bottle of water. I checked my watch: 12:07. I'd taken off my windbreaker an hour earlier, and I was considering untying the paracord on the back door so I could let some hot air out. But then I heard Jen shout, "Bandit! Bandit! Oh, please, where are you? Come here, boy." Her voice was getting louder as she approached the van. "Bandit! Excuse me, sir? Sir? Yes. My dog's run away. Have you seen him? He's black and white—"

"Just got outside. Ain't seen nothin."

"... medium-sized. Are you sure? I'm frantic. I'd do anything to find him." She was right outside the van.

"How long's he been gone?"

"I've been looking for twenty minutes, but I'm on foot, and I'm frantic. When I saw him last, he was running that way on 25th. I'm afraid he's going to get hit."

"Ain't in no hurry. Get in. I can help you look."

"Oh, my God, really? That's great. Thank you so much." The plan called for her to give him an enthusiastic hug of gratitude if he offered her a ride. The hug was to serve two purposes: To start him wondering if he might be one heroic gesture away from having sex with her, and to allow Jen to make as much contact as possible without obviously searching for a gun. I couldn't see their hug, but as Jen passed by the front window, she nodded her head once slowly, raised her right hand slightly, then dropped it to her right hip.

His door opened first. He slid into his seat and set the backpack on the floor in the large space between the seats. He turned to watch Jen get in, which she was supposed to do in whichever manner she thought would best keep his attention. I didn't look at Jen's side of the van. I'd made myself as small as possible behind his seat so he couldn't see me in the rear-view mirror. I'd removed the gun from its holster when I first heard Jen's shouts. As soon as she slammed her door, I came out of my crouch, moved to my right, stepped forward, grabbed his right wrist with my left hand, and slammed the muzzle of the gun between his eyes.

"Freeze," I shouted, as Jen grabbed the backpack and shoved it in the back.

"Wait, wait, no, no!" He started to turn toward the front, so the gun wasn't between his eyes, but I said, "Another inch and you're dead." He rotated his head back my way. He looked at Jen. I was about to yank his right arm behind him and the seat, which would've allowed Jen to grab his gun, but just as I was about to do that, he said, "Fuck you, bitch!"

I raked the barrel of the gun down hard on his nose, causing a crunching sound. Blood spurted onto the same dirty brown shirt he'd worn the day before. I quickly put the muzzle back between his eyes. He reached for his face with his left hand, while I held his right wrist down.

Then I remembered he was probably a lefty. If that was correct, either Jen got confused about which side his gun was on—she'd been facing the opposite direction when she'd surreptitiously frisked him—or this dumbshit wore his holster in what I called the Moron Mount, forcing him to reach across his body with his dominant hand, then pull the gun back across his body before finding his target. The smart money said Jen knew her left from her right, and this guy wasn't Einstein, so I let go of his wrist and dropped my left hand toward his right hip. My hand hit the grip of a handgun, with the butt facing forward. Moron Mount.

He moaned, clutching his nose. I elbowed him hard in the ribs, eliciting a grunt. I removed his gun. We had his coke and his weapon. He was bleeding profusely, and neither Jen nor I had sustained a scratch. I understood how easily the MLKs had hijacked his drug deal. But as I had that thought, I wondered why he was still in the mix. Why was he still a drug courier? Why hadn't he been sidelined, or killed, after he'd botched that transaction? He'd cost somebody a lot of money, but here he was, not far from a backpack full of cocaine that he would've delivered if we hadn't ruined his day. If I was right about why he was still a courier, I could use that to our advantage.

I grabbed him by his shirt collar and yanked him out of the front seat into the back.

"Bonnie," I said. "The drop cloth." I noticed she hadn't unbuttoned an extra button on her blouse to lure him. Instead, she'd buttoned them all to prove she didn't need to flash cleavage to secure his interest. Despite the situation, I smiled at her silent message.

"Got it, Clyde." She stepped into the back, grabbed the drop cloth, stepped up front, and spun both sun visors until they faced the doors. She carefully draped the drop cloth over the visors, blocking the windshield.

I pulled my wallet out and flashed him my P.I. license, including my firearms permit with concealed carry. I put my wallet away, set the gun behind me out of his reach, and pulled him upright so he leaned against the passenger's side of the van, against the sliding door, seated on the floor of the van. Jen passed behind where I was squatting and sat on top of the wheel-well on the driver's side. She pulled the backpack to her right side.

I picked up the gun and pointed it at his face. I said, "What's your name?"

"Kenny Slattery."

"Should I check your driver's license?"

"My name's Kenny Slattery."

"Okay, I could ask you a bunch of questions, and you could act tough by not answering them, but you'd get hurt again. Or I can tell you what I believe to be true, and you can let me know which parts I got wrong. I won't have to use further violence to detain you while you resist during this citizens' arrest."

The van had gotten very hot. The small crack created by the misshapen back door providing only a little fresh air.

"Does the AC work?" I asked.

"No."

"Then we'll have to keep sweating."

I pulled out my cell, started the recording app, and set the phone by my feet. I leaned against the side of the van on the driver's side, to Jen's left and directly across from him. "What do you think of my proposal?"

"Want to tell you to drop dead, but I ain't got no choice, do I?"

"No. We caught you with, what ..."— I reached over and lifted the backpack— "ten kilos?"

"Eight."

With the going rate for a key of cocaine in Los Angeles, the backpack's contents were worth about $160,000. The other backpack I'd seen Mike deliver that morning probably had the same amount in it.

I picked up a rag and threw it to him. He grabbed it and wiped the blood from his chin and neck.

"Here's what's going on," I said. "Workers in the San Felipe factory are adding coke to the raw materials that are combined to make the red Wave Skimmers. The boats in the other colors are legitimate, so part of the factory functions as other businesses do. But at least two people in San Felipe are involved with producing red kayaks. You're either contacted when new kayaks are ready, or you have a set schedule. Your organization has proven the concept works —Border Patrol and drug-sniffing dogs can't detect the coke—because there's no way the van goes through the checkpoint time after time without having its cargo searched by the dogs occasionally. But I'm guessing you've never been caught because you're sitting here and not in a cell. A chemist has perfected the amount that's undetectable. The amount per boat probably started low, but it's been increased to whatever it is today, still without detection."

He nodded.

"Based on your half of this shipment, I'm guessing eight boats per vanload, two keys per boat. That's about $320,000 per shipment, less expenses. Now that I hear myself say that, the money that needs to be washed simply gets run through the legitimate company, falsifying the books as needed."

"That's how I figure it."

"When the cocaine's been extracted, Mike picks it up and distributes it to you and another middleman, or at least one other, as he did last night. You sell it to da Uptown Posse, and the other guy sells it to the MLKs. The gangs step on it as hard as they can get away with and sling it on the street."

He nodded. "I need a verbal response," I said.

"Yeah, mostly. Ain't always eight boats and ain't no regular schedule. The gangs gotta sell their end, but it's pretty regular, about once a week, maybe every other. Think there's other couriers like me, but ain't sure. You got how it works."

"Good. Is film producer Marty Milford the kingpin, Mike's boss?"

"Until I got the shit jacked, I didn't know. Been doing this for almost two years now, and only deal with Mike. I wondered but wasn't stupid enough to ask. But, yeah, he's at the top."

"How do you know?"

"Because after I got my shit stole, they gave me a choice, but not really."

"They said you had to kill Chris Cerveris, or they'd kill you."

He nodded and looked toward the front of the van, trying to hide his tears.

"Speak your answers."

"Yes, they said they'd kill me. If I'm dead, my mom dies alone."

"What's that mean?"

"She got crap insurance, and she's dying from carcinoid tumors, practically everywhere. You have any idea how much money it takes for one night in a hospital if you got crap insurance? Or chemo treatments? I'm not exaggerating. It's more than most people make in a year. America, land of the free—free to go broke 'cause you get sick. That's why I ain't got shit to show for all this. Money goes to the hospitals and doctors all over the place. It's bullshit. I was actually a good person before this. Not educated—but not a crook. Ran a handyman business. Never made jack, but I was honest. Now I'm a murderer."

He cupped his bloody face in his hands and let his pain out. We listened to him cry for a minute. I looked at Jen. She was crying.

"People have done a lot of awful things for far worse reasons, Kenny," I said. "When my mom was alive, I'd probably have made the same choice you did, so I'm not judging you. But you threatened my life, so there's zero chance you're getting out of this, no matter how much sympathy I have for you. And you killed my friends Chris and Big Bill. And Jason Gilson."

"Yeah. I'm such a loser."

CHAPTER TWENTY-EIGHT

"Your position is non-negotiable," I said, "at least if you think you'll walk away without consequences. You won't. Now you determine whether you get put on death row, die of old age in general pop, or get killed soon by your organization. I don't see a fourth option. No, wait, I do. Maybe if you cooperate fully, you'll go into witness protection, but that's a longshot. You'll have to tie up Mike and Milford with a bow to have a shot at WITSEC."

He looked at his old Asics running shoes. He shook his head slowly but didn't speak. Sweat dripped down my back. I wiped my forehead with my sleeve and handed the gun to Jen, who hesitated before taking it. Her hands dropped from the unexpected weight of the gun, but then she leveled it at Kenny.

I stopped recording with my phone and called Game.

"Dawg, got an assignment for me?" he said instead of hello. "Summer boring as hell."

"I do. Be ready in thirty minutes. Jen will pick you up."

"Awwwight. Spy shit?"

"If driving qualifies."

"The Porsche?"

"Ford Taurus."

"For real? Okay, cool."

I continued to sweat with Kenny while Jen picked up Game, drove to the car rental agency, and returned her Versa. She drove the Range Rover to the van and took my place covering Kenny while I drove the Range Rover to the car rental agency, with Game following in the Taurus. Our shuttle complete, I drove us back to the van. I wouldn't have been surprised if Kenny had forced Jen to kill him by half-heartedly attacking her because death might seem to be his best option. But he had no fight left.

When we returned, Jen said he'd just sat there, resigned to his fate. Or maybe he was holding out hope he'd land in witness protection. For that to happen, he needed to behave, cooperate, and have his luck change dramatically.

Game was borderline giddy when he realized he was part of a citizens' arrest. He called it kidnapping because that's what it looked like and could legally have been. But Kenny seemed to understand we were saving his life, at least for now—until he was shanked in prison. I chose not to look at what we were doing as forcible abduction but as a life-lengthening, captive form of liberation. Of course, I'd shown Kenny my license, and I wouldn't have minded if he'd been under the impression that what was transpiring was perfectly legal under the California Penal Code.

While Game drove the van cautiously to West Los Angeles, Jen stopped at Versailles on Venice Boulevard and bought seven orders of the Cuban restaurant's unsurpassed Garlic Chicken. We were hungry, and we still had a lot to talk about. We'd likely be hungry again before we left the motel, so she purchased extra portions.

As Game drove, I didn't need to point the gun at Kenny because I could've broken him like a matchstick if he tried to overpower me—and he was already broken. When we reached the Wilshire Motel, Game moved the BMW to the street, then parked the van where the BMW had been in front of room twelve.

Jen cleaned Kenny's bloody face with the first-aid kit she kept in the Range Rover. If any of Milford's crew had been watching the room, they'd long ago figured we'd left through the window because there'd been no sign of life for days. So, we didn't have to sneak into the room because I didn't think we were being watched.

We scarfed down our meals, which included chicken, black beans and rice, buttered rolls, and fried plantains. Jen had also purchased a carafe of Cuban coffee.

When we were finished, we sprawled around the room, with Game sitting on the floor in the corner, leaning against the wall, and Kenny sitting in the desk chair that I'd placed in the center of the room. Jen and I sat on the bed, leaning against the headboard. I started the recording app and asked Kenny, "How many of you were there when you killed them?"

"Four. Me, two Posse, and Titan, that moron."

"Who's Titan?"

"Skinhead moron works in the shop."

"We had the misfortune to meet him," I said. "That's some team. A white supremacist, two Black gang members, and a white dude almost forced into being a criminal."

"Funny what money can do," he said.

"And funny what it can't," I said.

"Coulda used one more with the big guy. He was a real fighter. But we coulda did it with only two on the gay guy."

I laughed. "Gay guy? Because he dressed well?"

"He was watching a musical when we grabbed him. Hid outside. Grabbed him walking his little lap dog. That moron Titan broke its neck, threw it in the trash. He didn't have to do that. Someone woulda taken it, and it ain't like it could I.D. us."

"That's horrible on many levels," I said. "How'd you catch Chris unawares? He was neither old and distracted nor self-absorbed and clueless?"

"Milford said I had to kill him to work off the hijacked drugs. Then we'd be cool, but parta me knew he's lying, because then I'd have something on him, and he'd have something on me. At least I knew that much."

"How'd you do it?"

"Climbed over the security fence after dark. Thought he'd have motion detectors, maybe dogs. We moved around and waited, thinking we'd have to jump back over, find another way. But nothing happened. We snuck up to the house. Alphonse used his lighter on the trashcan full of leaves, made sure the fire took. We hid around the corner of the garage. He comes running out about ten minutes later when he smells smoke. Titan sticks the gun in his ear. Trash can melted, but the house was only scorched. Probably fire-resistant paint."

"How'd you get Big Bill outside with you?"

"Planned to do what worked later with the gay guy: Wait outside 'til he come out, but I saw a light down by the deck. That old house didn't have security. He was sitting in a beach chair next to a lantern, throwing sticks in a barrel. We snuck close in the sand, watched him. He got up, grabbed sticks, threw them again. We brung the rope, just like we done at the first one.

"When he got up the third time, we charged him from behind, threw the rope over his head, and hung on. That guy musta been something back in the day. Alphonse got an elbow in the eye, Deion broke a rib or two, Titan got knocked on his ass twice, and I took a kick to the balls. Dropped to the sand in agony, trying to catch my breath. That's when I saw the red kayak hanging there. It didn't make sense. Red Wave Skimmers only exist between the factory and the shop. The process makes them disappear, but there it was.

"The others don't know the process, I don't think, so I didn't mention it to them. Don't know how the big guy got it, but I guessed. Maybe he stopped by the factory late at night at the right time. He owned the place. I don't know. But he probably kept it as insurance. He could use it against Milford, prove what he was doing. I saw an opportunity, so after he was dead, hanging there, I drove them back to town and did what every jackass knows not to do: Return to the scene of the crime. I approached from the public entrance, unhooked the kayak, and had it back over the fence and in the van in a flash. Didn't take but seven minutes, tops."

"Where is it?"

"My apartment. Supposed to be my ticket out. Buy my freedom from Milford."

"It was leverage when Big Bill had it," I said, "an ace in the hole, or so he thought. But it didn't keep him alive, and now it's just another reason for Milford to kill you. You cost them their share of the $160,000 with the first stolen shipment. I was surprised you weren't killed for that, but he had other plans for you. Now that you've killed three men for him, you're a liability and their next target, and that was before a second shipment went missing." I patted the backpack. "No way anyone will believe you got a second shipment stolen without being involved."

"Damn straight." He stared at his shoes again. "Can't the kayak buy us anything?"

"Maybe. I'll have to figure out if we can make it work for us. You were surprised to see it that night, so Milford probably doesn't know it was there, either. Big Bill wasn't targeted because he had the kayak, at least not that we know of."

"Don't think so."

"Milford was probably cleaning up loose ends. My guess is that Chris suspected Milford of smuggling drugs, or maybe he knew he was. They'd been partners for decades. Chris could've seen a dramatic difference in lifestyle, or—who knows?—stumbled upon a cash delivery. But what if Chris accused Milford while Gilson was present, at a party or while on set together? Milford had to get rid of the guy who just threatened to turn him in and the witness who heard the threat. Chris knew Big Bill. The three of us fished for halibut in Wave Skimmers a few times. Did Big Bill tip off Chris? Did Chris know that Big Bill had a red kayak filled with cocaine?

"It doesn't matter because Milford got spooked enough to eliminate everyone he thought could bring him down, except for Alphonse, Deion, Titan, and you. And my guess is you're all next. But Milford can't keep bringing in third parties to do the killing for him, or there will always be people who can turn on him. If I were Milford, I'd start looking hard at Mike because Mike knows how the operation works and can bring down Milford. It has to be Mike's job to oversee the lower-rung distributors."

"Milford take Mike out?" Kenny asked. "I don't know, man. They're a team. Mike had Milford's back this whole time."

"You're probably right, so I'm just speculating about what would happen if he weren't Milford's rock, if we made Mike appear to betray him or rip him off. That could be pointless because we already know they want you and me dead. Maybe pointing a finger at Mike is unnecessary. But if Milford doesn't turn on Mike, then Mike will be the one he tells to take out the four killers."

We eventually arrived at a plan that we thought had a chance to work. Jen suggested we turn over Kenny and the cocaine to law enforcement in the hope the D.A. would go easy on him for cooperating. But he was involved in three murders. He could turn over the red kayak to them, explain the process, and direct them to the shop where the cocaine was extracted. His story and eight kilos would be enough for a judge to issue a search warrant for the shop. But as she made the suggestion, I realized that Milford could dismantle the shop. If he did that and cleaned up any evidence of coke ever having been inside the San Felipe factory, the authorities would have nothing to charge him with. He'd protected himself by having Chris, Big Bill, and Gilson killed, and he could only be implicated in those murders if Kenny, Alphonse, Deion, or Titan testified against him. Or maybe Mike.

"With the best lawyers that money could buy, Milford could be painted as a grieving movie producer and the owner of forty-nine percent of Wave Skimmer whose luck had turned awful overnight. Losing two business partners—Chris Cerveris and Big Bill Watson—on consecutive days, then losing friend and fellow showbiz big-wig Jason Gilson immediately thereafter. It was all just so tragic. Poor

Marty Milford. To anyone hearing the details, this story would look suspicious, but suspicion rarely sentences anyone to life in prison or to death row. Not when they have good lawyers.

We needed proof to guarantee Marty would be locked up forever.

I asked Kenny if he had any written or photographic proof of Milford's cocaine-smuggling scheme. He'd traveled to San Felipe and back almost weekly for about two years but had no documents implicating Milford. Mike had approached Kenny with a fantastic business opportunity when Kenny was visiting his mother in Saint John's Health Center in Santa Monica. After Kenny had made a few trips back and forth and marveled at how much money he'd made just for driving a van, Kenny asked Mike if he was the first driver to make these runs. Mike told him no. "What happened to the last guy?" Kenny had asked. Mike responded, "He got curious."

Kenny continued to pay his mother's exorbitant medical bills with the money he earned, never watching how the cocaine was infused into the kayaks and never watching how it was extracted. If he'd been audited, he would've been sunk because even a highly successful handyman/house painter wouldn't be able to pay medical bills a tenth as large as his mother's were. But he took that chance because doctors were keeping his mother alive.

I put the gun under my pillow and asked Game to keep watch over us while we slept for a few hours. It was only early evening, but I'd hardly slept in days, and I was exhausted. I didn't think Kenny would try to leave, especially because I had the keys to the van and the BMW in my pocket, and Jen had the key to the Range Rover in hers.

Before I put my head down, I asked Game, "You let your mom know you're with me, right?"

"Yeah."

"Good. Wake me in three hours, please, or if Kenny tries to leave."

"Ain't going nowhere," Kenny said. "I'm a dead man for sure out there. At least here I can have more chicken, right?"

"Knock yourself out. But I suggest you try to sleep. The next two days could be wild, and if we're really lucky, our biggest concern will be our lack of sleep."

Jen wrapped her right arm around me and adjusted her pillow.

"And if we ain't lucky?" Game asked.

"We'll have no concerns at all."

CHAPTER TWENTY-NINE

The red Wave Skimmer sat to the left of Big Bill Watson's walnut casket in the chapel at Holy Cross Cemetery. Nearly every pew was filled. A three-foot-by-four-foot poster of Big Bill paddling a yellow Wave Skimmer sat on an easel to the right of the lectern at which Father Gerard gave the sermon. Kenny sat to my left in the fifth pew from the front on the right side of the chapel, and Jen sat to my right. I'd set two coats down lengthwise on the pew about fifteen minutes before the service so we could enter after Marty Milford and after Frank led in his mother, Sadie, and Frank's wife, Janet, and their two daughters. I didn't want Milford to see us as he walked to the first pew, so I'd left the coats. Mike Sherwood sat at the end of the pew, next to Milford, who wore his long red hair in a ponytail. Game waited outside in the BMW.

After I woke up in the Wilshire Motel, I'd gone outside, crossed the courtyard to Wilshire Boulevard, and called Frank, even though it was after midnight. I didn't want to wake Jen by talking in the room, and I didn't want Kenny to overhear my plan, on the small chance that he still thought his best bet was to remain loyal to Milford. I'd already involved Game in ways I probably shouldn't have, but when I figured out that Mike was instrumental in Milford's crimes, I wondered if Mike would consider Game a liability. What did Mike think Game and the MLK members knew about the distribution scheme? Had the supplier who sold to the MLKs mentioned who delivered the coke to him? I suspected I was probably rationalizing, but, after I learned that Amanda was using again and Mike was involved in the smuggling and the murders, I trusted no one except Jen, Game, and Frank. And I was on the fence about Frank.

The call that morning, however, reassured me that Frank was on our side. He wasn't bothered by the late call because he couldn't sleep, not with his father being buried later that day. I told him everything I knew about Milford's smuggling operation and distribution process, including the fact that Kenny had in his apartment what was likely the only red Wave Skimmer in existence. Frank was amazed and upset by what I'd told him, and he agreed to cooperate "in every way possible, including risking my life," he said. "There's no chance I'm going to let them get away with killing Dad."

"Great. My first request is to allow the red kayak to be placed alongside your dad's coffin."

"Sure. Everyone else won't think it's weird because Wave Skimmer was, is, and always will be Dad—his life's work. The kayak will let the bastards know we've got them."

"They'll know we're onto them, but getting them will take some luck."

"Right, but we'll get them."

"I hope so. Try to get some sleep because to make this work we'll be awake for a long time."

"Got it. See you there."

"You, too. Be careful. Watch your back. They don't know what we know, and that could cause them to strike blindly when they learn we're onto them. By tomorrow afternoon, they'll know they're in trouble."

I made one more call early that morning before I went back to the motel room. Then, later that morning, on our way to Jennifer's, we stopped at the Malibu/Lost Hills Sheriff's Station.

Because we entered the chapel after Milford and Mike did, I couldn't see their expressions when they saw the red kayak next to Big Bill's casket.

The funeral service was similar to nearly every funeral service I'd attended: The priest heaped praise on the deceased, whom he'd never met, and emphasized the close relationship that William had to Jesus Christ, although in the more than thirty years I'd known Big Bill, I'd never heard him called William nor heard him mention Jesus. Throughout most of the service, I didn't listen to what the speakers were saying because I was focused on finding a way to ensure that Milford and Mike didn't get away, while keeping Jen, Game, Frank, Kenny, and me alive.

But when Father Gerard said, "And now we shall hear from William and Sadie's only child, Frank Watson," I paid attention.

"First, I'd like to thank each of you individually for coming today," Frank said at the lectern, "but that will likely prove to be impossible, so I will thank you now collectively. Dad would've been impressed by the number of people who came to honor him, but those of you who knew him well would know Dad would've hated the fuss we're making over him. 'I'm just a simple chemist. I got lucky. Anyone with a test tube could've done what I did. I just happened to do it first,' he told me at least a dozen times. No, Dad, only you could've invented the Wave Skimmer and could've been the wonderful father to me, and the doting, attentive husband to Mom, and the understanding, fun-loving grandfather to our girls that you were. And it is because I know you so well, Dad, I feel very comfortable saying—regardless of what the official report eventually says—you were murdered, and the men responsible for your murder are sitting in this chapel now."

The murmurs started when Frank said the word "murdered,"

then turned to gasps of surprise and exclamations of "Oh, my," "No," and "Good Lord" when he said the murderers sat among us. People quickly glanced over their shoulders, some of them in both directions, as though they'd be able to spot the murderers and take the necessary precautions.

Frank said into the microphone, "Now we'll hear from one of the murderers." The expressions of surprise multiplied ten-fold. I heard the sounds of dress shoes running on the marble floor.

Kenny stood up and spoke loudly: "I know Big Bill was murdered because I helped do it." I heard more people behind me fleeing, but I didn't turn around to look because I stood and focused my attention on Milford and Mike, who were seated four pews in front of me. Both of them snapped their heads around to the left to see if what seemed to be happening really was. Kenny waved to them, as I'd told him to do if the plan played out as it was playing out.

Milford stood and started to raise his hand to point at Kenny and likely threaten him. He was furious, and his mouth seemed to be searching for words, but none came out. Mike grabbed Milford's arm and forced him down into the pew. Nearly all the mourners in the first ten pews must've seen Milford's reaction and contrasted it with their own. They were shocked, but he was seething.

Kenny said, "Most of you don't know Big Bill had a silent business partner. That partner was Marty Milford, famous movie producer." Milford jumped up and hustled out the nearest exit at the front of the chapel on the right side. "And," Kenny continued, "I've worked for him the last two years—as a drug courier. We deal cocaine."

The service abruptly ended as mourners hurried out of the chapel. An elderly woman in the middle aisle appeared to have fainted. I looked at Frank, who stood and watched everyone fleeing, and he was laughing hard. His poor mother, Sadie, who would have had a difficult time understanding what was happening at a normal funeral service, looked lost. She kept raising her hands, as if asking for a divine explanation. Next to me, Jen was laughing, too.

"It's on," she said.

"Looks like it. Let's hope Game and Titan do what they have to do."

Kenny sat down, looking exhausted. It took guts—and a solid belief in our plan—for him to confess publicly to murder and drug running. He'd resigned himself to a lousy future, but how lousy it would be had yet to be determined. Would it be the San Quentin, death-row kind of lousy? Or would it be the new-name, new-town, look-over-your-shoulder-for-the-rest-of-his-life kind of lousy provided by the witness-protection program? He hoped his cooperation would grant him the latter.

Before he headed out the front exit to his right, Mike turned toward me with a look on his face that seemed to express regret. He shrugged and turned his palms upward in a gesture I took to mean, "It is what it is."

Jen drove Kenny and me to her house in the Range Rover, with the red kayak strapped to the top. My guess was that not many people heard the words Father Gerard said at Big Bill's gravesite. I'm sure Frank and his mother were there, but probably only a few others, after that fiasco of a funeral.

Our plan was for Frank to meet us at Jen's as soon as he could. I'd deduced that Milford would have only one place to go after he raced out of the chapel: The Wave Skimmer shop, where he would eliminate all traces of his cocaine operation. I wasn't sure I needed Game to confirm Milford's arrival at the shop, but I wasn't sure I'd convinced Titan during our phone conversation early that morning of how screwed he was and how wise it would be for him to cooperate. I took a perverse pleasure in having concocted a plan that required Game to oversee Titan.

Titan was supposed to hit record on his phone's recording app as Milford entered the shop, then unlock the front door, if Milford remembered to lock it behind him. Game was supposed to wait until Titan texted him before Game entered the shop. Game would walk in while recording video on his phone. At worst, we hoped to catch Milford dismantling or destroying the vats, hoses, beakers, scales, and ovens required to extract the cocaine. With luck, Titan would get Milford to implicate himself in the cocaine ring, acknowledging he was the mastermind. And if we were really lucky—or if Titan decided to beat a confession out of him—Milford would admit to having ordered Titan, Kenny, Alphonse, and Deion to murder Chris Cerveris, Big Bill Watson, and Jason Gilson. The best-case scenario would be to catch Marty Milford implicating himself in these crimes on Titan's audio recording and on Game's video recording.

On the ride to the house, I asked Kenny about the herky-jerky motions he'd used while delivering the threats to Amanda's and Jen's mailboxes.

"It was Mike's idea. He wanted you to think I was trying to hide who I was because you might know me if I didn't."

"Are you a horror-movie fan?"

"Yeah. How'd you know?"

"Your *Hunchback of Notre Dame* walk. Not many people today could distinguish Lon Chaney from Dick Chaney."

"Yeah, me and Mom used to watch old horror movies together. She's a big fan."

Jen pulled into her driveway, and I heard the text chime on my phone. It was from Game and said: *Serious shit. Watch video. Call me after.* I positioned my phone so Jen, Kenny, and I could see it and played the video. We watched as Game crept silently through the shop, through the swinging saloon doors, and across the workspace. On the far wall was a door I had no reason to take note of during my visit. Titan was supposed to make sure it was unlocked, and he'd played his part because Game opened the door silently and stuck his phone inside to film the action.

"Faster, you stupid oaf," Milford said to Titan on the video. Titan was on the ground on his back, with only his legs visible, his torso out of view beneath a framework of pipes that supported two enormous beakers and a large pot. A track ran out of frame to the left, probably to set the kayaks on. The apparatus reminded me of a moonshine still. Titan was dismantling the apparatus. Milford lifted one of the large beakers, looked for a place to set it, then threw it against the wall out of frame to the right. Game's phone captured the sound of shattering glass but not the visuals.

"This is bullshit, Marty. They can't prove shit," Titan said, still on his back.

"The residue alone will screw us. There's no legitimate use for this shit."

"You're paranoid," Titan said, wriggling out from underneath the apparatus. "Are you doing blow? Is that it?" He stood and glanced over Milford's shoulder, looking directly at Game's phone poking through the cracked door.

Titan said, "We didn't kill those traitors so you could go soft on us. You said, 'They're threatening my millions, so take 'em out.' We did what you told us."

"Yeah, but that ship's sailed. Drake's screwing us. He's next. But you gotta finish here first. You're so goddamned slow. Are you fucking retarded?"

"Marty, I killed for you. What makes you think I won't snap your head off for calling me retarded?"

"This," Marty said, reaching into his jacket on his right side. His body blocked the video from showing the gun in his right hand, but it caught the muzzle flash and Titan's response to the impact. Titan staggered backward and fell. Game pulled his phone through the door and had the presence of mind to ease the door closed and release the handle, so the door closed silently, preventing Milford from knowing he'd been seen, let alone filmed.

Just after Game pulled his hand through the door, the sounds of three additional gunshots were captured on the audio. The video became a blur as Game ran across the workspace, through the shop, and out the front door, his Adidas moving quickly in and out of frame. The audio caught Game saying, "Go, go, go."

Instead of getting in the BMW, he kept running down the alley he'd run down while chasing the white van. I heard Game's strained breathing as he ran. Thirty seconds later, after he had rounded two corners, he turned the camera toward his face and said, "How's that for proof?"

"Amazing," Jen said as Kenny said, "Yes!"

"He did it. He really did it," Jen said.

"He sure did," I said. "The kid came through, that's for sure. Be in in a minute."

Jen and Kenny went inside, and I called the Compton Sheriff's Station to report the shooting of Titan, which was probably a murder, if Milford's aim was good. The officer working the switchboard insisted I tell him my name after I tried to remain anonymous. "Jack Drake," I said. "In a minute, I'll send you video of the shooting. All you have to do is find Marty Milford." I sent Game's video to the Los Angeles County Sheriff, Oakville PD, and the Malibu/Lost Hills Sheriff's Station.

"What you think, dawg?" Game said upon answering my call.

"You are a true champion, Game. The best. Great job. We can discuss it for as long as you want when you get to Jen's, but right now, you have only one job to do—to stay safe. Make sure Milford has left the shop before you go back for the car. If you have any doubt—"

"Heard him tear outta there when I was running, but I'll double-check."

"Good. Again, great job. You couldn't have done better, but don't let adrenaline affect your speed on PCH. You're still a sixteen-year-old African American driving a BMW through Malibu."

"Gotcha, dawg."

I went inside Jen's house and locked the door. Kenny was pacing, and Jen sat on a couch.

"We got him," Kenny said. "But Titan's probably dead, huh?"

"He's strong, but it doesn't look good. If all four bullets hit him, he doesn't have much of a chance."

Jen looked shaken. "I ... I can't believe ... I've never seen anyone killed in real life. That was a human being, not an actor. I hate this feeling, and I wasn't even involved. Other than Titan killing Milford, that was the best we could hope for, right?"

"I thought I'd run the possible scenarios through my head, but I couldn't picture Milford as a killer, as the guy who'd pull the trigger himself. Not the type to get his hands dirty. I thought there was a chance Titan would flip again because he didn't think Kenny's testimony against him would be enough to convict. That's why I considered following Milford, instead of having Game do it. If Titan flipped again, anything could've happened, including Game being in real trouble. But even a guy stupid enough to believe the racist garbage Titan believes should understand that when accomplices are squeezed—he had three accomplices—they'll finger their partners for lesser sentences. So, I gambled on that part of the plan and left with the kayak, hoping Mike, Milford, or their minions would see us carrying away the only hard evidence we had at the time. We're much better off than we were before Milford shot Titan, but we're not in the clear. We still need the rest of the plan to work, but I don't think all of it will be necessary now."

It was only 6:15, and all my experience said they wouldn't show up until early morning, probably between 2 and 4. They'd arrived at Chris' much earlier, about 11 p.m., but Chris hadn't known they were coming for him, and we did. I was willing to bet they wouldn't show up when we were wide awake. The best time to attack is 4 a.m., when night-owls have usually turned in, and early-birds aren't yet awake. My calculated guesses had been correct lately, so, after instructing Jen and Kenny to go over the plan again with Frank when he arrived, I acted on another calculated guess, one that could eliminate one of our potential attackers and could prevent the attack itself.

CHAPTER THIRTY

I'd never been to Malibu Serenity. The only difference between it and the other rehabs that Amanda'd been treated in appeared to be the size of the pool. I hoped the doctors and therapists there were more willing to deal in hard truths than the medical professionals at the other rehabs had been. Awe of celebrities extends to professionals in every field, and everyone has the right to be impressed by, inspired by, or enamored of celebrities. But when fandom interferes with doctors doing their jobs, lives can be lost.

Getting sober requires "doing the work" and "working the steps," as adherents of Alcoholics Anonymous enthusiastically declare, and no one who's "gotten sober" would say that doing so was easy. The psychiatrists at those other rehabs might not have compromised their professionalism while treating Amanda, but I saw signed headshots of her in two doctors' offices while she was still a patient in those facilities. As I drove to Malibu Serenity, I hoped this stay would be different for her, but when I saw Mike's Corvette in a space to the left of the entrance, I knew she hadn't changed and probably wouldn't.

Mike was sitting in the lobby, waiting for the residents to finish dinner. He looked up as I walked in, smiled, and said, "Well, look what the cat dragged in." He looked worse than I'd ever seen him—gaunt and exhausted. His pupils were huge, and his right leg was bouncing up and down like a needle in a sewing machine. We'd been as close as brothers—closer than most brothers, probably—since meeting during freshman orientation in college. We'd supported each other in a hundred ways over the years, so the emotional pain I felt when I saw him sitting there was extreme.

Normally we would've given each other a hug, but instead of approaching him, I sat in an upholstered chair ten feet away. I didn't respond for a while, trying to decide if he would reach for the gun I suspected he wore under the leather jacket he was wearing. It was mid-June in Southern California, so the jacket was overkill, although it made sense because he'd driven to the rehab facility with the top of his Vette down. I believed he had a gun, although I didn't want to believe he'd use it on me.

I said, "How long?"

"How long? How long, what, Jack?" he said, raising his arms and shrugging his shoulders. His overacting reminded me again why a man with his chiseled good looks would be relegated to modeling and roles without dialogue. With even a little acting ability, he would've been a star. But he couldn't act at all, so he'd become a teacher. Unfortunately, he aspired to the movie-star lifestyle but only had a public servant's income. This discrepancy, I was sure, contributed to us sitting in the Malibu Serenity lobby that night.

"You know."

"No, really, I don't. Please tell me, Mr. Detective."

"How long have you been sleeping with Amanda?"

The receptionist had given me an unfriendly look when I'd sat down without greeting Mike or acknowledging her. I'd entered a medical facility without being a patient or accompanying one. When I asked Mike that question, she picked up the receiver of the landline on the desk and punched in an extension. "Yes, I think so," she said into the receiver.

"More than two years, every chance we got," Mike said.

I wanted to yell, wanted to slug him, wanted him to reach for his gun so I could outdraw him and wipe the smirk off his face. Instead, I shook my head and inhaled and exhaled deeply four times, trying to calm down.

"How'd you know?"

"The Amex she used to cut the blow in the bathroom. It was yours."

"Shit. I must have hers. We weren't exactly of sound mind after inhaling a mountain of Medellín's finest and a trough of Maker's Mark. Not sure how we made it home from Loews."

I didn't know what to say. Mike had taken the deaths of his father and his sister, Michelle, very hard, and I'd worried often about his drinking. I'd always thought he burned too hot, pursuing his passions —sports, bourbon, and women—too fervently, letting his blind enthusiasm throw him off balance. But I never thought he'd lose himself so much that he'd order a murder, if not become a murderer himself. Addiction warps reality to whatever extent allows an addict to down the next drink, to snort the next line, or to shoot the next dose. My father had proven that—and was still proving it, which was why he wasn't in my life.

I looked at Mike, expecting to see sadness or self-loathing. Or maybe he'd be apologetic. But what I saw was contempt. His expression told me he was spoiling for a fight. I hoped I was wrong but readied my right hand in case I had to reach for the Beretta.

"Took you long enough. Hell of a detective you are." He laughed loudly.

"Why, Mike? Why would you do this to Amanda and me? She's a vulnerable addict, and I thought I was among your best friends."

"Why does anyone do anything, Jack?"

A heavy-set, thirtyish Latino security guard wearing a gray uniform walked across the lobby toward us. The nametag affixed to his left breast read: Luis. He didn't appear to be armed.

"You gentlemen mind taking this conversation elsewhere?" Luis asked, although he was telling us to move, not asking.

"No problem," I said. "Amanda has probably finished eating. Should the three of us talk somewhere?" I asked Mike.

"Nothing more to say." He stood.

"Gentlemen?" Luis said.

"You didn't answer my question. Why'd you do it?"

I looked to my right, past Mike, who was facing me, and saw Amanda watching us from the edge of the lobby. She waved at me but didn't move toward us. I didn't respond because I wanted to hear what Mike would say about them when he didn't know she could hear him.

"She was there, and you were clueless. Your head's in the sand, man, in love with an ideal. Jami was impressive, true, but she was still human, still flawed. Even if she'd been perfect, she's gone. You never moved on, and Amanda was attractive and willing. I've never needed more than that."

"That's it," Luis said. "I'm asking you both to leave." He took hold of Mike's right elbow with his left hand. Mike threw his arm in the air, forcing Luis to let go. Mike stepped away and swept the right side of his jacket back, revealing his gun. Mike and I both heard Amanda gasp. He turned toward her for a few seconds. I removed the Beretta from its holster and leveled it at him. The receptionist ran from behind the counter and stood next to Amanda, about thirty feet away from me. Ten people were now fanned out around Amanda. Mike, still holding his jacket back, took his eyes off her and looked at Luis.

"Relax, sir," Luis said. "No need for that. Calm down, or I can call the sheriff if you'd like."

Mike laughed and glanced at me. He saw my gun aimed at him. "Yeah, we could do it that way, Jack. Sure. A blaze of glory. Or I guess it would be gory. A blaze of gory. It would make the papers, CNN." He laughed again, louder this time, with the sound transforming from laughter to a howl. "But that doesn't feel right. I'm gonna set my gun down slowly, like this."

He removed the blued revolver from its holster and set it on the floor next to his right foot. Luis took two steps toward Mike and picked up the gun. I was about to re-holster mine but thought doing so wasn't worth the risk. Mike was a great athlete and very quick, so I only lowered the gun, then said, "Call off the attack, Mike."

He smiled, and for a few seconds I saw the friend I'd known and loved for decades. Mike was still there somewhere, albeit addled by coke and bourbon.

"Maybe your head's not as far in the sand as I thought," he said. "I wouldn't have sent Game with you if I'd known you were suddenly going to re-enter the world of the living. Shit, your cluelessness was why I sent him. I knew he wasn't in a gang. I mean, look at the kid. His tough-guy act is ridiculous. I had to bite my tongue to stop from laughing at it. He got an A in my class. Bangers don't bother to show up, let alone study hard and ace their tests. If they show up, it's to socialize, not learn. I needed him out of the way so Rachelle and I could spend a whole night together. It's absurd how she dotes on him, not willing to leave a sixteen-year-old alone at home. The park shooting was the perfect excuse. Mama trying to protect her son, the so-called banger. I didn't have to work hard to convince her. And you? Shit. You've been a pushover for years. But here we are now, with you afraid you'll shoot me and me afraid you won't."

"Call off the attack."

"Okay. You win." He pulled his iPhone from his jeans and scrolled through his contacts. "Clever Jack Drake, rope-a-doping us for a decade, only to deliver the knockout in the late rounds. Bravo." He tapped out a text and sent it.

"Done," he said. "I can't vouch for Milford or Titan, but they won't get help from da Posse when they come for you."

"Milford shot Titan. Game caught it on video."

"Shit. Didn't think he had it in him. Marty pulling a trigger? Wow. Guess you probably won't need this, but just in case." He handed me his phone. "Pass code's 1207, Michelle's birthday. In the Voice Memos app, you'll find enough to put Milford away."

"Thanks," I said, taking his phone and putting it in my windbreaker.

He nodded, turned, and walked to Amanda. He opened his arms wide to hug her, and she put her arms around him, inside his jacket. He whispered in her ear as she put her head on his shoulder. I waved my arm to get Luis' attention. He saw me, nodded, and walked over to Mike and Amanda.

"Okay, we're done. Hand it to me, Ms. Bigelow."

"What? What are you talking about?" she asked, removing her arms from Mike's jacket and bringing them behind her back. She threw a Baggie of coke behind her. It hit a female patient in the leg and fell to the floor. Luis shouldered Mike out of the way and held Amanda at arm's length as he bent to pick up the Baggie. He turned to Mike and said, "You give me no choice, sir. If you leave now, you might miss the sheriff."

Mike looked at Luis and Amanda and bowed deeply, flourishing his right arm upward, then sweeping it in an arc toward the ground. He turned, walked toward me, and opened his arms for a hug. I thought he might make a play for my gun, so I held it tightly in my right hand, then wrapped that arm around his left shoulder as he embraced me.

He asked, "Did I ever tell you I was one of the Fruit of the Loom guys?"

"Nope."

"Yup, the purple grapes. The pinnacle of my acting career."

"Impressive," I said.

He let go, stepped back, and looked in my eyes.

"Take care of yourself," he said. "And Jennifer. I'm truly happy for you both."

"I will."

"And I'm sorry. Really."

"I know you are. I forgive you."

CHAPTER THIRTY-ONE

But I haven't forgiven him. Not for most of what he did—although I'm trying.

After Mike left Malibu Serenity that night, the director of the facility and Luis escorted Amanda to her room and watched her pack. Apparently, receiving smuggled cocaine while in rehab was against the rules. While she was upstairs, I unlocked Mike's phone and listened to the two recordings Mike had made of Marty Milford giving him instructions.

The first one said: "I carried Chris from the beginning. He and I both know that, and everyone else in the business suspects it. He's good with people, fine. So are hostesses and hookers. He couldn't organize a garage sale, but he's gonna threaten me? Gonna turn me in? Really? Fuck him. Two pictures in a row he championed, just had to do 'em. But they tanked. Total flops. But he's gonna tell me how I can make my money? What are we, nuns? I need you to take care of this. I want him dead, now."

How could Mike have gone through with the order? He'd calmed me down when I was drunk and wanted to attack the cop who'd pulled us over after we'd learned of Jami's bike accident. Mike had been the voice of reason that day. How had that man turned into this one? How long had coke been hobbling him while I'd wallowed in self-pity, not noticing his pain and addiction?

I played the second recording: "The old, fat slob thinks he can get away with that? He can ruin me? Really? Is he threatening me or shaking me down? What the hell? The guy'd be homeless if it weren't for me. Screw him and his dying wife. He invented a kayak. Yippee. I saved his business and found a way to do some real business. Take him out. Chris brought no heat. Do it the same way. Sad old guys off themselves all the time."

I forwarded both recordings to the Malibu/Lost Hills Sheriff's Station. I sent the second one to Frank, along with a text that said: *The video should be enough, but this could help land Milford on death row.*

I had no choice that night but to drive Amanda to her fifth rehab in Malibu, called Moonlight. As we drove down from the top of Latigo Canyon, where Malibu Serenity was located, toward PCH, I asked her, "When did you start using again?"

"I'm sorry, Jack, I really am, but I never really stopped. Maybe for a couple weeks after the last one, but I ran into Jason at Ralphs. We talked about our latest projects, and he looked loaded, so I asked if he had any left. None on him. He'd just snorted the last of it in the Ralphs bathroom. But he made a phone call, and we sat in Starbucks and talked, and in like an hour, Mike shows up. I was surprised, but nothing in this town surprises anyone, does it? I mean, really? Look at Weinstein and Cosby and Michael Jackson and Robert Blake. Shit, what's his name? Specter. So, I was surprised but I wasn't. Mike had always flirted hard with me, but I thought we were just having fun. He's your friend, so I thought we were flirting. When Jason finally left our room in the Malibu Beach Inn, loaded to the gills, Mike made it clear he wasn't just flirting. It started that night. Mike and I actually get each other, but I don't expect you to believe that."

"Apparently, I'll believe anything."

We drove in silence down Latigo. When I saw the firetruck,

ambulance, and two sheriff's patrol cars near the edge of the road where it turns sharply left, I knew what had happened. I didn't have to look down the cliff to know a convertible Corvette Stingray was at the bottom. When Mike handed me his phone, instead of forwarding the recordings to me, we were saying our final goodbyes.

"What happened?" Amanda asked as we passed the emergency vehicles.

"Someone missed the turn. Probably distracted."

She didn't find out about the accident for a couple days when a fellow Moonlight patient, a car buff, mentioned that he'd seen a picture of the destroyed Vette on the news. "It had a vanity plate," he said while eating dinner with the other patients, she told me when I visited her. "What does LOOM mean?" the patient had asked.

But Mike wasn't at the bottom of the canyon. I knew it as I drove by the scene. He was a fighter to his core, so he would never surrender. He would exhaust every option and wouldn't quit. He wanted me and everyone else to think he'd been thrown from the open convertible as it plunged hundreds of feet over the cliff, hurling his body into unreachable terrain or high in a tree that clung to a treacherous slope.

The next day's *Los Angeles Times* quoted a Los Angeles County Sheriff's press liaison as saying: "For the safety of the search and rescue teams searching for Mike Sherwood, a beloved English teacher at Oakville High School, the search was suspended because of darkness and the difficulty the terrain presents to the dedicated team searching for him. We'll begin again in the morning. We feel confident Mr. Sherwood will turn up."

Yes, Mr. Sherwood turned up, intact and unscathed physically but still jacked on cocaine.

Before he handed me his phone at Serenity, he forgot to delete his texting history. His oversight was understandable, considering I'd been pointing a gun at him. While Amanda packed, after I'd listened to the recordings of Milford telling Mike to kill Chris and Big Bill, I looked at the texts Mike had recently sent. The last one, the one in which he was supposed to call off Alphonse and Deion, said: *It's a go. If I ain't there, go without me. Good luck.* The one before that was to Amanda and said: *On my way, baby, with everything you need.*

My visit to Serenity had confirmed that Mike and Amanda were together and he was complicit in everything that had happened. But I'd hoped my visit would allow me to call off the plan that Jen, Game, Kenny, and I had put in place during our long talk in the motel. Mike's faked suicide was meant to get law enforcement to stop pursuing him for the murders and to pin them on Milford, but Mike's plan was also meant to get me to let my guard down. If I believed Mike and Titan were dead and Alphonse and Deion had been called off, no one would be left to come after me because Milford was on the run and Kenny had turned himself in, although Mike wouldn't have known that. He did know, however, that Kenny wouldn't have acted alone. With no one left, I would scrap the plan to defend ourselves, Mike was hoping. He'd given me the phone to get me to believe he would kill himself, to believe he was getting rid of his possessions and doing the right thing by providing evidence that would lock Milford up.

But his inability to act not only cost him his acting career, but it also tipped me off to his plan. When he'd made that showy bow, flourishing his right arm upward, then sweeping it toward the ground, as if he were a dandy on an Elizabethan stage, I knew the gesture felt wrong. At first, I thought the mountain of coke he'd consumed had influenced his elaborate choreography, but when he hugged me and mentioned Fruit of the Loom, instead of expressing contrition or regret, I knew he was playing a role. Poorly.

He wanted me to think he was about to kill himself, but I'd been on that ledge, and his emotions were wrong. While standing at the brink, considering whether to step into darkness forever, he should have been looking inward—his self-loathing and guilt should have been eating him up, devouring whichever positive traits he possessed, allowing him to see only the worst of himself and the world. But he chose to make two external gestures—the first a flourish for everyone in the room, and the second an inside joke to me.

After I left Amanda at Moonlight, I made a few calls to confirm our plan was still on.

I drove to Jen's house, parked in the driveway, and went inside. We turned on the lights that were usually on in the evening, then slipped out the back. We walked on the wet sand to Amanda's. I knew Amanda was too far gone to have changed the security code or changed the locks. If she wanted to try to get me charged with trespassing when she got out of rehab, good luck to her.

For however long it took for the attackers to arrive, Jen was supposed to manipulate the lights, stereo, and televisions in her house with her phone via Apple Homekit while she stood on the sand. She was supposed to live like a mouse in Amanda's house, providing no indication that anyone was home. After Game had dropped off the BMW, Frank had driven him to Oakville, where he broke the news to his mother about Mike being a drug dealer and complicit in at least three murders.

I'd turned the eight-kilos of cocaine over to the sheriff, making law enforcement agencies eager to cooperate with us. They greenlighted the parts of my plan that met with their objectives and nixed those that didn't. Two deputies and three DEA agents entered Jen's house from the sand and made themselves disappear throughout the four stories.

Although I cooperated with law enforcement, I didn't tell them everything. While they waited for Alphonse, Deion, and whichever other Posse members would arrive to kill me and anyone with me, the deputies and agents didn't know I wouldn't be with Jen at Amanda's, as the plan specified.

My gut had exposed the smuggling ring and helped to gather enough evidence to convict Marty Milford. So, when my gut told me that Mike hadn't driven off the cliff and wouldn't participate in the attack on me, I listened to it and knew it was up to me to catch him.

From the moment I passed the emergency vehicles parked on Latigo, I wondered how I would fake my death, if I had to. No one could fake his own death spontaneously and hope to get away with it, so Mike would have needed a plan, one that included plenty of money to help him escape and live a long time without an honest source of income. He couldn't make a bank withdrawal after he'd supposedly launched himself into the void. He'd need a sizeable go-bag—filled with cash, clothes, food, falsified documents, and anything else necessary to assume a new identity, probably in another country that didn't have an extradition treaty with the United States. And he'd have to stash the go-bag somewhere accessible enough to grab it at any hour. But it would have to be hidden well enough so that no one else could find it. His world would end if he needed to disappear but his go-bag had been stolen.

Where would he hide it? Not at his house. And he couldn't risk that Game or Rachelle would find it at their house. U.S. train stations and bus stations almost never have lockers anymore because terrorists could use them to store explosives for an attack. Gyms have cameras in them and aren't all twenty-four hours, so their lockers wouldn't be ideal, and safe-deposit boxes were out. He could bury a bag anywhere, but the land would have to be accessible twenty-four-seven, and could he afford to spend time digging it up while being chased?

Mike had probably squirreled away a lot of money in various accounts, likely overseas. But dead guys can't initiate wire transfers, so he'd probably opened those accounts under an assumed name, or more than one. He'd still have to have a lot of cash somewhere. Or cocaine.

He'd been Amanda's supplier for two years, and they'd snorted lines together in Loews a few nights before. But because I'd lived with Amanda, he wouldn't have risked hiding his stash or go-bag at her house.

But then it hit me.

The red kayak that had hung under Big Bill's deck wasn't Big

Bill's insurance—it was Mike's nest-egg. Or part of it. And maybe leverage against Milford, evidence that Mike could turn over to authorities if the situation had played out differently.

How had Mike convinced Big Bill to secure it under his deck? Had he approached the sad, old man as a stranger and said something like: "I heard you invented the Wave Skimmer, sir, but I bet you've never seen a red one like this? Someone must've screwed up at the factory, got the mix wrong. I tried it, but it's not my thing. You can have this one, if you want it."

Or had he let Big Bill in on the smuggling, promising to cut him in? "This will go a long way to paying for that full-time care your wife needs." Or did he simply threaten him? "Keep this for me, old man, until I need it. If it's gone when I get here, I'll kill your wife first, then your son, making you watch me stab them both. Then I'll kill you slowly."

Of course, I didn't know that Mike had anything to do with the red kayak until, late on the night he faked his death, I found a brown, extra-large canvas duffel bag secured with half a roll of brown duct tape above the pressure-treated brown beam that held up one side of Big Bill's deck. Even in daylight, the bag would have been out of sight from below. Only moonlight brightened the area outside of the deck, so the fifteen-by-fifteen-foot space was in near-total darkness. I spent ten minutes moving an overturned whiskey barrel from one spot to the next, standing atop it, then feeling blindly for what my gut told me would be there. Finally, it was.

I cut the bag down, tore off the tape, and unzipped it. Inside were four kilos of cocaine bundled as the ones that Jen and I had taken from Kenny had been, $100,000 in one-hundred-dollar bills, bound in bricks of $10,000, three changes of clothes, including a pair of work boots and a pair of flip-flops, and a Moroccan passport with the name Andrew Holton next to a photo of Mike Sherwood.

I closed the duffel, carried it in the dark across the sand to Amanda's house, removed $80,000, and set the duffel on the yellow Wave Skimmer hanging below her house. I pulled down the blue kayak, opened the hatch, put the eighty grand inside, closed the hatch, and hung the kayak back on its hooks. I went back to Big Bill's deck to get ready.

I hauled both whiskey barrels to the corner under the deck across from the corner in which the duffel had been hidden. I set the barrels against each other on the diagonal—the hypotenuse to the right-angles of the corner. I'd created a wall that a man could crouch behind after slipping through the small opening on the left side. I smoothed out the circular marks the barrel had made in the sand as I'd searched for the duffel in the rafters.

I'd carried the Mossberg shotgun, the Beretta, the Ka-Bar knife, and the night-vision goggles with me. I didn't want to use the weapons, but Mike was fighting for his freedom and his life, so he'd kill me without hesitation if he had to. I promised myself I'd do whatever was necessary to continue breathing.

He arrived at 2:15, carrying a revolver in his right hand, with a backpack slung over his left shoulder. He walked through the soft sand slowly, stopped, and looked around, apparently seeing nothing because he pulled a flashlight from his leather jacket. He shined the beam around the space, looking for the whiskey barrels so he could move one beneath where he'd stowed the duffel bag.

When he moved the beam to his left, he saw the whiskey barrels and the black muzzle of the shotgun. I'd wedged the shotgun between the barrels where their downward curves met, with the black barrel aimed into the middle of the space, about where Mike stood.

He fired five shots into the barrels, trying to hit the fool stupid enough to ambush him from behind them. He probably knew I'd be that fool.

But I wasn't behind the barrels—I was above the far rafter, where the large duffel had been. I was tall enough to jump up and grab the beam without needing to stand on a barrel, and I was strong enough to pull myself up. I wore the night-vision goggles, and for the last two hours had been listening carefully and lowering my head and right arm every so often far enough below the beam to see if he'd arrived. As he fired the fifth shot, I leaned down far enough to take aim, holding the rafter with my left arm, and fired a bullet into his left calf.

He fell to the sand as his screams mingled with the thunder of the gunshot. He dropped the gun and flashlight and grabbed his calf, writhing in pain. I swung off the rafter, badly scraping my left forearm as I fell. I took three steps toward him, grabbed his gun, and stepped away.

He looked up at me and winced, but then he managed to smile. I heard sirens in the distance, and I knew the deputies and the DEA agents would arrive by foot any second.

"Subterfuge," he said. "A real-world fumblerooski. I'm impressed."

I didn't say anything. So much adrenaline coursed through me that I felt my racing pulse in my temples.

"Kind of bullshit, though," he said. "Technically, I wasn't aiming at you."

I walked over behind the barrels and crouched behind them for a second. "Yes, you were."

When I stood, he was holding a knife in his right hand. His left still tried to slow the bleeding in his calf.

I aimed the Beretta at him and said, "What are you going to do with that, dice vegetables?"

I saw beams of light bouncing wildly out on the beach, then heard the sounds of law-enforcement officers running toward us. The first deputy and two DEA agents reached the area in front of the deck. Mike raised the knife in front of him and said, "There's something you should know."

Three shafts of light shined on Mike and glinted off the knife. He faced me, perpendicular to the light beams coming from his left.

"Drop it," the three law enforcement officers said almost simultaneously, aiming their weapons at him. Two others arrived with guns drawn. The sirens now sounded stationary, meaning more deputies and agents were running toward us.

"I slept with Jami."

No, you didn't, I thought. Not a chance.

He was trying to provoke me, so I'd shoot him. I had a better chance of being Miley Cyrus than he had of sleeping with Jami. She'd always been polite, even friendly, to him, but she'd told me he gave off a vibe she didn't trust. She'd been a better judge of character than I had been.

My pulse slowed, the adrenaline dissipated, and the danger to me had all but passed. Instead of excitement and anger, I felt extreme sadness. What had I done to cause him to hate me?

"Fine, don't believe me," he said. "You got the best of me here, I'll give you that, but you're still kind of clueless. You didn't know about Amanda, so what makes you so sure about Jami?"

Shouts of "Drop the weapon" and "Drop it now" came from the officers and agents on the beach.

"Listen to me, Jack," Mike said. "Here's your chance to prove you aren't a coward, a failure. Prove you're a man."

The Beretta was still aimed between his eyes. His revolver sat on the barrel to my right, with the shotgun between the two barrels.

"She was up for almost anything, but she loved it when I degraded her. You know, the stuff you wouldn't do to her."

He drew the knife behind his head, and more than a dozen bullets from five guns tore him to pieces. He died instantly.

But I didn't kill him.

CHAPTER THIRTY-TWO

The authorities questioned how I'd shot Mike in his calf, apparently from a high angle, but I told them he'd lost his balance while shooting at me, then spun around, falling backward toward me when the bullet hit him. They seemed not to believe me because all five of Mike's bullets had missed me while I was supposed to have been crouched behind the barrels, the ones riddled with bullet holes. But the authorities weren't going to consider charging me because their shoot was bad, and they knew it.

The eighteen bullets that tore through Mike supported this argument. If Mike had thrown the knife, it would have missed me. I'd ducked when he'd lifted his arm. Letting the shoot disappear quietly made sense to them because they didn't have to kill him, even though that's what he wanted them to do. Because I'd ducked, I didn't see him get torn apart. I only saw what was left of him.

Both the Los Angeles County Sheriff's Department and the Drug Enforcement Administration received plenty of press for dismantling a major drug ring and for capturing the murderers of Chris Cerveris, Big Bill Watson, Jason Gilson, and probably others. I was mentioned in two articles and on one news broadcast. Amanda was dragged into it because of her relationship with me, although I didn't read any stories connecting her to Mike. Because the world is fascinated by famous people, especially those who fall, news vans soon parked in front of Moonlight, which didn't help Amanda's battle to find sobriety. Someone had leaked her presence there.

Marty Milford awaits trial. The video of him killing Titan was sent to every Southern California law enforcement agency, then was leaked to social media, along with a description of his maroon Mercedes-Benz SLC 300 roadster. The footage of him being chased onto the USC campus and being surrounded by cop cars played on every news station. He didn't pinch the grip of the revolver between his index finger and thumb when the cops told him to put his hands outside the car. He presented his left hand holding the gun as though ready to fire it, with his index finger on the trigger. The cops yelled at him to drop his weapon. He didn't. They yelled again. He didn't. Eventually, a cop shot the driver's-side rear tire, and the impact and surprise caused Milford to drop the gun.

I didn't envy Milford's defense attorneys, not with the prosecution having a video of him killing a man, in addition to the recordings of him contracting two hits. The red kayak we'd turned over would likely make a courtroom appearance, along with whichever expert witness the prosecution found to explain the chemistry behind the smuggling scheme.

Jason Gilson's murder bordered on being gratuitous. He'd probably been in the room when Chris had threatened to turn Milford in, but believing that Gilson had enough backbone to rat someone out made about as much sense as a soup sandwich.

Kenny isn't likely to make it into witness protection. He lost his leverage when Mike was killed and Milford was apprehended. Kenny couldn't hand a big fish to authorities. Even though I understood the financial difficulties his mother's medical bills were inflicting on him, I couldn't let him get away with helping to kill two of my friends, so I sent the recordings of him confessing to the district attorney. Kenny's cooperating with authorities, so he may get out of prison one day.

His mother, Mildred Slattery, will not likely see her son again. I told him I'd help with her medical bills. The $80,000 I'd received from Jami's life-insurance policy had been sitting in my safe for nearly nine years. I'd been unable to think of a use for it that was worthy of Jami's memory. But Jami would have supported using the money to help a woman fight carcinoid tumors. After I washed the $80,000 that I took from Mike's duffel through the Bicycle Hotel & Casino and the Commerce Casino, I added the remaining $65,000 to the fund for Mildred.

Alphonse and Deion never showed up at Jen's, or if they did, something tipped them off before they barged in. So far, no charges have been brought against them for the three murders, and I'm betting nothing will ever stick. I think the park shooters have a fifty-fifty chance to beat the multitude of charges brought against them. My guess is that the workers in the Compton Wave Skimmer shop and the guys Jen and I saw in the San Felipe factory have vanished. I won't lose sleep if they got away because they were all pawns in a game rigged against them. Jen is teaching me how to focus on the present and the future while giving the past its due but never trying to change it.

She fixed up a room on the bottom floor of her house for Game, who spends weekends with us about once a month. Rachelle joined her son here for a weekend last month. She can't stop thanking me for saving her son's life and for giving him direction, but I owe Game far more than he owes me. I realized how close I was to the edge when I handed the Beretta to him that night and gave him permission to shoot me. The sliver of self-awareness that presented itself thereafter allowed me to see who I was, who I wasn't, and how much of myself I'd been throwing away.

Game's participation in solving the murders—all but assuring Milford's conviction—has given him a goal in life: He wants to become a private investigator, my partner, despite my suggestion that he pursue another career path.

But it could have been worse: He could have wanted to direct movies.

The cases I've had in the last five months haven't required the assistance of the now-seventeen-year-old neophyte gumshoe with the ability to crack wise and to pass a basketball, but I'll find him something.

"However," I told him, "I'll only think about making you my partner if you graduate from college."

"You got it, Dawg."

Every morning, I sit at my antique rolltop desk in our library filled with novels, histories, biographies, and science journals to write the book I abandoned long ago about baseball great Ed Delahanty and other unsung heroes, such as Moses Fleetwood Walker, the first Black man to play Major League Baseball; Major Taylor, the first Black cycling world champion; and Josh Gibson, the best all-around hitter in baseball history who played for the Homestead Grays and the Pittsburgh Crawfords in the Negro Leagues.

I write longhand on yellow legal pads with the Montblanc pen Jami gave me. On the desk sits the baseball card Amanda gave me of Big Ed Delahanty, wearing a light-blue uniform with red stockings and belt, and a blue-and-red striped cap. The title of the book is: *Only the Winners*. That was the headline of the article I'd sold to *Esquire* many years ago. The editors changed the headline to "At All Costs," but Jami had come up with the original title, so that's the one I'll fight to keep if a publisher wants to publish the book after I finish it.

Before I lost my wife to an accident, lost my mother to cancer, lost two friends to murder, and one to suicide-by-cop, I'd believed I could complete a well-researched, intriguing book. But I lost confidence in myself, lost my way, and lost hope. Now, however, with Jen having taught me how to love again and Jami whispering encouragement, I still could become the man I hope to be. I'm getting closer every day.

∼

Amanda shouted to me over the sound of the breaking waves two mornings ago from her deck, while Jen and I drank coffee on ours.

"Jack! Hey, Jack!"

"Yes?"

"Got a proposition for you." She slurred the "s" in proposition. It was 9:15.

"What is it?"

"What do you say you write my autobiography? Probably done with acting, and I know a lot of dirt. A lot."

"Don't doubt it, but I can't write your autobiography. You have to, by definition."

"I mean ghostwrite it, stupid."

"No, thank you, but I'll lend you my pen."

"Oh, screw you, Jack, you fucking fuck."

"You always had a way with words," Jen said.

"You fuck off, too, Little Miss Jennifer."

Jen turned to me and said, "I've been called a lot of things in my day. Oddly, that's now one of them."

"With language skills such as hers, how could her autobiography not fly off the shelves?"

∼

Jen made it to ninety meetings in ninety days, and she attends at least four meetings a week. She found a sponsor whom she likes and respects, and they're working the steps together. I'm very proud of her.

We've settled into a kind, supportive, laughter-filled, mutually fulfilling relationship. We paint, cook elaborate meals, and exercise together, and we generally feel good about our future.

But trouble intruded into our lives again last night. After dinner, while I was reading on the couch next to Jen, she said, "I could be paranoid, but I think someone's watching me."

"Where?"

"Pavilions yesterday morning and the rocks on the point in the afternoon, with binoculars. I mean, he could be just a normal pervert getting his jollies by staring at me."

"What did he look like?"

"Couldn't tell on the point. Too far away. But I got a good look at him at the market because he kept walking slowly past me in each aisle in the opposite direction. I know that happens while shopping, but he didn't have a basket and didn't buy anything."

"What did he look like?"

"White guy. Maybe sixty-five. Six feet, jet-black hair, obviously works out. Giant silver sunglasses and a handlebar mustache, like he's Elton John in the Old West."

Not good.

"Did he say anything?"

"Only 'Ain't you that model?'"

"You get that all the time."

"Yes, but this felt different."

"How?"

"I don't know. I guess the back-and-forth without him really shopping and the intensity of his stare. At one point he walked into a kid because he was staring at me. By the time I got to the alcohol aisle, I thought about buying something."

"I'm sorry. You shouldn't be tested like that. Did he have surgery scars on his neck?"

"Not that I noticed. Why?"

"Probably my dad."

"Great. Just what we need."

This morning while I was writing, my cell rang. I let it go to voicemail because I didn't recognize the number. I listened to the message:

"Looks like you're doing good for yourself, son. Not bad for a cop's kid, huh?" He sounded drunk. "Saw you on TV. And that's some girlfriend you got. Yowza. Your mom never looked like that, not on her best day or in her dreams, rest her soul. Well, anyway, you got my number now. The past is the past, as they say. Can't change none of it. Your brother still won't talk to me, but he's always been sensitive like that, holding grudges, acting all wounded. Thought I'd try you. I miss my boys. We had some good times, didn't we? Give me a call sometime."

Shit.

The End

ACKNOWLEDGMENTS

My wife, Sedonia, is my everything, so I owe my writing success to her. She believes in me when I don't, and it's amazing how powerful her belief can be while I'm stumbling through the fog of self-doubt.

As usual, my beta readers were invaluable. They pointed out my errors and let me know which aspects of this novel worked well for them. Thank you, Andrew Balmat, Jessica Carroll, Colleen Friesen, Biz Lyon, Mary Ellen Lyon, Jen Mauerman, Jenny Raith, and Sedonia Sipes.

Eva Spring employed her impressive talents to create the cover. Thank you, Eva.

I'd like to thank my mother, Barbara Leonard, my brother, Brett, my sister, Brigette, and my late father, Bruce Sr., for the support they've shown me for decades.

Please stay tuned for the second Jack Drake Mystery: *Stronger at the Break*. But it may be a while before I write that one because I'm currently writing a thriller, and I'll follow that up with the fifth Hadley Carroll Mystery — *Quilt City: Safety Second*.

If you enjoyed *Hard Exit*, please leave a rating and/or a review on whichever platform you prefer.

This novel took me decades to write, and I never would have completed it if readers hadn't responded so positively to the Hadley Carroll Mysteries.

So, I thank you for your support.

ABOUT THE AUTHOR

Bruce Leonard earned a B.A. in English with a creative-writing emphasis from UCLA. He has been a travel writer, a magazine- and newspaper editor, an owner of a bakery, and a guinea pig for the U.S. Government. He writes the award-winning, bestselling Hadley Carroll Mysteries, the first of which, Quilt City Murders, was named Best Mystery of 2022 in one contest. The fifth installment will be titled, Quilt City: Safety Second.

The second Jack Drake Private-Eye Mystery will be Stronger at the Break.

Quilt City Murders, the first Hadley Carroll Mystery, named Best Mystery of 2022 by the National Indie Excellence Awards
    Quilt City: Panic in Paducah, the second
    Quilt City: Measure Once, Cut Twice, the third
    Quilt City: Proving a Negative, the fourth
    Quilt City Cookbook, a companion book narrated by Hadley at her funniest and most vulnerable

Bruce's website is: https://bruceleonardwriter.com/, where his books are available. While there, please sign up for his infrequent newsletter, in which he keeps readers informed about upcoming releases, and you can look at a smattering of the thousands of photos he took when he was a travel writer.

Happy reading!

Made in the USA
Monee, IL
03 August 2024